THE GOOD, THE BAD, AND THE AUNTIES

JESSE Q. SUTANTO

BERKLEY
An imprint of Penguin Random House LLC
penguinrandomhouse.com

Library of Congress Cataloging-in-Publication Data

Names: Sutanto, Jesse Q., author.
Title: The good, the bad, and the aunties / Jesse Q. Sutanto.
Description: First edition. | New York: Berkley, 2024.
Identifiers: LCCN 2023040027 (print) |
LCCN 2023040028 (ebook) | ISBN 9780593546222 (trade paperback) |
ISBN 9780593546215 (hardcover) | ISBN 9780593546239 (ebook)
Subjects: LCGFT: Novels.
Classification: LCC PR9500.9.S88 G66 2024 (print) |
LCC PR9500.9.S88 (ebook) | DDC 823/.92—dc23/eng/20231004
LC record available at https://lccn.loc.gov/2023040027
LC ebook record available at https://lccn.loc.gov/2023040028

First Edition: March 2024

Printed in the United States of America
1st Printing

Book design by Tiffany Estreicher

*To my readers. Thank you for adopting
the aunties as your own.*

THE
GOOD,
THE BAD,
AND THE
AUNTIES

1

The wind is a constant song in my ears, the air so cold and refreshing it sparkles against my cheeks as I whoosh down the ski slope. I can't believe this is the first time I've tried skiing. Growing up, Ma and the aunts had forbidden me from doing any "dangerous sports," which included anything more physically strenuous than chess or piano. When I was five, I suggested that I wanted to try out for the girls' soccer team. In response, Ma smacked her palms to her cheeks and wailed, "Aiya, the ball will hit you in the head and you will get brain hemo-hedge!"

"What's a brain hemo-hedge?" Images of a hedge growing out of my head swirled through my mind.

Ma waved her hands around her head, opening and closing her hands. "Is when all the blood come out of your head. *All the blood.*"

My mind replaced the hedge bursting out of my head with

buckets of blood exploding from it in a red geyser. I swallowed, feeling ill. "Wait, so this is a thing that happens when people play soccer?"

Ma nodded sagely.

My mouth dropped open in horror. "Jenny plays soccer!" I couldn't believe that Mrs. Andrews would let Jenny play such a dangerous sport.

Ma nodded again, this time somberly. "Ah yes. This because Jenny is middle child. You should be grateful you are only child."

After that day, I hugged Jenny tight whenever I could, because the poor thing had no idea she was (1) this close to having her head explode like a watermelon on the beach, and (2) unloved due to her fraught position in the family as a middle child.

Soccer was the first sport to be deemed too deadly by Ma, but over the next few months, she and the aunties added to the growing list.

Softball: The ball will smash right through your chest and come out the other side!

Basketball: The ball will decopitot you! (Decopitot: verb. To have something hit you in the head so forcefully that your head is replaced by that thing. Highly probable when playing high-velocity, high-strength sports like basketball in first grade.)

Swimming: There will be a shark in the water, and it will eat you! "But we would swim in the pool, not the s—"

"Are you talking back to your elders??!"

I joined the chess club. I was the worst member in the club because I wasn't actually into chess, but there wasn't a possibility of an errant projectile hitting me and making my head spontaneously combust, so there was that. It wasn't until college that I met Selena, who dragged me to the school gym and introduced me to the wonders of exercise. I found that I liked the rush of endorphins, and later, when I went into wedding photography, it became necessary to start lifting weights so I could carry around my heavy camera equipment without injuring myself. Of course, Ma and the aunts still nagged at me, telling me I was going to give myself a hernia or pop a blood vessel by doing weight training. If they knew that part of my honeymoon with Nathan was a ski trip to Val Thorens, the highest ski resort in France's Trois Vallées, they would freak out like never before. Probably even more than when I accidentally killed Ah Guan, or when we thought that my wedding vendors were mafia.

I'd been resistant toward the idea of skiing before, due to the aforementioned upbringing of doom and disaster when it came to sports, but Nathan had convinced me and enrolled us in a two-day beginners class with a kindly instructor. That was five days ago, and I graduated from bunny slopes to green, and later, to blue slopes. Today is the last day of our trip, and I'm making the best of the remaining time I have here by skiing down my favorite blue slope, Gentiane. It's a wide slope that's so gentle I'm surprised it's a blue and not a green, and because most people prefer the more exciting reds and blacks, Nathan and I are the only two people on the slope for ages.

I glance at him now, skiing next to me. My husband. The term still sends a delightful little shiver down my back. Reflexively, the corners of my mouth quirk up into a smile. I'm sure that down the road, the words "my husband" will lose their sheen and I'll be able to say them without experiencing that little glow of joy, but for now, I still savor the words. It still takes me a moment to let them sink in. I'm married. To the

One That Got Away. The man I've ached for since college. My one true love, who's covered up literal murder for my sake and done so much more to ensure the safety of me and my family. I'm so glad we capped off our tromp across Europe with this ski trip. It's been the most amazing month spent venturing into museums and actual castles complete with battlements and crenellations and old armor, not to mention eating our way through Europe. Thanks to all the incredibly rich cheese and silky chocolate we've been having, the waistband of my jeans feels a tad snugger than I'm used to.

A shrill, familiar jangle tears through the peaceful, snowy calm, shattering my focus. I startle, my right foot slips an inch to my right, and that's all it takes to overturn my balance. My skis swerve precariously, and the world tips sideways as I try—and fail—to stop myself from falling over. Luckily, the snow is as soft as a pile of feathers, and I barely feel it when I land very ungracefully on my side. Dimly, I can hear Nathan calling out my name. Moments later, he skids expertly to a stop and crouches down next to me.

"Are you okay?" His gloved hands cup my face, brushing away snow and gazing with open concern down at me.

I blink and try to catch my breath. "Yeah, nothing's broken, aside from my dignity."

Nathan's shoulders sag with relief, and he pulls me up into a hug. "What happened?"

As though in answer, the ringing starts up again. I grapple for my phone, tucked somewhere into one of the many pockets in my bulky ski jacket. My fingers are half-numb from the cold and clumsy due to my padded gloves, and it takes an eternity to locate the phone and pull it out. When I finally see the screen, my heart sinks. "It's Ma."

Nathan frowns, a crease folding between his eyebrows. "That can't be good."

I nod. Ma and the aunties have made a big show of not calling me on my honeymoon because, as Ma had said, "Don't spend time talking to me on your honeymoon, you must spend all your time and energy to make me grandbabies, okay!" I'd almost pointed out that we would hardly be spending all of our waking moments making babies, but then my sense of self-preservation had kicked in and I realized that this worked in my favor, since I didn't exactly want my mother calling me at all hours of the day while I was on my honeymoon. Still, throughout our trip, Nathan and I have been dutifully check-ing in on the family WhatsApp group every morning. He had been invited to join the family chat group the very next day after our wedding, and to my slight annoyance, he fit right in, even diving into the inane emoji game with gusto. He had al-ready checked in with them this morning to assure them that we're okay and haven't been kidnapped by the same people who took Liam Neeson's daughter in *Taken*, so the fact that Ma is calling right now must mean there's legit bad news.

Ever since the unfortunate incident involving Ah Guan, fol-lowed by the appearance of his (understandably) vengeful fam-ily, every time Ma or the aunties call instead of using WhatsApp, I get this jolt of electric fear running through my entire body, jump-starting my heart rate into a gallop and making me break out into a sweat. God, I hope nothing's happened to them.

I struggle to pull my gloves off and hit Accept. "Ma, is ev-erything okay?"

Ma's face fills my phone screen. As usual, she's holding the phone right up against her face, so all I can see is one eye and a nostril. "Aduh, Meddy, disaster!"

My stomach plummets. There it is. I just knew that Stephanie and her family wouldn't be able to let go of the fact that we'd killed their beloved Ah Guan. They only pretended to accept it so they could regroup and come back to get us with a better, deadlier plan. I can practically feel the blood draining from my head, making me dizzy. Next to me, the crease between Nathan's eyebrows is so deep it looks like a crevasse, but he grabs my free hand and gives it a reassuring squeeze. "It'll be okay," he mouths, though clearly, neither of us believes it. There are too many skeletons in our closet for anything to be okay. It's always been a matter of time before my past caught up with us. I'm only sorry that I dragged Nathan into all this mess. My sweet, loving, unfortunate husband.

Somehow, I manage to find my voice. "What is it, Ma? Wait, tell me in Indonesian," I add as an extra precaution, though Nathan and I are still alone on the piste.

Ma's face scrunches up into a picture of sheer anguish. "Mama ngga keburu beli Porto's cheese rolls."

I blink. Narrow my eyes at her. "Come again? Say it in English this time, just so I know I'm not mishearing."

"I come to Porto's too late. They are out of cheese rolls!"

Only a few seconds ago, I'd felt like all of my blood had rushed out of my head and I was ready to faint. Now, I can feel a river of blood rushing up to my head. I'm about ready to blow a gasket. "Ma." It's a struggle keeping my voice even. "Why are you calling me because of Porto's cheese rolls? I thought we agreed that while I'm on my honeymoon, phone calls are for emergencies only?"

"This is *emergency*," she snaps, glaring at me so hard her gaze is like a laser shooting through the phone screen. "I promise everyone in Jakarta Porto's cheese rolls. You know how everyone love it so much. Every year I come back, I bring cheese rolls. Everybody love it. Now, if I don't bring cheese roll, I will lose face!"

"You're not going to lose face just because you—"

"And you know Fourth Aunt always trying to up me one. Last year, she bring Ladurée macarons for everyone. *Ladurée*. You know how expensive they are? Is so obvious she just want to up me one. I say to her, I say, Aiya, why are you so norak? Ladurée in Singapore also have, why you need to bring all the way from LA? And she say—you know what she say?"

"Let me guess," Nathan says with a smile, "she said the ones from LA are different from the ones in Singapore?"

"*YES!*" Ma cries with indignant triumph. "As if she can tell the difference. Is a franchise, of course they will all taste the same. But you know how Fourth Aunt is, keep talking and talking nonstop until everyone agree with her. Wah, they all say, yes, the macarons from LA very different from the ones from Singapore." She sniffs. "Now I will have to go back empty-hand, no face."

A vision of a handless, faceless Ma swims to my mind, and despite myself, I have to stifle a laugh. Argh, what is it about Ma that makes me want to hug her even while she infuriates the heck out of me?

"Well," Nathan says, "lucky for you, we're actually in France right now. At Val Tho—"

I nudge him in the ribs. Hard. Ma and the aunties aren't supposed to know we're skiing. I'm even being super careful with how I hold my phone so she can only see my face and the sky and that's it. If Ma and the aunties knew we were going skiing, they would zoom here in a chopper and yank us all the way back to LA by our ears, while lecturing us about the multitude of ways that one could get themselves killed by skiing.

"Ow. Uh, I mean, we're in Versailles. And we'll be flying out of Paris tomorrow, so how about we bring back a gigantic box of Ladurée macarons? Then you can tell your relatives that these aren't from Singapore or LA, they're from the original Ladurée shop."

Ma's mouth gapes open as she takes in a sharp breath. She leans even closer to the phone, so now all I can see is one eyeball. "From the . . . original Ladurée shop?" Her voice is furtive and soft with reverence, like she's referring to the crown jewels.

"Yep. The flagship store. I believe it's on rue Royale."

My eyes widen. How in the world does Nathan know this? As though reading my mind, he shrugs like, *I don't know, I'm just guessing here.*

"The flagship store," Ma breathes. The one visible eye is practically glittering at the thought of one-upping Fourth Aunt with macarons from the original Ladurée store. Then she throws her head back and cackles. A literal witchy cackle. Nathan and I exchange a glance. Uh-oh, Ma has ascended to her final form. "Yes!" she positively shrieks. "Oh, Fourth Aunt will be so embarrass. *So* embarrass. Nowhere to put her face!" She cackles again. "Buy the biggest box, okay? Everyone will want one."

"Ma, do you know how expensive those things are?"

Nathan waves me off. "We'll buy the biggest box of macarons they have. And a few other treats for you as well."

"Aiya, you no need to waste money on me."

Before Nathan can reply, I say, "Okay, we won't buy you anything."

Ma stops short and stares at us. There is a pregnant pause. "Yes, don't waste money on your own mother. I always tell you, no need to buy me any gifts. Other people always asking their children to buy gifts, but no, I say, I don't want to burden my daughter. As long as she happy and healthy, I am okay. Don't need her to make fuss over me or anything like that."

"Yep, we won't get you anything." I bite back the smile that's threatening to take over my face. Next to me, Nathan is giving me WTF looks, but I ignore him.

"Good, good," she mumbles, looking like I've just punched her in the heart.

I'm torn between laughter and frustration. My whole life has been a series of mixed messages from Ma, and though I know it's cruel to trick her, I want her to get a taste of what it would be like for her if I were to follow her every instruction.

"Ma, of course we've bought you a lot of souvenirs," Nathan blurts out. Goddamn traitor.

I can't help but laugh out loud. "Of course we haven't forgotten to get all sorts of presents for you, Ma."

"Aiya!" she cries, her face incandescent with joy. "Why you waste money? I tell you not to buy me present already."

I roll my eyes. "So we shouldn't have gotten you an Hermès bag? Fine, I'll give it to Big Aunt."

"Eh!" Her shout is so loud I wonder if it would trigger an avalanche. "An Hermès bag? A real one?"

"I promise you they don't sell fake Hermès bags in France. I think it's an actual felony," I laugh. The shock and delight on Ma's face is everything.

"You shouldn't waste money like that," she snaps again, but she's also grinning as wide as a hyena, probably already plotting how to drop the Hermès bomb on Fourth Aunt. She still hasn't forgotten how Fourth Aunt cut her out of the family Louis Vuitton luggage set.

By the time we hang up, Ma is still beaming and muttering "Aiya, shouldn't have wasted money" over and over. It's like she's stuck on a loop, torn between sheer joy and the Asian tradition of scolding your kids for spending money on you. My breath releases in a relieved huff, steaming in the cold mountain air, as I stuff the phone back into my jacket pocket.

Nathan is still smiling.

"What are you smiling about? We're about to lose a small fortune in Laduree macarons. God, those things are so overpriced. I can't believe she's willing to spend money on them. This is the same woman who haggled with bus drivers to give her a discount on bus fares."

He laughs and pulls me close. "It's just—her glee over one-upping Fourth Aunt. Come on, that's so funny. I love it."

"Try growing up with it, then you wouldn't find it so adorable."

He leans close and kisses me on the tip of my nose, then grimaces. "I think I got a bit of snot there."

"Yeah, don't kiss people's noses on ski slopes, genius."

"Lesson learned. Shall we keep going?"

I gaze up the slope, toward the peak of the mountain, and sigh wistfully. "I wish we could just stay here forever."

"What, on this slope? It'd get pretty cold."

"Tch. I mean, do we really have to leave for Jakarta tomorrow? We could tell them we're snowed in. That's believable, right?" I gesture around us. "Look at this view. Look how blue that sky is, and how fresh the air is. Every breath I take is like drinking straight from a mountain spring, it's so refreshing. And I love skiing, and—"

"And you don't want to see your family again."

Smart-ass. I narrow my eyes at him. "Okay, that's inaccurate. I love my family, I just—I'm not ready for our honeymoon to end."

"Hey," he says softly, putting his arms around me. Of course, we're bundled up in so many layers that our arms can't go all the way around each other. "It hasn't ended yet. We're going around Pulau Seribu, aren't we? There's still an adventure awaiting us."

"True," I admit. "But before Pulau Seribu, there's going to be Jakarta and my family."

"Your family is wonderful. Just like yourself."

I shudder. "Okay, never, ever say that to me. I am nothing like my family."

Nathan bites back a grin. "Really? You mean you're not going to tell our future kids not to waste money buying you gifts and then give them a hard time when they listen to you?"

"Ugh, never!"

"Because I think that's kind of really cute."

"Oh god," I groan. "Only you would find that cute."

Nathan looks deep into my eyes, and despite myself, I melt against him. "It's going to be okay," he says softly. "I can't wait to go to Jakarta and meet everyone and experience the whole Chinese New Year celebration with you, your mom, and your aunts. It's going to be great."

I want to remind him that when it comes to my family and big, over-the-top events, we kind of have a terrible track record. But I don't want to spend the last day in Val Thorens arguing, so I close my eyes and lose myself in a long kiss, and I remind myself over and over that this time will be different. That this time, I have my husband (!) with me, and we will weather anything and everything together, as a single family unit.

2

The last thing I want to do after flying for eighteen hours is to meet everyone in my greasy-faced, matted-hair state (Nathan, of course, somehow manages to remain fresh-faced and smelling of clean laundry), but that's exactly what greets us at the Jakarta airport. There's Ma, hopping up and down and waving madly at us even though we've both waved back to indicate that yes, we saw her. And behind her are not only Big Aunt, Second Aunt, and Fourth Aunt, but about half a dozen of my other aunts and uncles.

"We could turn around right now and fly back to Paris," I mutter as Nathan pushes our trolley, which is piled impossibly high with souvenir-stuffed bags, toward the gaggle of waving, grinning aunties and uncles.

"You'll be fine. Look how excited they are to see you."

"You mean how excited they are to see *you*?"

Nathan has just enough time to say, "Why would they be

excited to see me?" before we walk through the glass doors and are immediately swarmed by my family.

Instinct takes over and I raise my arms to shield my face as they stampede toward me, but instead of the fierce, over-whelming hug I expected, they rush past me. "Wha—" I turn around. And stare.

I was right. They truly do not give a shit about seeing me. It's all about Nathan, the golden boy; the chiseled, Captain America–jawlined hero.

"My son!" Ma cries happily, throwing her arms around him.

Fourth Aunt pinches his cheek, nearly taking out an eye with her viciously manicured fingernails. Meanwhile, Second Aunt has picked up one of his arms and is holding it up for the other aunties and uncles to admire.

"Look, so muscular, ya? I tell you, such a strong lad."

The other aunties and uncles *ooh* and *aah.* "Wah, yes, so healthy. Will give you good, strong grandchildren."

Second Aunt simpers as though they've complimented her arm and not Nathan's. "Is because I teach him Tai Chi."

Big Aunt snorts and rolls her eyes. "I think Nathan already working out before you rope him into doing Tai Chi with you."

"Er—" Nathan's eyes ping-pong back and forth between Big Aunt and Second Aunt before going to me with a silent plea for help. I smirk at him, enjoying the fact that:

1. For the first time, I'm not the center of attention.

2. He was so confident and smug about everything being fine in Jakarta, so he can very well deal with them himself.

Is that mean? I should probably come to his aid or something, shouldn't I? I shouldn't leave my newlywed husband (!) at the mercy of my family.

With a sigh, I walk up to them and wave weakly. "Hi, everyone."

As though she's just remembered the existence of her only daughter, Ma whips around. "Ah, Meddy, there you are."

"I've been here the whole time. You literally walked right past me."

"Aduh, you look so tired." Ma places her hands on my cheeks and squeezes. "So pale. Why so pale? You not feeling well? You too skinny! You need to eat more. Aiya, must be the food in France no good, that's why you get so skinny, you eat more, okay?"

"But not too much," Second Aunt says, "otherwise later you get high cholesterol."

"Yes, don't eat too much," Ma agrees. "But do eat more, you see, otherwise your face is so peyot." She sucks in her cheeks to illustrate just how peyot—sunken—my cheeks look. "Like old hag," she adds, just to drive her point home.

"Mm." Second Aunt nods. "But remember, not eat too much, otherwise blood pressure spike, then you will die."

"Uh. Right." I take an inhale and smile at them. "I'll eat more, but not too much more, okay."

"She is pale, right?" Ma says to the others, still not mollified by my answer. They all nod in agreement.

"Maybe she enter wind," one of the uncles suggests.

"Enter wind?" Nathan says.

I gently pull Ma's hands off my face. "It's an Indonesian phrase—masuk angin. It means catch a cold. And no, I don't have a cold. I'm just tired because, you know, eighteen-hour flight and all that. Anyway—" I'm desperate to change the subject. "Ma, didn't you guys arrive only this morning? How are you so . . ." I gesture around for a bit, looking for the right word. "Perky?"

"Aduh, of course is because of my TCM," Ma announces with pride.

My stomach drops. Oh god, the woman can't possibly be foolhardy enough to bring marijuana into Indonesia, a country with the harshest penalties for drug abuse.

"Don't worry, I made sure it's legit TCM," Fourth Aunt says with a roll of her eyes.

I breathe a sigh of relief. "Thanks, Fourth Aunt."

"I substituted the THC with Ambien. We all slept through the entire flight."

"What? Ambien? Isn't that prescription only?" My mind spins, trying to keep up with my mom and aunts and their drug use.

"Yeah, we all got a prescription for it," Fourth Aunt says so simply, like she's talking about the weather.

"Big Aunt talk in her sleep the whole time," Second Aunt snickers. "Keep on shouting orders at the flight attendants in her sleep."

Big Aunt harrumphs. "I think you making that up."

"I'll show you video later," Second Aunt says to me. I give her a weak smile.

"Enough of that. Come, Nathan, you have to meet the rest of the family!" Ma grabs my arm and Nathan's and pulls us toward the group of aunties and uncles, who are all smiling and staring openly at us. "This is Auntie Yuli, she is our cousin from Nainai's side, and this one her brother, you call him Uncle Ping, okay, and this one Uncle Mochtar, he is our second cousin from . . ."

I glance at Nathan as Ma presents each aunt and uncle to him. I still remember the first time that Ma took me back to Jakarta, when I was a kid, and how overwhelming it was. It took me two more visits to remember every aunt's, uncle's, and cousin's name. Poor Nathan. He must be so overwhelmed.

"Auntie Yuli, Uncle Ping, Uncle Mochtar, Auntie Wati, Auntie Sheren, and Uncle Ong," Nathan says, nodding at each one with a warm, open smile.

What the hell? Did he seriously memorize all of their names just like that?

The crowd of aunties and uncles erupts into huge grins. The uncles reach out and slap Nathan fondly on the back, and the aunties grab his arms, yammering the whole time about how handsome and well-mannered he is. Together, the throng leads him toward the exit, leaving me behind. Nathan turns his head and gives me a wide-eyed, helpless look, but beneath it is warm amusement. He's totally enjoying this, the ham. With a laugh, I jog after them, catching up with Ma and linking my arm through hers. Maybe Nathan's right. Maybe we'll actually have fun in Jakarta.

The family home is a huge, ostentatious mansion in Pantai Indah Kapuk, north Jakarta. Like many of the other towering mansions in PIK, when the aunties and uncles renovated the house five years ago, they chose to go baroque, the most over-the-top architecture that has ever been architectured. I'm talking about a literal giant crown built atop the roof of the house, like that's going to fool anyone into thinking we're actual royalty.

"Wow," Nathan breathes as we get out of the car and tilt our heads back, and back, and back to take in the behemoth of a house in front of us.

I grimace. "I know. But this house has like, four different families living in it."

It's the Chinese-Indonesian way; traditionally, most children live with their parents, even after they get married, so you'd often get three whole generations living in a single house. Most Chinese-Indonesian families are huge, comprising more than six children, so usually some of the children would move out after they got married, but more often than not, at least one or two of them would remain in the family home. Our family home is no different; though Ma and the aunties long ago emigrated to the States, Auntie Sheren and Auntie Wati, their cousins from their mother's side, have remained in the family house with their respective families.

"Wow, four different families?" Nathan raises his eyebrows.

"There's Auntie Sheren and her husband, Uncle Ping and his wife, and then there's Auntie Sheren's son and his wife, and Uncle Ping's daughter and her husband, and all their kids. So . . . I think there are fourteen people living here? Plus their live-in helpers." I hate having to explain this stuff to non-Indonesians, who always seem to be horrified by the concept. I can't help but feel judged whenever I tell them that no, it's not actually part of our culture to move out of our parents' house, because nine out of ten times, people would react with shock/horror and make comments about how infantilizing our culture is.

But Nathan nods slowly before grinning. "Sounds like a blast. Can you imagine how much fun the kids must have? I was always so lonely growing up as an only child. I would've killed to live in one single house with my cousins."

My chest loosens. I hadn't even noticed it tightening.

"Ayo, masuk!" Uncle Ping gestures jovially, ushering us through the massive double doors.

Nathan and I go inside and are almost blinded by the crystal chandelier cascading from the foyer ceiling. It must be about a thousand watts of light and is a total showstopper. Grecian statues flank the foyer, staring down at us impassively while wrestling dolphins. Next to them are Ming vases as tall as Nathan. My insides squirm at how ostentatious everything in here must look to Nathan. I mean, it's as though my family raided the British Museum.

"Masuk, masuk!" Auntie Wati pushes us along, deeper into the house, and suddenly, there are shouts and stampeding feet and we're attacked. Well, by hugs.

The kids jump around us like little pups, and I laugh and hug them all.

"Cici Meddy!" they shout, throwing their little arms around my shoulders and tugging affectionately at my hair and telling me how pretty I look (aww) and how bad my breath smells after my long flight. Then they look at Nathan and gasp. "Is he a movie star?" my five-year-old niece, Jeassyka, wonders aloud, her eyes wide.

"No," I laugh.

"But he can be," Ma adds loyally, patting Nathan's arm and beaming up at him with fondness. "He is as handsome as Thor, ya?"

The kids nod, their eyes never leaving Nathan's face, which has turned an interesting shade of red.

"But better," Big Aunt sniffs. "Because he is Chinese. Chinese Thor better than American Thor."

"Okay, first of all, Thor isn't American," I say, but my voice is already drowned out by everyone talking at once.

"Oh? Then what he is?"

Embarrassingly, it takes me a moment to figure it out. "Uh, I wanna say . . . Norwegian?"

"Aiya, all these Caucasian country all the same," Big Aunt says with a careless flap of her hand.

"Big Aunt, you can't say that. That's offensive."

"Is it?" She looks at me like she's genuinely surprised. "Why?"

"Because . . ." I struggle to figure out a way of telling Big Aunt about diversity and cultural identities, and finally mumble, "Um, because they're all different?" Wow, great job, me. I really need to get better at thinking on my feet.

Big Aunt sniffs, clearly unimpressed, and turns her attention back to Nathan, who's completely surrounded by my family.

Why do I bother? I sigh and smile as I gaze at my poor husband. The little ones are literally climbing onto him. Already he's got the smallest kid, my two-year-old nephew Herrisan Ford, on top of his shoulders. The other littles are hopping around him, shouting, "My turn! Me next!" and "Let me show you my room! I've got the biggest princess castle in there! And my Barbie has a sword! It's named Skull Crusher!"

"Skull Crusher?" I cock an eyebrow at my cousin Jems. Jems is one of my favorite cousins because not only is he into photography, but both our names have been so unfortunately spelled that it's impossible not to share a certain kinship with him.

Jems shrugs with a rueful smile. "She came up with the name all on her own."

I laugh and we hug each other. "It's so good to be here again."

"How was your honeymoon?" my cousin-in-law Elsa says,

putting an arm around my shoulders and squeezing. "Think you made a baby yet?"

I groan. "Not you guys too."

"Just kidding!" Elsa laughs.

"But not really," Jems says. "My mom told us that we have to talk you into starting a family like immediately."

I roll my eyes. "Figures."

Jems and Elsa take me to the dining room, where to the surprise of no one, there is a humongous feast large enough to feed an entire army battalion. The dining table has run out of space for food, and there are dishes placed on the side tables as well. Platters piled high with seafood noodles, topped with deep-fried quail's eggs, braised sea cucumber and meaty shiitake mushrooms, crunchy tofu skin rolls, sliced abalone, fist-sized fried pork balls, and literally a dozen other dishes.

"Our parents might have lost their minds a little bit when you guys announced you were coming back for Chinese New Year," Jems says.

"They really wanted to impress Nathan," Elsa adds.

"Oh, he will definitely be impressed."

I was right. Once Nathan joins us, along with everyone else, in the dining room, I can practically see his mouth salivating from the sight of all this food. Shouts of "Makan!" fill the room. A plate is thrust into Nathan's hands, and immediately after that, there is a mad rush as everyone lunges forward to pile food onto his plate.

"Here, have the sea cucumber," Ma cries, slapping a large sea cucumber on his plate.

Before Nathan can thank her, Uncle Ong heaps a thick slice of steak next to the sea cucumber. "This is wagyu, you know wagyu? We order special from Japan."

"Wow, amazing, I love wag—"

"Eat more veggie-tibbles," Auntie Wati orders, heaping a large ladleful of bok choy atop the steak.

Second Aunt does some fancy Tai Chi stretch and overturns a bowl of fried rice on top of the almost overflowing pile of food. Nathan's biceps are now bulging as his plate gets heavier and heavier.

"Should I save him?" I mutter to my cousins.

"God, no," my cousin Sarah says. "Take this chance to grab the food you actually want and eat in peace. He's our sacrificial lamb. For once, no one is paying attention to us and nagging at us to eat this or that."

"True." But when Uncle Ping plops a whole fish head on top of the mountain of food, I feel too guilty and hurry over, placing myself between Nathan and the aunts and uncles. "I think he's got enough on his plate. Literally." I hold up my hand to stop Auntie Sheren, who's threatening to put what looks like a whole chicken onto Nathan's plate. "We'll come back for the chicken when he's done with all of this, Auntie. Thank you, though. You're so kind, really." I gesture at Nathan to escape to the cousins table but am too slow to stop Auntie Sheren from smacking the chicken onto my own plate.

"You better eat that, Meddy!" She wags a finger in my face. "You too skinny. How you going to make a nice, fat baby if you so skinny?"

Her words act as a signal for the other aunties and uncles to swarm around me and pile food onto my plate, all of them telling me I need to eat more so I can give my poor, long-suffering mother the chubby grandbaby she deserves. By the time they're done, I swear my plate weighs more than all of my camera equipment combined. I stagger with it to the cousins table and slide into a seat next to Nathan.

"Thank you for saving me," he murmurs, squeezing my hand.

"Ah, newlyweds," Sarah sighs. "That was very selfless of you, Meddy."

"Yeah, we told her to leave you to the wolves," Jems laughs.

Next to our table, the "grown-up" table is in full party mode, all of the aunts and uncles cackling as they exchange crazy stories. Even Big Aunt is laughing uproariously at something Uncle Ong is saying. On the other side, the kids squeal and giggle at their little table. I can't help smiling as I watch everyone, loving the noise and warmth that fills the entire house. It's no wonder that Ma and the aunties make sure to come back every year. They seem younger here somehow, more vibrant and filled with life.

"I love this," Nathan says, echoing my thoughts. "This is so lively. I can see how everyone living together under one roof really works for your families."

Elsa laughs. "Oh, trust me, we get into our share of arguments. But yeah, on the whole, it's really great, and the kids are never bored or lonely."

"I've always wanted to be part of a big family." Nathan's dimples wink at me, and I smile back.

"Well, you'll meet the big family tomorrow morning, on Chinese New Year."

"The 'big' family?" Nathan says.

"Yeah, this isn't the whole family, it's only a small portion of it. Everyone else will come here in the morning to bai nian." Bai nian, done during Chinese New Year, consists of going round to relatives' homes or congregating in the house of the oldest relative to wish everyone a happy new year.

Nathan's eyebrows disappear into his hairline. "Whoa, this is only a small portion of the family?"

"Yep," Sarah says through a mouthful of noodles. "There are about eighty of us in total."

"*What?*" Nathan sputters.

Again, my stomach knots. Maybe it's too much, too overwhelming. I shouldn't have brought him here for Chinese New Year, the biggest holiday for our family. I should've brought him here on a normal day and had him meet everyone in a slow, manageable trickle.

But Nathan only beams wide, eyes alight, and says, "That's amazing. I can't wait to meet everyone."

Honestly, I don't deserve this man. I lean over and plant a chaste kiss on his cheek.

An insistent tinkling of metal against glass catches our attention, and we look over to the next table to see Fourth Aunt tapping her fork against her glass with flourish. Next to her, Ma is rolling her eyes, like, *Of course she's calling all of the attention to herself.*

When Fourth Aunt is satisfied that all eyes are on her, she sets down her fork and places her hand on her hip. "I'd just like to say thank you to everyone for welcoming us home, and I am *so* excited about the Chinese New Year celebration tomorrow."

"Hear, hear!" Jems calls out.

Ma rolls her eyes so hard I wonder if she'll give herself a migraine.

Fourth Aunt's fire-engine-red lips stretch into a playful smirk. "Aaand, I've prepared a very special surprise for tomorrow."

Uh-oh. My stomach drops. I hate surprises. People often say they hate surprises, but see, the last time my mother and aunts surprised me, I killed that surprise, so when I say I hate surprises, I really mean it.

As though reading my mind, Fourth Aunt frowns and flaps her hand at me. "Meddy, I see that look of horror on your face. Don't worry, it's not a surprise for you, okay?"

"Oh." Okay then. I sag with relief. Nathan squeezes my hand again, and I mouth "phew" at him.

"Who's the surprise for?" someone calls out.

Fourth Aunt grins slyly before miming zipping her mouth shut. Everyone groans good-naturedly. I'm surprised Ma's eyes are still working after all the rolling they've done. Dinner lasts for hours. By the time we finish up with dessert, the kids are all asleep, except for little Jeassyka, who's still yammering on to Nathan about how she's planning on using her red packet money to buy a real lightsaber for her Barbie. Somehow, against all odds, it seems that everything is going well, and I find myself looking forward to finding out what Fourth Aunt's surprise is tomorrow.

3

Crash! Bang!

The noise jerks me awake and I leap up, my body flinging itself into motion before my mind can catch up. My mouth, too, works on its own accord, shouting before I even realize what the words are. "Nathan. Nathan! Wake up."

Crash! Honk!

It hits me then. We're in the volcanic belt. Indonesia has—uh, I don't know what's the exact number, all I know is that it's a *lot*. A lot of volcanoes. One of them must have erupted, triggering an earthquake. "Earthquake!" I blurt out. "Nathan!" I grab his arm and shake it.

"Mrrfgl?" He blinks slowly awake just as another deafening crash judders through the house. How in the world can this man sleep through all that noise? "Whassat?"

"Earthquake!"

"What?" He jumps up, fully awake now, and looks around, blinking owlishly.

I'm already running toward the makeup table in the far corner of the room, my hands clasped over my head in case the ceiling caves in. "Take cover!" I yelp as another crash thunders through the room.

Nathan frowns. Instead of running after me and hiding under the table, he gazes up at the chandelier, because of course there's a chandelier in every bedroom.

"What are you doing?" I hiss. "Take cover."

"It's not moving."

"What?"

"The chandelier. Look, the crystals aren't swaying. It's not an earthquake, Meddy."

I glance up at the chandelier, and sure enough, it's completely still. "Wha?" I rub at my eyes. "Then what's all the commotion about?"

Nathan opens the curtains and peers out of the windows. He unlocks one and slides it open, and immediately, noise spills into the room. Cymbal crashes, trumpet blares, and other whistling, hooting sounds made from instruments I don't recognize.

"What the hell?" I clamber out from my hiding spot and join Nathan at the window. And gape at the scene unfolding below.

There is a—there are no other words for it—cavalcade of sleek black cars, each one equipped with flashing blue lights, like cops, and each one with people hanging out the windows, playing some musical instruments with gusto. I count at least ten cars in the procession, snaking up the driveway like a black dragon. A black dragon of explosive music.

"Is this a regular part of Chinese New Year here?"

I shake my head. "Well, at least I don't think so." I search my mind for memories of the last Chinese New Year I spent in Jakarta. Nope, definitely no cavalcades then.

As we watch, the sunroof of the first car slides open and a man emerges from it. From this distance, I can barely make out his face, but I do spot a mustache and slicked-back hair. The man lifts his hands dramatically, and the noise is immediately silenced. And I do mean immediately; even the trumpet stops mid-blow. Wow. Despite myself, I'm impressed. Whoever this guy is, it's clear he commands respect. He lifts a loudspeaker to his mouth, straightens up, and begins speaking.

"Enjelin Chan." His voice, magnified by the loudspeaker, booms across the courtyard. It's a deep, rich voice, brimming with confidence. A shiver runs down my spine.

"That's Second Aunt," I whisper. Why am I whispering? "He's calling for Second Aunt."

Just as I say that, the window next to me slides open and Second Aunt peers out, her hair still in rollers. When she spies the man, she squawks and jerks back inside her room. A moment later, Ma leans out the window and waves at the man. "Hallo! Please wait a second," she says in Indonesian, "Enjelin is just making herself presentable."

"Enjelin," the man says into the loudspeaker, "please, you are exquisite just the way you are."

I press the knuckles of my right hand into my lips to keep from laughing. This is . . . this is delightful. Apparently, this guy has come here to court Second Aunt.

"Oh, Abi, you always know the perfect thing to say," Ma calls out.

Abi? That sounds familiar. I narrow my eyes as I scour my

memories for a mention of his name. When the memory does resurface, it hits me like a tank filled with rifle-touting men. Because Abi is the freaking mafia lord that my mom and aunts had told me about back when we were in Oxford. Abraham Lincoln Irawan, the guy who was infatuated with Second Aunt when they were teens and joined the mafia to impress her. Oh my god. Why in the world is Abi, a literal gangster, here in our front yard? I look at the procession of black cars again, and this time, they stop being impressive and are instead terrifying. Of course he has a cavalcade with him. They've probably got guns and all sorts of weapons inside each vehicle.

"Are you okay?" Nathan places a hand on my back and rubs gently. "You look so pale."

"That's ah—that guy is a mafia lord."

Nathan frowns. "Uh. What?"

"Yeah, exactly." I don't have time to explain before Second Aunt pops her head out the window again, this time sans hair curlers.

"Abi, what in the world are you doing here?" she yells in Indonesian.

Abi spreads his arms wide and says, "Your sister Mimi told me that you're back in Jakarta, so I have come to pay my respects for Chinese New Year. I had to see you, look upon your beautiful face once again, my darling Enjelin."

Wow, he's really laying it on thick. I can't help but grin at that. Then I feel insane for smiling, because hello, the guy's literally called the "Scourge of Jakarta." Also, after the awful mess that was our wedding, I have had enough of anything that might even come close to being illegal.

"Aw, he's a romantic," Nathan says, wrapping his thick

arms around me. I lean back against him, taking comfort from his warmth.

"He's a mafia lord," I remind him.

"You're ridiculous," Second Aunt snaps, but her grin is visible miles away. "Go home to your wife!"

Abi looks affronted. "I don't have a wife. I've been in love with you all my life. When you left the country, you took my heart with you."

"Tch," Second Aunt snorts, flapping fiercely at him with one hand while primping her hair with her other hand. She sniffs, turning away to hide the smile that has taken over her face. In a weird way, the scene is reminiscent of the iconic balcony scene in *Romeo and Juliet*, and I can't help but go a bit soft inside at how obvious Second Aunt's glee is.

Then another window slides open and Big Aunt's head pops out. "Who is being so noisy?" she booms.

Even from all the way in my room, I can see Abi tensing, straightening up. "Uh, greetings, Dajie," he says, using the Chinese honorific for "Big Sis." "I'm sorry for disturbing you—"

"He's here to pay his respects to me," Second Aunt snaps. "Nothing to do with you."

Big Aunt seems to swell up in size, her ample chest ballooning as she draws breath. I feel Nathan's chest stiffening. Everyone must be holding their breath right now. I for one am glad that Big Aunt's displeasure isn't aimed at me.

Abi hurriedly says, "Ah, I'm here to pay my respects to all of you. Dajie, please accept this token of my respect." He waves a hand, and black-clad men climb out of the second car, each one carrying a hamper piled high with an assortment of gifts. He turns to Second Aunt and his face softens. "And for you, my lovely angel, Enjelin." He waves again, and yet more car doors open, a stream of gift-bearing men striding toward the house.

Second Aunt's mouth purses and she bats her eyelashes demurely while Big Aunt scoffs. Next to Big Aunt, a huge puff of hair pokes out, followed by Fourth Aunt's face moments later. "Dajie, I asked him to come here. Would it be okay if he comes inside the house? Join our family for Chinese New Year?"

Big Aunt can never say no to Fourth Aunt. With a long, dramatic sigh, Big Aunt nods. Then she calls down, "But no hanky-panky, you hear me? There are children about."

Nathan laughs. "Hanky-panky? Haven't heard that one in a while. And isn't Second Aunt in her fifties? Surely if she wants hanky, it's fine."

I sigh. "When will you learn that you're never too old to be scolded like a child by Big Aunt?"

In the driveway, Abi is nodding vehemently and saying, "Of course, we will be so well-behaved." He comes out of the car with a triumphant grin. Flanked by the staggering procession of gift-bearing men, Abi Lincoln Irawan, the Scourge of Jakarta, walks up the front steps and into our family home.

The next few minutes are spent in a flurry as Nathan and I rush to get dressed for the Chinese New Year celebration. Ma has prepared outfits for us that she deemed appropriate: a qipao for me and a button-down shirt for Nathan, both of them made out of the same red batik cloth. I love batik, I adore how every piece of batik cloth is unique, each one hand-painted with painstaking detail. This particular one is illustrated with a golden dragon, swirling like smoke and adorned with plumerias.

"Wow," Nathan says when he's zipped me up, his eyes riveted on my chest.

"Stop staring, you perv."

"But—I—but you look—wow." He swallows.

I smack his hand, laughing. "None of that. We need to go downstairs and meet everyone now." I wiggle a bit, trying to get comfortable in my dress. All that rich French food hasn't done my waistline any favors.

Nathan gives a rueful sigh. "Okaaay, if we must."

Noises come through the wall and I shush him. Together, we go to the wall and press our ears against it. Next door is the guest room shared by Second Aunt and Ma, and evidently, they are having some sort of crisis.

"Aduh, I can't believe Mimi didn't tell me she asked Abi to come!" Second Aunt is wailing in Indonesian.

"Typical Mimi," Ma says.

"How do I look?"

"You look very good, Erjie."

"Only 'very good'?" Second Aunt wails again. "I need to look more than just 'good.' I need to look . . . you know, effortlessly gorgeous."

"But you do. You always do."

"Aiya, I messed up the eyeshadow!" Second Aunt cries.

Poor Second Aunt. I bite back my laugh as I straighten up. "I've never heard her this excited." Not even when she found out I'd accidentally killed Ah Guan. It's really nice, seeing my mom and aunts in a tizzy over something that, for once, has nothing to do with me. "I'm going to go help out. I'll see you downstairs?"

"Okay." Nathan kisses me and makes his way downstairs as I head into Second Aunt's room.

It takes another fifteen minutes of fussing before Ma and I manage to convince Second Aunt that effortless gorgeousness has been achieved. By the time we're done, the noise from downstairs has reached fever pitch. Apparently, in addition to Abi, the rest of our huge, overbearing family and all of the kids, hopped up on Chinese New Year sweets, have arrived. There are merry shouts and loud laughter booming through the large house. Second Aunt brushes down her emerald-green qipao and stands ramrod straight. Ma and I flank her on either side, and as we walk down the stairs, there is a hush. Eyes ping-pong back and forth from Abi to Second Aunt. When I look at him, my heart melts. The only way I can describe the expression on his face is reverent. He's gazing at Second Aunt like she's every daydream of his come true. It's humbling.

It's also kind of fun to see this side of Second Aunt. Even Ma, her arm linked with Second Aunt's, seems to be reveling in the glow. They both look suddenly young, their faces bright and flushed with color. Second Aunt's cherry-red lips are pursed into a shy, repressed smile, but Ma is openly beaming, so obviously joyous for her sister. I want to hug them both. It feels like Ma and I are giving Second Aunt away at her wedding or something. Below us, Big Aunt is standing with her arms crossed and an expression of disapproval, but her eyes are twinkling, and I have a feeling that she won't stand in Second Aunt's way of a happily ever after. Next to her, Fourth Aunt is grinning like the Cheshire cat, clasping her hands below her chin so that her newly manicured talons are visible. Behind them is the rest of the family, over eighty people all clustered together, looking up at us.

When we finally reach the bottom step, there is a collective *ahh*, and Abi rushes forward, his eyes glued to Second Aunt, and clasps her hands. For a moment, they both stare at each other, unspeaking, and the amount of emotion and history between them is so thick it's almost solid. In a flash, I see them as teenagers, both of them gangly and awkward, exchanging shy glances at each other, him watching her as she cycles home from school.

"Enjelin." Abi's voice is hoarse with emotion.

"Abi." Second Aunt gives him a slight, coy smile. God, who knew she had it in her?

"You look beautiful." Without taking his eyes off hers, Abi leans down and brings Second Aunt's hand up. His lips lightly graze her knuckles. The world turns soft and warm, like the entire universe has just gone "Awww."

Even through her thick makeup, Second Aunt's cheeks are visibly red. She turns her face ever so slightly away from him, fluttering her eyelashes, and scolds him. "Oh, you're so full of it."

"It's true. I don't know how, but you've hardly aged at all. Or rather, you have, but like a limited edition Patek Philippe." Interesting metaphor, could use a bit of work, but the sentiment behind it is sweet, I guess.

"Or maybe like a fine wine?" someone in the crowd suggests.

"I think a vintage Patek Philippe is better," someone else says.

"I prefer Chopard myself."

"Ahem." Big Aunt narrows her eyes at them, and everyone falls silent.

They both look over at Big Aunt. "Is that all you have to

say to my sister after all these years? Is everything just based on her looks?"

Abi quails slightly before turning back to Second Aunt. "Of course not." He clears his throat. "Ah, uh." My heart goes out to the poor man as he visibly struggles to find something appropriate and meaningful to say to Second Aunt in front of Big Aunt's unwavering glower. "Xin nian kuai le," he says finally.

Seriously?! Two lovebirds reunited after decades, and all he can come up with is "Happy New Year?" It's such a lolsob moment. Nathan catches my eye, and it's obvious he's barely holding back his laughter.

"Xin nian kuai le, Abi," Second Aunt murmurs quietly, and goose bumps erupt across my arms, because though she's just said the same thing back to him, there is so much hidden meaning behind it. Again, I see them as teens, having to hide their affection for each other for whatever reason (probably Big Aunt) and heaping all of their emotions into a single, loaded sentence. Second Aunt and Abi exchange a glance. Electric.

"Xin nian kuai le!" Fourth Aunt hoots. The charged atmosphere breaks, everyone laughs and claps, and conversations resume. People shout well wishes at one another in Mandarin.

"Gong xi fa cai!"

"Nian nian you yu!"

Nathan walks toward me, and together the two of us make our way through the crowd, our hands clasped in front of our chests, one fist encircled inside the other in the traditional Chinese New Year greeting.

"Gong hay fat choi," Nathan says to Elsa and Jems in perfect Cantonese.

"Oh my, your Cantonese is amazing," Elsa says.

We're immediately joined by more cousins, all of whom are dying to meet Nathan. "He's gorgeous," my cousin Sofia says in my ear. I laugh and nod, gazing fondly at Nathan as he rattles off a string of flawless Cantonese new year greetings at the behest of the others.

The kids slip between people, clasping their little fists in front of their chests and shouting, "Gong xi fa cai! Hong bao na lai!" Wish you a prosperous year! Give us our red packets!

Growing up, this was my favorite part of the holiday. Married couples have to give out red packets filled with money to unmarried people and children. My cousins and I had a ton of fun going around wishing people a happy new year before demanding our red packets. The grown-ups would purse their lips and tell us off for being rude, but no one could resist our cuteness, and we would end the day by opening our red packets and counting the spoils of war.

I reach into my prepared bag, filled to bursting with red packets, and give half of the stack to Nathan. The rest of my cousins do the same, and we all hand out red packets to the kids, who hug us before running away to find more victims to extort red packets from. Abi's voice booms above the clamor.

"I have brought red packets also!" He waves with flourish, and one of his henchmen—er, assistants—staggers forward under the weight of a humongous gift basket piled high with red packets.

The kids shriek with joy and there's a mad rush, but their parents manage to grab them and hold them, their little legs kicking in the air. "One by one," one of the parents scolds.

"I technically can't give them out because I'm unmarried," Abi says, emphasizing the word "unmarried" with a wink at Second Aunt.

Big Aunt nods. "Meddy, Nathan, since you two are the newlyweds, you can give them out."

Nathan puffs out his chest and I roll my eyes. It's honestly adorable how eager he is to please Big Aunt. We each take a pile of red packets, and one by one, the kids are loosened from their parents' grips and they scurry toward us, shout "Gong xi fa cai!" in a single rushed breath, grab a red packet, and run off. The older kids are more reserved, walking instead of running, and smiling shyly as they mumble their well wishes to us. I can't believe how much my nieces and nephews have grown since the last time I saw them. I barely recognize many of them, and my heart squeezes at the realization that I've missed out on so much of their lives. I try to sear every face into my memory, taking the time to hug each one of them before they can escape.

When the last red packet has been handed out, we all go to the dining room, where once again, every available surface has been covered with plates of food. This time, there are a lot more desserts than usual, because sweet foods signify a hope for a sweet year ahead.

There is a mix of Chinese and Indonesian sweets. Lapis Surabaya, a notoriously rich Indonesian layered cake that uses no fewer than thirty egg yolks per loaf; nian gao, a caramel-brown sticky rice cake that's been cut into thin slices and deep fried to crunchy, chewy perfection; fried sesame balls the size of my fist; and about a dozen other sweet dishes, each one more decadent than the last.

"Ayo, makan," Fourth Aunt calls out. "Dajie made a lot of these cakes."

Big Aunt nods with barely suppressed pride.

"Big Aunt, how in the world did you have time to make them? You arrived in Jakarta only yesterday morning," I gasp.

Big Aunt's chin lifts. "Discipline, Meddy. If you got discipline, you can do anything."

Why does even an innocent question get the kind of reply that makes me feel chastised? But my cousins are around me, and they all laugh and share a look with me, and I feel my heart expanding because I'm not alone. Nathan squeezes my hand, and when I look up at him, I find him gazing at me with complete understanding, and I know then that we both feel like we've found our home.

The rest of the day passes by in a blur of eating, games with my cousins and the kids, one hour melting into the next in a haze of laughter. At some point, Abi leaves, saying he has to pay his respects to his family, and Second Aunt deflates like a punctured balloon until he assures her that he will be back first thing in the morning.

Right after lunch, Big Aunt and a few of the other aunties march into the kitchen to prep the dishes for dinner, even though all of us have been soundly defeated by lunch. I insist that I can't eat another bite, but dinner turns out to be so delicious that we all end up stuffing our faces once more.

Later that night, when everyone has gone home, Nathan and I slump on the couch, my head nestled against his arm, both of us muttering and laughing softly as we rehash the events of the day. Everyone else has retired to their bedrooms for the night, and I'm ready to pass out from exhaustion, but at the same time, my mind is buzzing from endorphins, from the sheer excitement of everything. I hadn't dared to hope that introducing Nathan to my larger family would go so well, but everything has far exceeded my expectations. My cousins and aunties and uncles adore him, and he sees them as the family he's always wished for.

"Maybe we should move here," he says.

I snort and glance up at him. He's only half joking, I realize. "Seriously? But what about your work?"

He shrugs. "I travel to Asia for work half the time anyway. It would make sense to use Jakarta as my hub. And your family is amazing, and the little ones . . ." He sighs, smiling, and rests his chin on the top of my head. "Seeing all of your little nieces and nephews running around, playing with one another . . . it made me realize that that's the kind of childhood I want to give our kids."

Warmth floods my chest. "Nathan—"

The rest of the sentence is cut short by a frantic hammering from the front door. Something about the knocking jars me, piercing straight through the satiated haze. I jump up, all of my instincts screaming. Something is wrong. This isn't the kind of knock that people use when all is well. Nathan must have come to the same conclusion because he's already halfway to the door. He pauses, turns to look at me, and gestures at me to stand behind him. I almost laugh out loud. After everything we've been through—the accidental murder, the so-called mafia scare—he still feels the need to protect me. I can't decide if it's infuriating or endearing.

Together, we approach the front door. I jump when the banging starts again. Whoever's outside really wants to be let in. God, I wish we weren't the only two people left down here.

"Who's there?" Nathan calls out in his deepest voice.

"It's me, Abi."

"Oh." Our breaths release in a relieved whoosh. It feels as

though all of my muscles have turned to water, and a small, shocked laugh startles out of my mouth. Nathan unlatches the lock and opens the door. I feel silly to have been so scared just moments ago. But then Abi strides into the house, his face awash with naked, primal fear, and my insides clench up, a steel grip seizing them with ruthlessness. No one would wear that expression unless something was very, very wrong. And when Abi speaks, the words confirm my worst nightmares.

"You must help me," he gasps. "Otherwise we're all doomed."

4

This can't be happening. It can't be. But wait, what *is* happening?

These are the thoughts swirling through my mind as I creep up the staircase, careful not to wake anyone up. I knock softly at Ma's door before going inside. Ma and Second Aunt are sitting in their beds, hair rollers on, both of them scrolling through their phones, probably watching one of the dozens of fake health news videos that they will then forward to the family WhatsApp group with the caption: "You see, if you want to be healthy, avoid sunlight for one hundred days!" The normalcy of the scene weighs me down. I wish I could lie and say "Just wanted to wish you a good night" and then leave them alone.

But just as I think that, Ma glances up, catches the expression on my face, and lowers her phone. "Aduh, Meddy. What now?"

"Yes, who you kill this time?"

"Nobody! Why's that always your first assumption?"

Second Aunt narrows her eyes. "Every time you call or you come into our room late at night, wearing that miserable face, is either someone die, or someone about to die. So, which one is it?"

I put my hands on my hips. "Well, you'll be glad to know that for once, none of this is my fault. Abi's downstairs, and he says he's in trouble."

Second Aunt shoots straight up like a meerkat. "Abi is in trouble?"

I blink, and she's out of the bed, leaping out of it with the fluidity and speed of a ninja. Wow, I guess Tai Chi really does keep you young. She moves like a whirlwind across the room, tearing off the curlers from her hair. When she reaches the makeup table, she swipes on a lick of lipstick, slaps some rouge onto her cheeks, and steps back, glaring at the mirror. "Okay. Let's go. Quick!"

Ma is still struggling out of bed. Second Aunt tuts at her. "Why you move so slowly? Cepat!"

"Iya, iya," Ma sighs as she finds a robe and shrugs it on. "Okay, ready."

Second Aunt side-eyes her. "You not even bothering to put on lipstick? Tsk. Don't blame me if Abi thinks you are the older sister." She primps her hair and slinks out of the room. Is it my imagination or do her hips sway more exaggeratedly than usual?

I exchange a glance with Ma, who smiles softly. "Been a while since I see Second Aunt act like this."

I bite back my smile. I know so little about what Ma and the aunties were like when they were younger. There are only a few faded photos retained from their youth, so every time I get a glimpse at what they must have been like back when they were still living in Jakarta, it's a priceless moment that I like to savor. I can see Second Aunt in her teens, walking past Abi's house on her way to school. I can see her giving him a half-shy, half-flirtatious side glance that would set his heart racing. She would've noticed the way his Adam's apple bobbed up and down as he gulped at the sight of her, and she would've laughed a little and swayed her hips ever so slightly, feeling his eyes on her as she walked away. Oh, Second Aunt. Who would've thought?

But now, there are far more pressing issues at hand. I link arms with Ma and the two of us make our way out of the room, past Big Aunt and Fourth Aunt's room. Their door is ajar, the room empty, so I guess they've gone downstairs as well. I grimace. Big Aunt is probably already deep into a lecture, telling Abi off for showing up so late at night. We hasten our step and hurry down.

As it turns out, they're not in the living room but in the study, and all of them are looking very somber and worried. Immediately, my anxiety spikes. It's okay, I tell myself. This time, it's not my problem. I mean, of course it's something I would help out with, but it's not actually anything I've done. Or is it? No, there is no way that this could be related to me. I haven't killed anyone, I haven't hired anyone . . . I'm clean.

Ma joins Big Aunt and Fourth Aunt on the sofa, while Second Aunt is perched on the other sofa, next to Abi, her hand on his arm. Nathan leans against the back wall. I go up to him and he puts his arm around me. "It'll be okay," he whispers, as though he could sense just how anxious I am. I nod and try for a smile, but it feels heavy and forced.

Abi clears his throat before speaking in Indonesian. "I'm very sorry for disturbing all of you."

"Eh, wait," Ma says, waving her hand at Abi. "Can you speak English? So my son-in-law can understand."

My heart swells. That's so sweet and thoughtful of Ma.

"Ah, yes, of course," Abi says in flawless English. His accent is vaguely British. "As I was saying, I'm so sorry for disturbing all of you. I wouldn't have come here like this, in the middle of the night, if I had any other choice."

Big Aunt shakes her head. "I knew it." Her voice is sharp with disapproval. "I knew you are bad egg, Abi. Even when you are kid, I already know, very bad egg, always up to no good."

I'm surprised her face doesn't melt under the furious heat of Second Aunt's glare. Second Aunt shifts, straightening up, her chest ballooning and her nostrils flaring. "Some people," Second Aunt declares, "cannot help but jump to crazy conclusion. Is a bad habit. They are always wrong, but they think they so smart, keep on jumping to very embarrassing conclusion."

Some terrified survival instinct kicks in and I blurt out, "*Anyway.* What's the matter, Om Abi? Anything we can help you with?"

Abi nods vigorously, his face a mixture of gratefulness and fear. His gaze skitters to Big Aunt before dropping to his hands. "Ah, well, there has been an unfortunate mistake. The gift baskets that I brought over earlier today . . ."

"Aha!" Big Aunt barks. "I knew it. You want them back, right? You cannot have them back. You already give out the gifts, how you can ask for them back? So lose face."

"No, not at all," Abi says quickly, raising his palms in front of him, as if to shield himself from Big Aunt's wrath. "They are all meant for you and your family, of course."

"Hmph," Big Aunt snorts, deflating slightly.

"Ah, well, all of them, that is, except for one." Abi wrings his hands, looking like he would die to have a hole to crawl into and hide. "One of the baskets, you see, was actually meant for somebody else."

This time, it's Second Aunt who snaps. "What?! You going after some other hussy? Hanh? You come here and give me all this gift, then you go to her house, give her more gifts?"

"What? No. It's not like that at all, wait—"

"You tell me which hussy is it now. Aha, I know, must be that Halena, right? Ever since we young, she is always drooling after this boy and that boy. I haven't seen her in over thirty years, but I bet you she is just as genit as before."

Abi looks at the rest of us with panicked eyes. He's so obviously out of his depth that I can't help feeling sorry for him. "Second Aunt," I call out, "maybe it's worth letting Om Abi explain?" *Before jumping to conclusions*, I silently add.

Abi nods. "Yes, please, Enjelin, it really isn't what you think."

Second Aunt takes an enraged breath and releases it dramatically. Abi reaches out for her hand, but she yanks it away. "Fine. You continue," she snaps.

Big Aunt is openly beaming at this.

Abi clears his throat. "So as I was saying, one of the baskets was meant for somebody else. That person is the director and majority owner of the Ruo Fa Group."

Nathan releases a low whistle.

"What is it?" I frown at him.

"That's a major multinational corporation. Some of my partners are vying to do business with them."

"Yes," Abi says, "they're sort of a big deal." He laughs weakly. "So you see, that's why I had to come back here to get the gift basket—"

"Aiya," Ma says, "you were here, you can see for yourself that all the gift baskets are all taken apart and give away already! Why not you just get a new gift basket for this Ruo Fa Group director? We can help you with it. My Dajie can even bake her masterpiece cakes to put inside the basket. No one can resist Dajie's cakes."

Big Aunt harrumphs again, but she's also smiling slightly at that.

"Er, well, you see, it's about what was inside the gift basket." Abi scratches his chin, looking utterly miserable. "That particular gift basket contained all the red packets. And before you offer to give me money for it, it's not about the money. One of the red packets contains a title deed to a large plot of land. Land that's very strategically located in Jakarta. Ruo Fa Group has been gunning for it for almost a decade now, but I've held fast to it all this time. But now, after all this time, I've reached an agreement with their director, and I am giving her the land as a show of good faith."

This is greeted by a moment of shocked silence.

Then Second Aunt hisses, "Her? I knew it was a she."

"Really? That's your takeaway from all that?" I mutter.

"Aduh, all the red packets given away to the kids," Ma says.

Abi nods forlornly. "I know, I was there." He pinches the bridge of his nose. "Trust me, I've replayed the scene in my mind countless times. All those red packets going out to dozens of children . . ." He ends the sentence with a defeated groan. "I really, really need that title deed back, otherwise . . ." His voice wavers with a note of fear bordering on shrill panic.

Ice tingles down my spine. Sure, from a business stand-point, this sounds bad. But Abi is positively fearful. I mean, his hands are actually shaking, for god's sake. That's a little bit over the top, right?

"Om Abi," I say, "can I ask, what's the worst thing that can happen if you fail to give the title deed to this Ruo Fa Group director?"

Abi's eyes meet mine, and the chill spreads from my spine to the rest of my body. My scalp crawls. His eyes are filled with pure, animalistic desperation. "I—I don't dare to think of the consequences of that, my dear," he whispers. He tries for a smile, but it ends up a ghastly grimace.

What the hell is going on? What am I missing here? "If it's a business deal, then surely the worst that can happen is that the deal falls through?" I look around the room at the various expressions everyone is wearing.

Big Aunt appears triumphant. Second Aunt is pursing her lips at Abi, and I'm not sure if it's meant to be disapproving or coquettish. Ma is looking very worried, and Fourth Aunt is watching with horrified glee, her eyes wide and shining. The last time Fourth Aunt had that look was when she was about to look at Ah Guan's body. Oh god. It clicks into place then.

They'd said, hadn't they, in Oxford, that Abi was a crime lord. A mafia. A gangster. I don't know, whatever the terms are here. But all that talk about Abi being a criminal was no exaggeration.

"Oh my god," I whisper. "This is a mafia thing, isn't it? The head of the Ruo Fa Group, she's also some—I don't know—some cartel leader?"

"Whoa, whoa," Abi cries, holding up his palms. "We're definitely not gangsters. We're all law-abiding citizens here. There is no such thing as a crime syndicate here in Jakarta."

He glances around the room, as if searching for a hidden camera, and says, loudly, "We all respect and follow the law. We are very law-abiding. I don't even jaywalk."

We all stare at him. This is the most unconvincing thing I have ever heard.

"Weren't you referred to in newspapers as the 'Scourge of Jakarta'?" I point out as politely as I can. "I'm sure I've seen articles about how you've had people murdered. Not that I'm judging or anything," I add quickly, in case I accidentally offend him and he has us killed.

Abi laughs. "Oh god, no. Those aren't newspapers, my dear, they're tabloids. They also write about women giving birth to half-goat demons, and family curses, and all sorts of rubbish. My competitors, they like to feed these lies about me to the tabloids to tank my reputation." He gives Second Aunt a pleading look. "I promise you, I am a law-abiding citizen. All of my businesses are legit."

I take in Abi's tattooed arms, noticing how a bit of tattooed skin peeks out from above the collar of his shirt. I can totally imagine his entire torso and back and arms covered in a dragon tattoo. It's too easy to see him holding a cigarette casually while ordering someone to be tortured or killed. Despite his civility and his fear, he exudes an aura of strength, a certain rough quality that hints at a life of danger.

The uneasiness spreads across my entire being, and I place a hand on my stomach, feeling ill. There's a sensation of needing to get as far away from Abi and his terrifying problem as I can. "I don't know if I want to be involved in this—"

"I don't want any of you involved in this," Abi says quickly. "But the thing is, the Ruo Fa Group will know that this was where I lost the title deed, and they will send men to—ah, ask for it. Unless we find it first."

The way he says "ask for it" triggers alarm bells. Somehow, I don't think he meant people politely asking where the title deed might be. Visions of my family, of my little nieces and nephews, screaming with fear as their loved ones are tortured in front of them, swim across my mind, and my knees nearly give out. I clutch at Nathan, and he keeps a firm hold on me. His jaw is clenched. I know he has sensed the danger as well.

"Okay, simple," Ma says, with a clap of her hands. "In the morning, we call everyone and see who got the title deed. No big deal!"

Abi nods eagerly. "Yes, that's a wonderful plan. Wonderful! But ah . . ." He stretches his mouth into a terrified grin, glancing at Big Aunt before glancing away again. "We need to go to the Ruo Fa Group director's house now to apologize and beg—ah, I mean, negotiate—to have more time to locate the title deed."

"What?" We all say this at the same time, and Abi quails under our collective surprise.

"Yes, er, you see, it's important that we don't anger her, because—"

"Because she's a mafia lord and might kill us if we anger her?" I cry.

Abi laughs, a shrill sound. "No! Of course not. Oh, you kids are so dramatic. Ha. Ha-ha." He clears his throat. "She might—you know, just—be a bit offended, that's all."

"And what happens when she gets offended?" Nathan says.

Abi's mouth opens and closes. Opens again. "Ah . . . nothing good." He laughs weakly. He looks like he's about this close to peeing himself, this man who's all ropey muscles and fearsome tattoos.

"Okay," Second Aunt says, looking resolute. "I go with you. I explain to this woman what happen."

"I'll come too!" Fourth Aunt pipes up. She's still wearing that expression of horrified glee, grinning like a kid on Chinese New Year. "I'm not going to miss this for the world."

Big Aunt frowns. "I come also."

"Yes, me also," Ma says.

For a split second, I see myself saying No. *I won't come. I'm staying out of it.*

The thought lasts less than a heartbeat. Because of course I will come. How can I possibly not, when my mom and aunts have had my back at every unfortunate turn of events? They never even questioned it; they were all immediately in for the ride. Guilt gnaws at my belly for even hesitating to go along with them.

But why do they need to get involved here? The whole thing smells bad. It smells of danger. No matter how hard Abi insists that there's nothing fishy going on, it oozes of hidden perils. The smart thing to do here would be for all of us to wash our hands of it.

"Would it be possible to have a chat with my family before we decide on anything?" I say to Abi.

A shadow crosses his face, and for just a moment, it looks thunderous. My heart stops. He looks every bit like the mafia lord he claims he isn't. Every part of me wants to run away and disappear from his sight.

"Meddy," Ma scolds, "so rude. Don't be so rude to our guest, ya?"

I fight all of my instincts and stand firm. My skin crawls,

as though it's trying to get as far away from all of their disapproving stares as possible.

Then Abi smiles. "It's fine. Yes, of course, I'll leave you all
alone to discuss. But I do have to remind you that we are running out of time." With that, he stands and leaves the room.

I release my breath.

"Why you do that?" Second Aunt hisses. "You see, now
you offend him. So disrespectful to your elders!"

"Sorry, I—I just—look, I feel really awful for Om Abi, I do.
But it sounds really fishy."

There's silence for a moment, then Big Aunt starts sniffing
the air. "Mm, yes, there is bad smell in here."

Second Aunt sniffs too. "I think moldy. Maybe the curtains
not washed regularly, aiya, so dirty."

"No," I groan. "I meant—ah, don't you guys find it suspicious? Do you actually believe Om Abi when he says he's not
a mafia lord?"

"Oh, he is for sure one hundred percent a gangster," Fourth
Aunt mutters.

"Right, exactly!" I cry.

"Tch, don't listen to Fourth Aunt." Ma rolls her eyes. "She
think everyone is bu san bu si because she is like that. Abi say
he is law-abiding. If he is not law-abiding, why he say he is
law-abiding?"

Second Aunt nods vigorously.

I flap at them, flabbergasted. Are they seriously this naive?
"Because he's trying to lure us into a false sense of security?
No bad guy is going to be like, 'Oh yeah, I'm a bad guy.' Of
course he'll say he's a legit businessman. But I'm telling you, I
sense danger. He's telling us to go to a rival mafia group's estate. Does that not strike you as massively unsafe?"

"Aduh, Meddy," Second Aunt sighs. "Why you so drama?"

"Yes, you always overly reacting," Ma agrees. "Everything so over-the-top all the time, Meddy. Honestly, is very tiring, you know."

"*What?*" I feel as though my head is about to burst from all the oh-hell-no going through it. Nathan, who is very low-emotion and down to earth, maybe has the right to tell me I'm over-the-top in comparison. But my *mother* and my *aunts?* Hell to the no. I struggle to keep my voice even. "All of my life, you guys have been overreacting to every little thing that happens. I've always been the level-headed one."

Big Aunt frowns. "I don't think so, Meddy. I think we all are always so wise, guiding you to become proper person."

I grind my teeth so hard I swear my back molars crack. "I—yes, you've always guided me well, but you've also always done it in the most melodramatic way possible." They all start to say something, and I quickly add, "Not that it matters now. I don't even know why we're talking about this. What matters now is that this feels really shady and dangerous."

Second Aunt says, "I tell you, all this is normal Indonesian business. Nothing illegal. Right, Nathan?"

All eyes are suddenly on Nathan, who stiffens under the sudden onslaught of attention. He tugs at the collar of his shirt and clears his throat. "Um . . . I mean, I'm not sure that I have enough information to make a judgment call here . . ."

"Tch," Second Aunt tuts. "Yes, but you are businessman, so you must know all about businesspeople. What you know about Abi's business?"

Nathan scratches his chin. "Well, I do know that Ruo Fa Group is highly sought after by many of my business partners—"

"You see?" Second Aunt says triumphantly.

"But I know nothing about the director as a person," he finishes, but no one is paying attention. Second Aunt and Ma are already nodding and getting ready to leave.

"Meddy, you coming or not?" Ma says, almost as an afterthought.

Oh god, if only I could say no and still live with myself. I try one last time. "I don't think any of us should go. I think we should let Abi handle this, and in fact, I think we should fly back to LA tomorrow, because this feels really wrong."

"Will be okay, Meddy." Big Aunt pats my arm kindly. "I be there, make sure they don't get in trouble."

I want to scream at all of them, remind them that they're elderly aunties, for crying out loud. What's Big Aunt going to do when faced with a houseful of gangsters? I glance with desperation at Nathan, who raises his eyebrows at me. The words are unspoken, but I know him well enough by now to know what he's saying: *It's up to you.*

There's no choice. I exhale, my shoulders slumping with defeat. "We'll come. Of course we will." There is no way I'm about to let my mother and aunts stroll into a potential mafia lord's house without me around to get them out.

5

Ma and the aunties chatter excitedly as they pile into Abi's minivan. From the way they're clucking about how eager they are to see the director's estate, which must be very grand, you'd think they were on their way to see a friend and not someone who might potentially have us all killed. Once we're all bundled in, Abi tells his chauffeur to go, and I gaze longingly at our house as we get farther and farther from it. Nathan rubs my arm.

"It's going to be okay."

"I wish I could believe that."

He gives me a sympathetic smile. "I know, but chances are, it'll be fine."

"When it comes to my family, chances are, it won't be fine." I raise my eyebrows meaningfully, and I see the past two years replaying in Nathan's mind. Ah Guan's death, followed by his family taking their revenge during our wedding. He grimaces.

"Well, maybe third time's the charm," he says finally. I love him for trying to comfort me despite the odds.

I clear my throat and raise my voice to be heard above the aunties' chatter. "So, should we come up with a game plan for when we arrive?"

"What this game plan?" Big Aunt says with a sniff of disapproval. "Why you talking about playing video games like a kid?"

Damn it. I shouldn't have said "game plan." Big Aunt is very against video games. She's convinced they're the reason for everything bad with the younger generations. "Sorry, I didn't mean 'game' as in 'video game.' I meant more like, a strategy. We should have a plan in place."

"Yes, Meddy, good idea," Ma says loyally. She turns to Big Aunt. "Meddy doesn't play video game, you know she is very good girl. I raise her well. I tell her, don't waste time playing video game, later your eyes go blind."

"Um, yeah. Anyway, so what should we do when we get there?"

"I would suggest letting Om Abi do all the talking, since he knows the director personally?" Nathan says.

"Oh no." Abi shakes his head like a terrified schoolkid. "If it were to come from me, I think she might suspect me of lying. It would be preferable if you folks could explain to her what happened."

Once again, alarm bells go off in my head. Abi is so jumpy, and what kind of business dealing would occur between two untrusting parties? But I don't have a choice, so I might as well make the best of it. "Okay, well, maybe Nathan and I can explain to her—"

Big Aunt waves me into silence. "Have you kids be the one

explaining? Very insulting. I will talk. I am head of family, I explain."

"Why you?" Second Aunt snaps. "Is my—" She hesitates, glancing at Abi, and I feel the word "boyfriend" almost slithering out of her mouth before she swallows it back. "Abi is my friend," she says finally. "So I will explain."

Big Aunt snorts. "You? You will just end up insulting here and insulting there. No, I am best at explain."

Oh god, this isn't going well. "Nathan and I will explain!" I half shout. "Because . . . ah . . . ." I scour my mind for possible excuses as to why it should be us and not them. "Because it'll show that you've all done such a great job bringing me up. I'll be so, so respectful, I promise."

Nathan squeezes my hand and adds, "Yes, we'll do it. We'll make you all proud."

Ma reaches over and pats him on the cheek. "Oh, Nathan, we all so proud of you already."

I don't know why they're proud of him but not of me, but whatever.

"Thanks, Ma," says Nathan the suck-up. "We'll just apologize to her, explain what happened, and assure her that first thing in the morning, we'll find the title deed and personally deliver it to her. Sound good?"

We all nod. His plan sounds so simple and straightforward that I can't help but feel bolstered by it. Short and sweet and to the point. She can't possibly take offense to that. We can do this. We'll be home and in bed within the hour. Right, yeah.

But then the car arrives at the front of the estate, and my newfound confidence falters. In front of us is a gilded, ornate gate. The chauffeur opens his window and speaks into the intercom. "I have Mr. Abraham Lincoln Irawan here."

There is a buzz, and the gates swing open, revealing a massive sprawl of manicured lawn, complete with a Grecian water fountain and about half a dozen black-clad guards milling about.

"Are those rifles?" I croak. "They are, aren't they? They're actual rifles. She's got actual armed guards."

Abi laughs. "Oh, my dear, they're fake rifles, of course. Firearms are illegal in Indonesia, don't you know? Only authorized personnel are allowed to have them."

I stare at him. "Why would anyone have guards carrying fake firearms?"

"To deter potential burglars, to impress visitors, all sorts of reasons." He waves at us to get out of the car, and with growing apprehension, I climb out and stare at the behemoth of a mansion before us.

I'd thought that our family home was big, but this house dwarfs it completely. At least five stories high, it looks like an actual Indonesian castle, complete with beautiful stonework. No doubt its grandiosity is supposed to humble visitors, and it works. I feel completely out of my depth, and painfully aware of the discrepancy in power. Compared to the owner of this house, I am nothing but an ant, easily squashed and forgotten. I'm about to beg my family to turn around and go home—no, not even go home, but speed all the way to the airport and jump onto any plane leaving the country—when the front doors open.

A woman wearing a gray pantsuit, her hair tied into an elegant ponytail, stands before us. "Good evening, Mr. Irawan. Ms. Handoko is expecting you. Please, follow me."

We enter the foyer, where we are presented with a neat row of house slippers. We fumble to take off our shoes and put on the slippers, after which we are led into the main hall, so large that it feels like a stadium. It feels as though every available surface is adorned with a beautiful carving, or draped with rich velvet, or hung with a priceless painting. It's the most decadent room I have ever been in. The marble floors are so shiny that they reflect the many chandeliers hanging from the ceiling. As we are led deeper into the house, I jump when I pass by a marble pillar and spot yet another armed guard.

The rifles are fake, I tell myself. The problem is, I also do not believe myself at all.

We're led into a private elevator, because of course this be-hemoth of a house has a private elevator. The doors of the el-evator slide shut, enveloping us in uneasy silence. I look down at my feet to avoid making unwanted eye contact, and shrill laughter bubbles up my chest. With a huge amount of effort, I swallow it back down and force myself to take a deep breath. Keep it together, Meddy. So what if we're going deeper inside the abode of someone who is very likely a mafia lord? So what if we're surrounded by maybe-armed guards? We've done nothing wrong. Any sensible person would be able to see that we're Average Joes, harmless and sincere and well-meaning.

Okay, well, Average Joes who have murdered someone, but that was an accident, so it shouldn't count. Should it?

I glance around at the others, wondering if they look as nervous as I feel. Nathan is watching the numbers on the screen intently, his eyebrows knitted together in a thoughtful expression. I've often seen that same slight frown on his hand-some face, usually when he's trying to work out a knotty busi-ness deal. A small smile melts across my lips. Whenever he wears that expression, he'll come up with some brilliant solu-tion that nobody else would have thought of.

Big Aunt is glaring, eyes narrowed, at Abi, who is pretending not to notice the death glare she's giving him. Second Aunt is—oh! Is she? She is. She's holding Abi's hand. Ah! I want to grin, but it seems highly inappropriate given the situation, so I bite it back, wrestling my mouth into a neutral position. I probably look like I'm having a stroke. Ma is wringing her hands, obviously very anxious. Poor thing. She's probably wishing she could take a swig of her TCM right about now. Only Fourth Aunt looks like she's enjoying herself, smiling as she studies her ridiculous nails.

There's a *bing* and the doors slide open. We all pile out, obviously relieved at not having to be cooped up in such close quarters with one another. We're on the fourth floor, and as we walk out, our footsteps are swallowed by a lush, thick Turkish carpet. We're led down the beautiful hallway to a set of double doors at the very end. Our guide knocks softly at the door.

"Masuk," a voice calls out languidly.

Our guide opens the door with reverence, stands aside, and nods at us to go in. Big Aunt squares her shoulders, lifts her chin, and starts to stride forward, but Abi places his hand on her arm and murmurs, "Let me go in first." Big Aunt frowns, but acquiesces, and Abi adjusts the collar of his shirt and walks in. Big Aunt follows closely, striding in with her usual confidence, and the rest of us hurry after her like ducklings. Here goes nothing.

The room is massive and decorated in the lavish style of an eighteenth-century French palace. Lush carpeting, silk upholstery, baroque furniture, and huge vases of fresh flowers that fill the vast space with their spicy-sweet scent. Atop a grand sofa sits a woman in her late fifties. She's striking, her hair an icy silver that makes her look fresh and alert instead of old. It's puffed up, of course, in the usual huge Chinese-Indo hairstyle that defies gravity. Despite the fact that it's nearly midnight, her makeup is flawless, her lips colored in perfectly and her eyelids lined so sharply they could cut someone. She's giving me serious Michelle Yeoh vibes, including Michelle Yeoh's deadly martial arts ability.

Abi lowers his head in deference. "Julia, thank you for seeing us."

Julia lifts her chin and regards us slowly, almost lazily. But there is nothing lazy about those sharp eyes of hers. As they rove over me, I get the sense that she's reading all of my innermost thoughts and missing nothing at all. She waves her hand to one side and says, "Sit."

This is a whole new level of commanding presence. Not even Big Aunt dares to defy her. We all hurry to find a spot on the sofas opposite her. When we're all settled, Julia's lips quirk into a polite smile.

"Thank you for coming to my humble abode," she says in Indonesian. Then she seems to notice me straining to follow her words. She looks pointedly at me, then at Nathan, and without prompting, switches to British-accented English. "I said, thank you for coming to my humble abode."

"We're honored to be invited here," I blurt out. Then I mentally kick myself. Technically, were we even invited here? But it felt weird to not say anything.

"Mm." Julia's gaze slips over Ma and the aunts one by one, taking them all in.

Abi leans forward. "I wish to explain—"

Julia gives him a sharp look, and he falters before mumbling an apology. After a moment of excruciating silence, Julia says, "I'm pleased to make your acquaintance. I'm Julia Child Handoko. You may call me Julia Child."

Of course. She can't just be Julia Handoko. She's got to be named after some famous white person. I have to stifle another bubble of hysterical laughter at this. Everything about this is so unreal.

"So," Julia Child continues, "I understand that Abi here has failed to bring the title deed that I was promised."

Abi jerks up. "I didn't fail, I will bring it, but it might take some time—"

Once again, Julia Child silences him with a single look. When she does speak, she directs the question to us. "You all strike me as honest people. Not businesspeople." She gives a humorless laugh. "Save me from businessmen, each one is a bigger snake than the last." She levels her gaze at Nathan. "Well, obviously you're a businessman, but you're still young, still uncorrupted. Now, which of you will tell me the truth about what happened?"

For a moment, we all exchange panicked glances at one another. Then, true to our family's structure, Big Aunt nods and turns to face Julia Child. "I'm Friya Chan, head of the family," she says in Mandarin.

"A matriarch," Julia Child replies in equally smooth Mandarin, delight clearly written on her face. "Carry on."

"My family and I are only visiting for a week for the Chinese New Year celebrations. We have no connections to you or Abi, no loyalties to either party." Big Aunt shoots Abi another deadly look. "I don't even like Abi. Never trusted him."

"What?" Second Aunt cries. She turns to Julia Child. "She's just saying that because she's jealous that he likes me and not her."

Oh god. This can't be happening. Part of me wants to lunge

forward and tackle Second Aunt, but Ma is faster than I am. She pushes Second Aunt back and smiles at Julia Child. "So sorry about my older sister. She's a bit emotional because of . . . ah, her menopause."

Julia Child's eyebrows quirk up. "Oh? I've got lots of remedies for that. I'll have someone bring them up here."

Ma goes, "Ooh!" and looks utterly delighted. "What sort of remedies? Jamu?" Jamu is Indonesian traditional medicine, something Ma sometimes looks into as a side hobby.

"Some jamu, some traditional Chinese medicine, some Western medicine too."

"Wah!" Ma claps her hands together, her eyes lighting up like a kid entering Disneyland. "Yes, please, have someone bring up your collection. I would love to see it. I'm a bit of an expert in TCM, you know. I even subscribe to *Traditional Medicine Monthly* and I've been trying to—"

Fourth Aunt clears her throat. "Maybe this isn't the best time to talk about your drug habit?"

Ma glares at her. "It's not a drug habit, it's—"

Fourth Aunt flaps her hand at Ma and turns to Julia Child, pointedly ignoring Ma. "As my big sister was saying, we're only here for a visit. Now, I admit that maybe this was all triggered by me, because I was the one who called Abi to let him know that Erjie is in town. He came by the house this morning with all these gift baskets, which he generously gave to our family."

"*So* generous!" Second Aunt croons, smiling at Abi, who grins bashfully, scratching the back of his head like he's all of twelve years old.

"But so badly organized," Big Aunt sniffs. "It turns out one of those baskets was meant for you."

"The basket that contained the title deed," Abi adds. "It was in a red packet, nestled among other red packets. They were all meant for you, as a token of my respect."

Julia Child looks on impassively. "And what happened to all those red packets that were meant for me?"

I raise my hand. "We, um, we gave them out to the little ones."

"So you gave my red packets away." Julia Child's voice is icy cold with finality.

My mouth shuts, dread suddenly crushing me from all sides. I take a breath to say something else, some words of explanation or apology, but nothing comes out.

"I'm so sorry," Nathan says in his smooth, rich voice. "Meddy and I—it's our first Chinese New Year as a married couple, and we were so excited to finally be able to give out red packets to the kids. I might have rushed her into doing it."

I can't decide whether I'm grateful or frustrated at Nathan for taking on all of the blame for us. I stare up at him, wanting to hug him and kiss him, and also smack his gorgeous face.

Julia Child's gaze lands on him, and it's like she's taking him in for the first time. Her eyebrows rise just a smidgen, and her mouth stretches into a smile that reminds me of a shark. "What's your name, boy?"

"Nathan. Nathan Chan."

Her head tilts to the side. "Nathan Chan. Are you by chance Frederick Wong's business partner?"

Nathan nods, smiling with obvious relief. "We have a lot of deals together. He and I go all the way back to grad school."

"He's a snake," Julia Child says flatly.

Oh god. The dread solidifies into a fist and crunches into my heart. Nathan's smile disappears.

"I do not like smarmy young men who think they know more than I do about how to run my own business," she hisses.

"I—ah—I definitely don't think that," Nathan says quickly.

"Nathan is good boy," Ma pipes up in English. "Very good boy. Very filial and very respectful."

The other aunties all nod.

Julia Child narrows her eyes at Nathan. "Yes, I can see you're different from that greasy partner of yours. You need to keep an eye on him. He won't hesitate to stab you in the back, you know, you take my word on it."

Nathan nods. "I will. Thank you for the advice."

A corner of Julia Child's mouth quirks up. "I like you. Come here, boy."

With one last helpless glance at me, Nathan gets up and walks toward Julia Child. My insides clench, and I very nearly shout at him to stop but somehow manage not to do so. When he gets to her sofa, she pats a spot next to her, and he sits down gingerly, at the very edge of the sofa, as though he's ready to leap out and make a run for it at any moment. Julia Child's hand shoots out like a striking snake and grabs him by the chin.

"My, my," she muses, "they don't make jawlines like this very often." She turns his face this way and that. "Oof, very good nose. Very mancung." She smiles at me, her hand still clutched around his jawline. "He's a good-looking one, isn't he? He'll give you very handsome children, my dear."

"Aiya, this is why I always say, quickly have children," Ma cries with enthusiasm, seemingly having forgotten that her son-in-law is in the literal clutches of a mafia lord. "Very beautiful grandchildren."

"Yes, thank you." I force a smile. "Could I, um, could I have him back, please?"

Julia Child lets go of Nathan, who sags with obvious relief. "I'm afraid not, my dear."

It takes a second for her words to sink in. "I'm sorry?"

Julia Child leans back, looking relaxed, completely unperturbed. "My dear, I've been in this business long enough to know who has a killer instinct and who doesn't."

"What—"

"You, my dear girl, have it. So does your family." She nods at Ma and the aunties, who smile like she's told them they have beautiful eyes. I want to scream at them that it's not exactly a compliment she's giving them. She nods at Nathan. "But this one doesn't. He's an innocent babe. Look at him, so pure."

Nathan squares his shoulders, trying to look—I don't know—manly? Julia Child scoffs. "Oh, I'm sure you're good at what you do, dear." She pats his knee. "But you're not a criminal."

"We're not criminals!" I cry instinctively.

Julia Child looks at me. Then she looks at Ma and the aunties very pointedly, and again, I get the feeling that she's somehow reading our innermost thoughts. Somehow, I get the feeling that she knows exactly every bit of our dark pasts. The literal skeleton in our closet.

"You will get my title deed back no matter what," she says with finality. "In the meantime, sweet Nathan here will stay and accompany this old lady." She smiles at Nathan and pats his knee again.

"No." I start to stand up, but Big Aunt grabs my arm and pulls me back down.

Julia Child laughs. "Oh, young love. So energetic. So full of drama. You remember what that was like, Abi?" When she asks the question, her voice turns cold, all of the laughter leeching out of it.

Abi shifts uneasily, looking down at his hands. "Yessss."

"Please," I beg, "don't—"

"I won't let anything bad happen to him," Julia Child says. "He's here as my guest. We'll spoil him, don't you worry. But you will get me my title deed, yes?"

Next to her, Nathan nods at me. He looks surprisingly calm, which is funny given I'm about to freak the hell out. But he pushes his mouth into a smile and says, "You can do this." And then he winks.

How is he so confident? I want to stay and argue, but already, the door is being opened, and the assistant who led us up here stands there patiently, waiting for us to go. There is nothing else to do but for us to stand up and leave. I turn my head as I walk out the door, and my heart clenches at the sight of Nathan in Julia Child's impossibly huge room. I will do this. No matter what it takes, I will get that title deed back and claim him from her. After all, how hard can it be to retrieve the title deed from one of our little nieces and nephews, right?

6

By the time we get back to the house, I feel about ready to collapse, but at the same time, my mind is too wired for me to get any sleep. It's as though my body and mind are at an impasse; one wants to dive back into bed, the other one is a caged animal throwing itself onto the bars of the cage, roaring with frustration and anxiety. It still can't comprehend just how the hell we ended up in this situation. For the umpteenth time, I walk myself back through the events of the night.

First of all, none of this was even supposed to be my problem. Hell, it's not even my family's problem. It was Abi's issue, Abi's ass on the line, and Nathan and I had only agreed to come along to show support for Second Aunt. And now, Nathan, my husband (ah!), is a freaking hostage. A literal hostage in a mansion full of "armed" guards. And are we even sure that the rifles are fake, like Abi said? Was Abi telling the truth when he said they're all law-abiding citizens here? But even if they weren't law-abiding citizens, if they really were mafia, he wouldn't exactly own up to it, would he? I don't know, do gangsters readily admit to being gangsters?

I rack my mind, coming up with all the mafia/gangster/cartel TV shows I've watched. There's *Narcos*. Pablo Escobar. I believe he did call himself a cartel leader. Up until he ran for government. Okay. What about *The Sopranos*? Oh yeah, they totally referred to themselves as mafia. Okay, so across the board, mafia members tend to be pretty open about identifying themselves as mafia, so the fact that Abi said that they're just normal businesspeople means—

Who am I kidding? Of course it means nothing. What kind of normal businessperson has armed guards in her estate? And takes people's husbands hostage? AAAH!

I don't realize that I'm just standing there in the living room of our family home staring into space and breathing hard until something touches my arm. My muscles explode into movement and I jump, yelping.

"Aduh, Meddy!" Ma cries, patting her chest. "You trying to give me heart attack, ya? Hanh?" She shakes her head and releases her breath.

"Oh my god, sorry, Ma." I blink several times, trying to clear my head and slow down my speeding heart. "I was—I didn't hear you coming in."

Ma sighs. "Come, come to the kitchen, we make tea. Everyone talking. Ayo. Don't just stand here like patung."

I'm only half-aware of her taking me by the arm and leading me through the massive dining room and into the kitchen. Unlike the rest of the house, the kitchen is somewhat normal-sized and therefore far cozier. The aunties and Abi are gathered around the island. Someone has taken out platters of leftover cakes and cookies, and someone else has brewed a fresh pot of tea. Despite the fact that my world has just fallen apart, the scene is comforting. This is what my family does best. We sip hot tea, eat sweets, and devise a plan together. We've weathered so much together. Surely, we can overcome this as well. By morning, everything will be okay. We'll get Nathan back and we'll laugh about the ridiculousness of everything together.

"Come, Meddy," Big Aunt says as she piles almond cookies and kue lapis onto a small plate, "you sit, okay." She pats the stool next to her and plonks the plate in front of it. "You eat. You look so pale, later you faint how?"

Second Aunt waves a hand and shakes her head in obvious disagreement. "I think maybe better you do exercise, ayo." She slips off her stool and raises her arms over her head. "Ayo, follow me, Meddy. Get blood flowing to your head, so you not so pale like ghost."

"Uh . . ." I'm so dazed that I follow her barked instructions without really thinking about it, and I find myself with my legs parted in a lunge and my arms above my head. And now my mind catches up with the situation and goes: *Um, WTF?*

Big Aunt must have caught the bewildered expression on my face, because she snaps her fingers at me and says, "Sudah. Ayo, sit. Eat. You need blood sugar, not exercise."

Second Aunt's chest puffs up like she's about to go into a tirade, but Abi rushes to her and pats her on the shoulder, deflating her. I quickly escape to the stool and sit down with a deep sigh.

"Come, eat," Big Aunt says again, pushing the plate closer to me even though it was already right in front of me to begin with. If I don't take a bite now, I swear she'll pick up a cookie and shove it into my mouth. I have no appetite whatsoever, but I force myself to take a bite of almond cookie to appease Big Aunt.

"Mm, this Lapis Surabaya is so good," Fourth Aunt moans in between bites of cake. "I wish you'd make them more often, Dajie."

Big Aunt gives one of her trademark I-don't-want-to-smile-because-it-looks-immodest-but-I'm-very-pleased smiles. Ma tuts. "Tch, is so unhealthy. Thirty egg yolks in just one cake. So wasteful. So expensive. You want Dajie to waste so much money just to make you cake? So ungrateful."

Fourth Aunt glares at Ma. "Unlike some people who spend their lives determined to be miserable, I know how to enjoy life while I'm still young."

Ma snorts. "Young? You? You middle-aged already ah!"

Fourth Aunt's fork clatters to her plate. She looks about ready to lunge at Ma.

"Enough!"

It's only when they all stare at me that I realize I've just shouted at them. Oh my god. I just shouted at my mom and aunties. My survival instincts kick in. "Sorry. I didn't mean to raise my voice . . ." I falter. Well, actually, I did mean to raise my voice, because my poor husband is stuck at a mafia lady's house and my mom and aunts are squabbling over, of all things, cake. I straighten in my seat, lifting my chin. "I think we all need to focus on how we're going to fix this and get Nathan back. Okay? Please, no more arguing. Poor Nathan is—" My voice wobbles.

Ma rushes forward, patting me on the hand and grabbing the teapot to pour me more tea. Big Aunt spears a piece of coconut cake and shoves it in my face, saying, "Eat, eat!" Second Aunt and Fourth Aunt squeeze their mouths into thin lines, looking abashed. Abi stares at the floor, the tips of his ears turning red.

"Okay," Big Aunt announces. She's got that voice again, the one that says she's ready to get to work and everybody had better listen the hell up. "Our Nathan is stuck in that Julia Child house."

My chest swells with the way she said "our Nathan." I love how readily they've accepted him as one of their own. There's no doubt in my mind that they would go to the ends of the earth to save him.

Her steely gaze burns through Abi. "Abi, he is safe, right? That Julia Child person, will she do anything to him?"

Abi starts, his eyes widening. "Yes, of course he's safe. No, she won't lay a finger on him." He hesitates. "Well, looks like she might have taken a liking to him, so maybe she will lay a finger on him? But not to harm him."

Great. But I trust Nathan, even though Julia Child is beautiful.

"As long as we get her the title deed," Abi adds.

My gut sours again. "What do you mean, as long as we get her the title deed? So she will harm him if we don't get it?"

"No, of course not," Abi laughs. "Because we will get her the title deed."

Frustration pounds on top of the growing panic. "And if we don't?"

"But we will," Abi says with a terrified smile. "So it's not an issue."

I gape at him. Why can't anyone here give me a straight answer? Are they mafia, or are they normal businesspeople? Is Nathan's life in actual danger or not? I feel like I'm about to scream, but luckily, Big Aunt's authoritative voice slices through the mess of thoughts flying around in my frazzled mind.

"Okay. We get the title deed. We make list, ya? All the children, all the single people."

"Right, yes." I hurriedly take out my phone and open my notes app, then I look expectantly at Ma and the aunties.

"Acai's grandkids," Ma says.

"Nelson's daughters, I think they are twins, ya? So pretty, ya?" Second Aunt says.

"Oh yes, they have such star power," Fourth Aunt pipes up. "I was chatting with them, and—"

"Hang on." I hold up a hand to stop them from getting derailed for the millionth time. "Let's do this methodically. We go from the eldest to the youngest. Otherwise we can't keep track of all of them."

"Yes, very smart idea, Meddy." Ma's eyes shine with pride, and she smirks at the aunties. "So smart, ya?"

They all nod loyally except for Fourth Aunt, who rolls her eyes as per usual.

"Should we wake up the others in the house?" I say. "Ask them for help? They know these relatives better than we do."

"No," Big Aunt says with finality. "They will ask so many questions, then we lose face."

Right, of course. Can't forget about saving face, not even now, when we're trying to save my husband.

"Okay, so." I take a deep breath, my thumbs hovering over my phone. "Let's start with your oldest cousin. That would be Uncle Ping?" They all nod. "Right. So his children are . . ."

For the next half an hour, my thumbs fly across the phone screen as my mom and aunts go through each relative and their children. Progress is painfully slow, as several times they disagree on which family member a particular child actually belongs to. There are so many of them, so many children we only see on Chinese New Year, and newborn babies popping into the family tree once every few months.

"Ashley is Aling's granddaughter!"

"No, that one is Zhenzhen's grandson!"

"Ashley is girl's name, how can be grandson?"

"In Ireland, Ashley is boy's name!"

Each time they get derailed by some petty argument, I have to swallow my growing frustration and gently but firmly lead them back to the pertinent question. By the time we're done, I feel thoroughly spent, like a hollowed-out shell, but in my hands lies a priceless list of names that everyone agrees is the most comprehensive family tree of our clan. I scroll down the endless list, marveling at just how humongous our family is. Everyone else is slumped back in their seats, obviously exhausted. My stomach roils with guilt. I've put them through this. No, wait. I haven't. Abi has. I glare in his direction, but the poor guy looks so rumpled and sorry that I can't even stay mad at him.

"Great work, everyone," I say.

Heads nod slowly. "Okay," Big Aunt says, stifling a yawn. "We go bed now. Then first thing in the morning, we call up everyone."

"Aduh, my son taken hos—host—hostake," Ma cries, "and you all go bed? How can? We call them now."

I nod in agreement.

Fourth Aunt frowns. "That's a terrible idea."

"Why?" Ma and I say in unison.

Fourth Aunt stares at us like we're complete idiots. "It's the middle of the night? Everyone will wonder what the heck is going on, and we'd have to explain, and my guess is that our friend Abi and Julia Child would rather this whole trade involving the title deed be kept quiet." She side-eyes Abi, who jumps to attention.

"Ah, yes." He grimaces. "Sorry, but yes, it's imperative that the trade involving this plot of land is kept under wraps, otherwise we might uh . . ."

My eyes are so wide they can't possibly open any wider. "Otherwise? What, you might get assassinated by another mafia family?"

Abi laughs weakly. "Of course not! But ah, well, it's sensitive. Very sensitive."

"See?" Fourth Aunt says with a smug smile. "And," she adds when Ma opens her mouth, probably to protest, "if we call everyone, waking them up in the middle of the night, it's so rude. We will lose face."

There is a horrified silence. Because worse even than the threat of death by mafia is the threat of losing face. Ma immediately sits back, nodding. "Aduh," she mutters, "this is true. Will lose face."

If not for the fact that Abi is being so cryptic about the actual consequences of not being discreet, I would've imploded right then and there. Because really, who cares a whit about losing face when Nathan is a hostage? But even as I think that, the exhaustion catches up with me. What little remaining adrenaline was left leaks out, and I feel like I could fall asleep on the kitchen floor. I'm only half-conscious of climbing up the stairs to the bedroom and murmuring good night to Ma and the aunties. I can't even bring myself to change into my pajamas before slumping into bed. A single tear drips from my eyes as I think of Nathan, my sweet, loving husband, alone in that big house, surrounded by danger. I close my eyes. We'll get you out. We will . . .

A knock on the door jerks me awake. I blink, confused by the sunlight streaming in through the window. What? I don't get it. It was nighttime only moments ago. I grope about for my phone and unlock the screen. Good gods, it's already seven in the morning. Somehow, I've slept for five hours. The knock comes again, and I call out, "Yeah?"

Ma's voice floats through the gap in the door. "Meddy, bangun," she says, even though I'm clearly awake already. "Come down and eat, ayo cepat." She knocks again, for good measure, before I hear her slippers slapping down the hall.

I bound out of bed and quickly wash up, slipping into a shirt and jeans and tying my hair back into a ponytail. I shake my head, trying to clear it, trying to get myself fully present in the moment. Last night couldn't have been real, could it? It felt like a nightmare, a horrible figment of my asshole imagination. But a glance back at the empty bed confirms it. No Nathan. The thought slams into me like a steel anchor. Or whatever metal anchors are made of these days. My stomach immediately bunches up into a tight fist. We've been in Jakarta only twenty-four hours and already I've lost my husband. I grip the edge of the sink and glare into the mirror.

Get. A. Grip.

Today will be the day we get him back. And how hard can it be, honestly? We'll call each and every single person who was here yesterday and find the title deed in no time. Actually, come to think of it, chances are, whoever it was whose kid got the title deed would probably call us this morning and go, "Yo, you gave our two-year-old a title deed to a plot of land. What the heck?" Then we can be like, "Ha-ha, that was such a silly mistake, LOL. Give it back now. Now. Give now." And we'll speed all the way to Julia Child's house, fling the title deed at her, grab Nathan, and speed away. Easy peasy.

Taking deep breaths, I stride out of my bedroom and down the stairs. To my dismay, the rest of the house is already awake, and the dining room is full of my cousins and aunts and uncles and nieces and nephews, all of them engaged in merry, raucous conversation as they have their breakfast. Argh!

"Good morning!" Jems is way too perky for seven o'clock in the morning. I hate him. But then he pours me a cup of freshly brewed coffee and I find that I hate him a little bit less.

"Meddy, ayo makan!" one of the uncles shouts. Why do Chinese-Indos always have to be so loud? I manage a weak smile as Auntie Wati grabs me a bowl.

Today's breakfast is a typical Indonesian fare: Bubur ayam. It's rich, thick congee topped with shredded chicken, roasted peanuts, fried onions, fried youtiao, and scallions. Auntie Wati ladles the porridge into my bowl and then tops it with so much chicken there's more chicken than porridge. She adds the other ingredients with a heavy hand, and by the time it's done, my bowl is basically a precarious mountain of food. She squeezes fish sauce, sesame oil, and a squirt of fresh lime on top of it and plops it down on the table in front of me. "Makan!" she orders.

The last thing I want to do is to eat, but Big Aunt catches my eye and gives me a small, sure nod, and the tightness around my chest eases a little. She gets it. She understands my anxiety to get out of the dining room and launch into action.

"Eat, Meddy," she says. Then she lowers her voice and adds, "We have interrogate the kids here. They are clean." I get a flash of Big Aunt interrogating my little nieces and nephews CIA-style, but the children seem perfectly happy, so I'm guessing she hasn't waterboarded them or anything. Next to her, Ma nods. Second Aunt and Fourth Aunt glance up from their various conversations to also nod (well, Fourth Aunt winks), and I almost burst into tears then, because as always, these women have my back. They're all having their breakfast and chatting with the others, but at the back of their minds, they're fully aware that they're about to get down to business right after this to help get Nathan out of Julia Child's house.

I sit down and prod at the tower of chicken and fried dough gingerly. I have no idea how to even start eating without accidentally pushing the entire mountain all over the table.

"Did you sleep okay?" Elsa says.

"You guys came up really late," Jems adds. "I heard voices down in the kitchen after midnight."

My breath catches in my throat. Excuses crowd inside my mind, but nothing comes out of my mouth.

"You guys must be so jet-lagged, huh?" Sarah says.

I nod quickly. "Yes, we are!" Jet lag, of course. "We all came down for a midnight snack."

Elsa gives me a sympathetic smile. "Ugh, jet lag's the worst. We got it really bad when we went to Vancouver last year, didn't we?"

Jems nods. "Yeah, that was rough. The kids' bedtime routine was completely destroyed. I almost started crying when the little one woke up at two in the morning."

"How long are you going to let Nathan sleep in?" Elsa asks, sipping her coffee. "If he sleeps in too long, he's never going to get to sleep tonight."

Oh god. I can practically feel my pores opening up and

sweat seeping out. Nathan. How the hell have I forgotten that nobody else knows that Nathan's not here? "Uh—" Quick, come up with a good answer! A believable answer! Anything!

"Tch, let the poor man sleep," Fourth Aunt laughs. "They're newlyweds, you don't want to know what those two get up to at night." She gives us an exaggerated wink.

"Ew." Jems makes a face. "Please, Auntie Mimi, don't put such images in my head."

"I'm just saying." Fourth Aunt shrugs. "If a newlywed husband isn't left completely wrecked in the morning, then something ain't right." With that, she cackles while Jems and Elsa make gagging noises.

I catch Fourth Aunt's eye and silently mouth "thank you," and she waves a manicured hand at me flippantly. Thank god for Fourth Aunt. As I spoon some porridge into my mouth, I mentally berate myself for not being prepared. I should've been able to answer such an easy question quickly, but I'd just frozen in the moment. This is the thing about my fight-or-flight response. It's completely broken. When most people either fight or run the hell away, I freeze like a hamster and hope that no one notices me because I'm so still. It never works, so I don't understand what sort of evolutionary glitch has led to this survival instinct.

The rest of breakfast is just as excruciating. Everyone seems to want to linger over the breakfast table, chatting about how wonderful it was to see the extended family yesterday. When Uncle Ping says, "And today, shall we all go to Grand Indonesia?" I blurt out, "No!"

Every conversation falls silent, scythed by my extremely rude outburst. Eyes turn to stare at me.

"Ah, sorry." I falter. My mind is a mess. What should I say

to them? I need to come up with an excuse that's polite and respectful, one that won't make Ma lose face.

Big Aunt clears her throat. "We're very excited to take Meddy around Jakarta. And Nathan. But this morning, I want to take Meddy to my old kitchen at the Ritz."

"Oh, wonderful," Auntie Wati says. "Can we come too?"

"No," Big Aunt barks. Then she hesitates and adds, "Ah, um, they limit the number of visitors who can go inside the kitchen. You know, for sanitary reasons. Anyway, it'll be hot and awfully noisy and we'll be back by lunchtime. Then we can go to Grand Indonesia."

The other aunties and uncles smile, though a couple of them look uncertain. Big Aunt doesn't leave any room for questions as she stands up abruptly and says, "Ayo, Meddy, we go now."

Second Aunt, Ma, and Fourth Aunt jump up as well, and we leave the dining room after saying bye to everyone. The back of my neck burns as we walk out. I'm sure that everyone thinks we're being really rude and weird, and my skin crawls with guilt because they've all been nothing but lovely toward us. Once this is all over, I'm going to be so, so nice to my poor cousins and aunts and uncles.

We go back up to our rooms to grab our purses, and when we exit out the front door, we find Abi waiting outside, with a huge minivan. Second Aunt primps her hair with obvious delight, and we all climb in.

"I've booked us a private dining room at the Formosan," he says as the minivan travels onto the road. "We'll be able to make all our calls without anyone overhearing."

I gaze out the window as we drive, my thoughts consumed by Nathan. I wonder if he's okay. I hate that his first visit here with my family has ended up this way. At the same time, I'm distracted by the sights of the city. Jakarta changes so rapidly, new skyscrapers popping up each time I visit, all of them behemoths made of steel and glass, looking very futuristic. And all the tropical plants growing in lush abundance everywhere, along the streets, turning it into a garden city. It's so beautiful it makes my stomach twist because Nathan isn't here to take in the gorgeousness with me.

By the time we arrive at Formosan, my insides are a writhing mess of snakes. We are greeted by a hostess, who leads us to a private dining room, as promised. The room is beautiful, decorated in a traditional Chinese style, with paintings of cranes and water lilies on the walls. The round dining table is already filled with cold dishes. The hostess bows and tells us to press a small bell if we require anything, then she leaves and shuts the door behind her. We're finally alone and ready to dive straight into business.

Phones are whipped out and brandished like weapons. Second Aunt takes out the master list of names we came up with last night and puts it in the center. Big Aunt regards us with the solemnity of an army general. "Ermei, you take these names," she announces, pointing to a bunch of names on the list. For once, Second Aunt doesn't argue. "Sanmei, you take these. Simei, you call these ones, and Meddy, you call these ones down here. Okay?"

We all nod.

"And remember," Abi pipes up, "you can't let them know that anything is amiss."

Big Aunt frowns at him, probably annoyed that he's interrupted her command. "I was going to tell them that."

Abi blanches. "Yes, of course. I'm sorry, Dajie."

"Hmph." Big Aunt sniffs and turns to us. "Let's begin."

Heart thudding, I look at the list of names I've been assigned and start dialing. Of course, as soon as we are connected, we find out another problem: the aunties are freaking loud, and they're all trying to talk over the phone in a confined space. This means that the volume in the room quickly climbs from normal conversation to shouted "Eh! Can you hear me? HELLO? HELLO AH HUAT! YOU HEAR ME OR NOT AH?" and the aunties all flap at one another, hissing at the others to quiet down, *can't you see I'm trying to have a phone call?*

I walk to the farthest corner of the room and dial the first number. I put my finger into my other ear to try to drown out the noise of Ma and the aunties. No idea how the person I'm calling, my cousin Frensin, is going to hear me, but I'll figure that out as I go.

Frensin picks up on the first ring. "Meddy? It's so nice to hear from you!"

"Ah, hi!" I wasn't expecting her to pick up so quickly, and now that she has, my mind is a blank.

"It was so nice seeing you guys yesterday. It's been way too long. We should do a cousins lunch to catch up with you!"

Guilt worms its way through my stomach. I swear, by now, I'm fueled by a mixture of anxiety and guilt. Those seem to be the main two emotions I have. "Yeah, totally," I make myself reply. "Ah, anyway, so I was wondering . . ." Oh god, this is so much more awkward than I had anticipated. "Um, have Ryan and Joen opened their red packets yet?"

"Ugh, are you kidding? First thing they did as soon as we got into the car was rip everything open and count their money." She laughs. "My kids are terrible. But you know what? I remember doing the exact same thing when we were kids, so I can't be too harsh on them."

I give her a weak laugh before gritting my teeth. How do I smoothly segue into asking if they found a title deed among the cash inside the red packets? "Was there anything weird in the red packets? I remember I once got an IOU in one of mine."

"Oh my god. I think that was from Uncle Lie. Yeah, oh gosh, I remember that too." She laughs again, her voice warm with fondness. "No, I don't think they got anything weird like that . . . they were screaming in the back seat about all the candy they were gonna buy with the money."

"Aww." Could they have been screaming about buying so much candy because one of the packets contained a freaking title deed? Nah, they're what, five and six years of age? They wouldn't understand the worth of something like a title deed. They would've been like, "Mama, WTF is this?" and Frensin would definitely tell me about it, especially since I'd just asked if there was anything weird in the red packets. Right. So this one's a no. Frensin is still chattering away, and now I need to end the call quickly so I can progress to the next cousin. Argh. I hate this. Another stab of guilt jolts through me as I say, "Oh, shoot, my mom's trying to talk to me about something. I have to go."

"No worries. I can hear her in the background. Say hi to her for me, and let's schedule our cousins lunch soon!"

"Yes, definitely," I reply feeling like a total shit. "Byeee." I hang up and sag against the wall, feeling all hollowed out. Just from a single phone call. Argh. And I have at least eight more to go. Somebody save me.

As I cross out Frensin's name on my list, I glance at my mom and aunts and listen in on one of their calls. Of course, they're all speaking either in Mandarin or Indonesian, so I struggle to follow their conversations.

Big Aunt: "You know how much that cheapskate Enjelin gave in her red packets? Just ten dollars. How embarrassing."

I wince. That's . . . very direct. But next to Big Aunt, Second Aunt is saying, "Hanh! I hear that Dajie gave twenty dollars per red packet. She is so wasteful, she's always been like that. Who gives a two-year-old twenty dollars? I mean, really now." They both pause to shoot daggers at each other with their eyes.

Then Big Aunt says, "But I just got off the phone with a friend, and someone had given her grandchild a lotto ticket in his red packet. Can you even imagine? Did your grandkids get anything like that? Anything that's not actual cash?" Her face switches from fake smile to intense narrowed-eyes glare, as though she could glare right through the voice call. A moment later, she grunts. "Hrmmh, okay, so nothing strange like a lotto ticket or a Starbucks gift card or a—ha-ha, title deed to a plot of land. Okay, sounds good. We'll talk more next time." She hangs up the phone and crosses the name off her list.

Second Aunt shakes her head at Big Aunt, sees me looking, and says in English, "Meddy, you got hear that? Big Aunt just say, 'title deed to plot of land,' you hear or not?"

"Ah . . ." I freeze like a rabbit that's heard the sudden rustling of leaves nearby and knows it's probably not another rabbit. "A little?" I don't know how one could hear something "a little," but I'm trying to be as noncommittal as possible here.

"Aha!" Second Aunt snaps, glaring at Big Aunt. "You see? Even Meddy say, she notice you saying 'title deed to plot of land.' That is so obvious. You want them to know is it? You want them to figure out what happen? Hanh?"

Dread overcomes my frozen instincts and I raise up my hands in a gesture of don't-shoot-me. "Hang on, I didn't mean that it was obvious or anything. I actually thought you did it really smoothly, Big Aunt."

Big Aunt's chest balloons, and her face glows with a smug smile. "Yes, Meddy is right. Very smooth. You hear? She say is very smooth, I agree. Is because I am businesswoman, always must know how to handle customer, how to make customer happy, make them feel special, not to worry, nothing is wrong."

Second Aunt snorts. "But in reality every time they go with you, always got something wrong with cake." She looks over at Abi and says, "Right? You remember when we were all young, Dajie kept baking this and baking that, nobody want to eat but she still baking here and there."

Abi looks like he's seriously considering digging a hole in the floor with his bare hands and hiding in it. "I—um—"

This time, Big Aunt balloons so much that I fear she might actually explode. "What?" she says, her voice dangerously soft, like a sword being slid out of its sheath. "Got what wrong with my cakes?"

"Nothing's wrong with your cakes!" I practically scream, lunging in between the two of them. "Your cakes are amazing. My friends are always raving about them. You've got a rating of 4.5 stars on Yelp. Your cakes have gone viral on Instagram at least four separate times!"

"*Aha!*" Second Aunt cries again. "You see? Your cake got virus. Everyone agree!"

"That's not what going viral means," I groan.

Fortunately, Ma and Fourth Aunt end their respective calls then and join in the quickly spiraling conversation.

"No luck with mine so far," Fourth Aunt says. "How are the rest of you doing? Any hits?"

Ma shakes her head. "Everyone talking about so happy, kids getting red packets. Nobody bring up anything strange."

Abi looks crestfallen. "Well," I point out, "we've still got a lot of people to call, so let's get back to work, okay? You're all doing an amazing job." I quickly go back to the far corner of the room before any of them has a chance to respond. This time, I feel far more ready, and I call my next cousin with more confidence than I had before. The calls go a lot smoother, with me getting into an efficient pattern of wishing them well, asking them how their family enjoyed the Chinese New Year celebrations, and then saying, *One of my friends' kids received a lotto ticket in his red packet, can you even imagine? The audacity! Did your kids receive anything strange like that? No? Oh, thank goodness. Yes, let's have a cousins lunch soon. I'll coordinate with the rest of the cousins. Byeee!*

In between each name, I pause a second or two to take a deep breath, then I hit Call. Rinse and repeat seven more times, and before I know it, I'm out of cousins to call. Not a single one of them says their children have found anything that isn't actual cash in their red packets. A few of them expressed wonderment at receiving a lot of money in the red packets, to which I could only laugh weakly and agree how generous Abi was. Okay, well, chances are that Ma or the aunties found something. I trudge back to the table and slump down into a chair and wait as one by one, the others finish going through their lists and cross out the last name. Ma is the last one to finish, and she shakes her head as she hangs up the phone. My stomach sinks. All of our mouths drop open. For a moment, no one says anything as we stare bleakly at one another.

"No luck?" Abi says.

We all shake our heads, our expressions still disbelieving. Big Aunt studies her list as though it could tell her something, then she frowns at us, a displeased North Korean dictator. I shrink away from her knitted brows. "How can?" she rumbles after a pregnant second. "No, this not possible. Must be one of you make mistake. Who is it?" Her glare sweeps across the table, scouring our skins as it passes each one of us. I feel my skin shriveling up under it, as though getting burned.

"How you know is not *you* who make mistake?" Second Aunt hisses.

Abi places a hand on Second Aunt's arm gently, and weirdly enough, even though things are looking really dire, I find myself liking Abi for a moment, just for that gesture alone. He's good for her, I think. Then I mentally kick myself for thinking that, because hello, we wouldn't be in this position in the first place if not for Abi and his shady dealings. Still, I appreciate that he's at least trying to keep the peace between Big Aunt and Second Aunt.

"Yes," Ma pipes up, "could be someone else, someone who spend her time on phone talking about her silly singing show that nobody watch." She side-eyes Fourth Aunt, as though none of us knows whom she's referring to.

Fourth Aunt glances up from admiring her nails. "Uh, I have forty thousand followers on TikTok, so obviously there are tons of people watching me sing. And *they* asked me about it, so of course I had to respond, otherwise they'd get suspicious. You can't blame me for being a TikTok star."

Ma snorts. "Hah! Just because you buy follower on the TokTok you think you a real star now?"

"Well, all I heard was you telling everyone how Meddy and

Nathan still haven't given you a grandchild yet," Fourth Aunt shoots back, "so I'm not the only one getting derailed, okay?"

I push the tips of my index fingers into my temples and close my eyes. I wonder if I could press hard enough to actually squish into my brain and put myself out of this misery. But no, I need to focus, I need to somehow lead them back to the topic and save Nathan. God, give me patience. But what use is patience? I have no idea what went wrong. Why haven't we found out where the title deed went?

"No choice," Big Aunt grunts, "we call everyone again."

My eyes and mouth open with dismay. *Nooo!* Oh god, my insides are curling up at the horrifying thought of having to struggle through another round of awkward conversations with my cousins. "They're definitely going to suspect something of being wrong," I moan. "I don't think we can just call them up again and ask them the same questions. That's just really suspicious."

"Meddy is right," Ma says loyally.

Big Aunt's mouth purses up and she takes a deep breath, looking thoughtful. "Then how?"

I must think of something. Maybe someone is hiding it? The thought hits like a punch to my stomach. I love my cousins. I love my aunts and uncles. I hate the possibility that one of them might have been dishonest. It fights me all the way up, but I finally manage to bring myself to say it. "Could whoever got it be hiding it from us? Because they realized how valuable the title deed is and they wanted to keep it?" God, just saying those words makes me feel filthy, like I need to rinse my mouth out with Listerine. Urgh.

Ma and the aunties look as horrified as I feel. They gape openly, their eyes as wide as some animal caught in a trap.

"Aiya, no lah!" Ma cries after a beat. "These people our family, you know. How can you say such thing? How I raise you, Meddy?"

I wince. "Sorry, Ma. I just thought—"

Ma isn't done with her tirade. "I always say to you, family first. Do I not always say to you that? Hanh?"

"You do, but—"

"And now you saying someone in our family—*our* family!—decide to put land first? Choi! Knock on wood. Why you say such bad luck thing, especially during Chinese New Year? Is supposed to be auspicious time, but you cursing our family. Aduh, what have I done to deserve this kind of daughter?" Her face crumples up into a sob.

"I'm sorry, I didn't mean to imply that." Of course, I did much worse than just imply, I literally suggested it. And now, my aunts are crowded around Ma, comforting her, and argh, how the hell did we get here? I need to think of a way to redirect this whole conversation, but how? I scramble through my mind, coming up with a myriad of ideas and rejecting them as quickly as I think of them. Then it hits me, the way a lightning bolt strikes and brightens the entire sky so abruptly. "The photos!"

They glance up at me.

I gesture at them excitedly. "The photos. We took so many of them. And you—" I say to Ma, who's frowning at me, "you took a ton of photos of Nathan giving out red packets—"

Her frown melts into a smile. "Oh yes, he looks so good giving out the angpao, ya? You can tell, you know, that he will be good father, ya kan?"

"Right. And I saw that most of the red packets have different patterns."

"Oh yes, most people use the ones that they're given by their banks," Abi pipes up. "But I had mine specially printed on high-quality paper, illustrated by an award-winning artist. And! The one that has the title deed is special. It's larger than the others and it's gold in color, with a pattern of water lilies."

"Aiya!" Big Aunt says. "Why you don't tell us that sooner, hanh?"

Abi shrinks back.

"Well, it doesn't matter. We asked about the title deed, and if anyone's kid had received one, I'm sure they would've said so," I say, feeling bad for Abi, the poor little mafia lord being bullied by Big Aunt. "Right, so it's easily recognizable. We'll go through all the photos from yesterday morning and see if we can't find it." My pulse is racing so hard that I'm getting a headache. Why didn't I think of doing this sooner?

Ma and the aunties are all staring at me. "Wah, Meddy, that is so smart idea," Second Aunt says.

Ma flushes with pride, as though Second Aunt had praised her instead of me. Seems like she's forgotten about how she was just scolding me moments ago, so I'm not complaining.

"Thanks, Second Aunt. Alright, everybody's got photos on their phones? Let's go through them." Hope flutters in my chest. This has to work. If it doesn't, then I honestly have no idea what the hell we can do.

7

It's not long before Ma shrieks, "*Nih!* I find the angpao! This one, right? Ya kan?" She waves her phone around crazily, brandishing it so close to our faces that we all have to lean away to have any hope of seeing the screen.

"Tch, you stop moving it a bit," Big Aunt tuts. Ma does as she's told and we all crowd around it.

Sure enough, there's a photo of Nathan holding a red packet that's larger than the usual size. The red packet is, as Abi described, a brilliant gold in color, with fat pink water lilies swirling across it. It's a stunning red packet, and the sight of it in Nathan's hands brings a pang to my heart.

"Yes!" Abi shouts. "That's it! That's the one!"

Fourth Aunt snatches the phone from Ma's hands. "Hey!" Ma protests, but Fourth Aunt ignores her and swipes to the left, going to the next picture, which shows a teenage girl beaming down at the red packet in her hands. There's a thoughtful silence. All breath hangs suspended in the air, and the room is so quiet I can practically hear myself blink.

"Okay," Abi says, breaking the silence, "so she's the one who received it."

"Hmm." Big Aunt rubs her chin. "Is that Ah Gui's eldest granddaughter?"

"Tch!" Second Aunt shakes her head. "No lah. Ah Gui's eldest granddaughter in Sydney. Masa you don't remember? Make us lose face ah, you don't even recognize your own family."

Big Aunt takes in a deep breath. "Oh, ya? So is mean you know who this girl is, ya? So? Who is she? Hanh?"

In answer, Second Aunt squints harder at the photo. After a while, she says, "Ah, yes, this is Katarina, is Meihua's second daughter."

"No, no," Ma says. "Meihua's second daughter is only twelve year old. This girl look like she maybe around fifteen, sixteen."

Fourth Aunt snorts. "Like you know what a twelve-year-old looks like nowadays. They're always trying to make themselves look older, haven't you heard?"

Ma glares at her. "That's just you. You think I don't remember? When you twelve, you putting on so much makeup, acting like you fifteen. Even when you so small you acting like a not-right woman."

Fourth Aunt rolls her eyes. "Oh right, and you as a teen were the saddest, most uncool thing ever. She was still wearing pigtails as a teen, did you know that?" she says to me.

I shrink back. No way in hell am I about to be dragged into this conversation. "Anyway," I say quickly. Time to lead them back to the actual subject at hand. "So none of us know who this girl is?"

"Well, she's got to be somebody's grandkid," Abi wails.

I empathize with his frustration. I, too, feel like wailing. This is the problem with families as huge as ours. We can't even keep track of who's who. I look down at my phone and swipe through the photos I took yesterday. There's that girl again. Except this time, she's standing next to a girl I do recognize. My niece Annabelle. They're standing very close to each other and both of them are laughing, so clearly they're familiar with each other. "Look," I call out, raising my voice to be heard over the sound of my family squabbling with one another. "Annabelle knows her. We can ask Annabelle who she is."

"Who is this Annabelle?" Second Aunt says.

"Aduh, how you cannot know who is Annabelle?" Big Aunt chides. "She is Selina's third granddaughter. Like that you also don't know? Is like you not even care about our family, how embarrass."

Before Second Aunt can fire off a caustic retort, I quickly jump in. "Auntie Selina's third granddaughter. Great job, Big Aunt. That would be my cousin Janis's daughter, right? Right, cool. I'll call Janis. I don't actually have Annabelle's number. Come to think of it, she should've been on the list of family to call, so good catch, Big Aunt." I locate Janis's name in my contacts list and hit Call before any of the aunties can say anything. I've had enough of them derailing everything with their petty arguments. Janis picks up on the third ring, and I quickly say, "Hey, Janis! It was so nice seeing you yesterday."

"Who—oh, Meddy? Hi! This is such a nice surprise. I heard from Jems that we're doing a cousins lunch?"

Wow, news travels fast. "Yes, yep, looking forward to it. Anyway, ah . . ." I falter. Now that I'm about to ask Janis for her kid's phone number, I realize that it's going to sound hella weird. Like, why in the world would I be asking that? I should've paused before making the call to think of a good excuse. Gah! I wrack my mind, trying to think of anything I know about Annabelle. She's sixteen. She . . . she asked me about photography. *Yes.* I pounce on it. "Yesterday, Annabelle mentioned that she was interested in photography, and I would love to chat with her about it. Could you WhatsApp me her number?"

"Ah, that's so nice of you. Are you sure it's not a bother? I told her not to bug you about it."

"Definitely not a bother!" My words come out so fast that they're all strung together into a single word.

Janis laughs. "Wow, okay. Yes, I'll send you her contact details right away. *So* nice of you, Meddy."

"No worries. I'll see you at the lunch. Okay, byeee!" I only exhale once I've hung up the phone. Phew. That went well. Thank god for shared interests. We all stare at my phone until it buzzes a few moments later. There it is. *Janis has sent you a Contact.* I click on it and hit Call Contact. Belatedly, I realize this is probably a faux pas as most teenagers say they hate talking over the phone. But whatever, we don't have time to waste.

"Put on speaker," Ma whispers.

The last thing I want to do is to put Annabelle on speaker, but Ma and the aunties are all goggling at me expectantly, so I do so just before Annabelle picks up the phone.

"Hello?" Her voice sounds wary.

"Annabelle? Hi, it's Meddy. Your ah, your aunt?" Wow, that's really weird, referring to myself as an auntie. God, I feel ancient.

"Oh my gosh, yeah, of course, hiii, Aunt Meddy."

Hearing the words "Aunt Meddy" come from the mouth of a teen makes me want to crumble into a pile of ancient ash. "Hey, it was so great to see you yesterday. You've grown so much." Oh my god, I'm even speaking like an old woman now.

Annabelle laughs. "Tell that to my mom. She still acts like I'm two."

I laugh politely. "So anyway, I was looking through the photos from yesterday, and there's someone I don't recognize, and"—I give an apologetic grimace—"well, I feel awful about not knowing all of the members of my own family. Can I send you a photo? And maybe you can tell me which of my nieces she is?"

"Oh. Sure!"

I locate the photo in my gallery and send it to her. From the other end, there's a sharp intake of breath. "Annabelle? You got it?"

"Yeah."

"Is that—ah—" I'm distracted by Big Aunt flapping her hand and mouthing, "Ah Gui's granddaughter." And next to her, Second Aunt hisses, "It's Meihua's granddaughter." I shake my head, ignoring them, and say, "Is that Uncle Ah Gui's granddaughter? Or maybe Auntie Meihua's granddaughter?"

"Oh no," Annabelle laughs. "That's my friend Rochelle. She came over to borrow a qipao and decided to stay for a bit to get some red packets. She's a hoot."

I look up at the ceiling. Why can't anything be straightforward when it comes to my family? How did we get to this point, where the person who got the one red packet we're looking for isn't even our family? Struggling to keep my voice calm,

I lean closer to the phone and say, "Ha-ha, yeah, she sounds great. Um, so, listen, we actually gave her the wrong red packet and we kind of—ah—need it back? But of course we'd be happy to replace it with a proper red packet."

"A fat one," Ma calls out.

"Oh, hi! Is that . . . Grandaunt Natasya?"

"Hallo, Annabelle, yes, it's me. You so pretty now, ya, what a young lady you are."

"Aww, thank you, Grandaunt. Anyway, yeah sure, I'm texting her right now."

There's a few moments of silence as Annabelle types out her message. It feels as though the seconds are crawling by, each one clawing to remain instead of passing by. A glance at Ma and the aunties and Abi tells me they're just as anxious and jittery as I am. Big Aunt is glaring at the phone like she could intimidate it into behaving, Second Aunt is endlessly massaging the back of her neck, probably wishing she could lunge into a Tai Chi position, Ma is wringing her hands, and Fourth Aunt is—well, Fourth Aunt is pouting into her mirror while applying more lipstick, so I guess maybe she's not too bothered by all of this. Next to her, Abi is standing with a clenched jaw, a vein pulsing in his forehead. Despite how reverent he's been, especially toward Big Aunt, he's oozing danger. It makes my skin prickle.

Annabelle's voice makes us jump. "Oh." She sounds taken aback.

"What is it?" Big Aunt barks.

"Uh, she says—wait, is that Grandaunt Friya? Um, hi, Grandaunt Friya. Didn't know you were there too."

"Yes, is me. Now tell us, what she say? Quickly."

"Oh, ah, she says: 'Sorry, but no.'"

Our breaths collectively catch in our throats. A scream very nearly rips its way out of me, but somehow, I manage to swallow it down. "What do you mean, no?"

"Um, I think it means she wants to keep the red packet she got from you guys?"

I imagine myself putting my hands around this kid's neck and squeezing. Whoa, okay, Meddy. Take a step back.

Second Aunt grabs the phone and hisses right into it. "Why she say that? Such no manners girl. What kind of not-right kid is this? Hanh?"

"Uh. Hi, Grandaunt Enjelin. Gosh, how many of you are there right now?"

"Doesn't matter!" Second Aunt is hitting pitch levels that would make Mariah Carey, or a pterodactyl, jealous. "You tell her right now that she need to be respectful of her elders!"

"Okay. Yes, I'm doing that."

We all glare at the phone as Annabelle types a message, our chests rising and falling rapidly. A few seconds later, she says, "Rochelle says: 'Nope.'"

I don't think I've ever seen my aunties looking this enraged. If there's anything Ma and the aunties cannot abide, it's teenagers being rude toward their elders and betters. Each of them swells up, their faces turning pink, then red, their nostrils flaring. Part of me shrinks down to the size of a small child, and I have to resist the urge to find a rock to hide under.

"Annabelle," Big Aunt booms in the Voice of God, "we are go your house now. We pick you up, then you come with us to this Rochelle house."

"Wait, what?"

"We come now." She stabs at my phone, disconnecting the

call in the middle of Annabelle saying, "Hang on—" She nods at us. "Come, we go now."

I wish I could simply agree and rush out with the rest of them, but I have to point out the obvious: "I don't know that we should storm some teenager's house. Are there laws against that? Would it technically be breaking and entering? Or harassment? I don't know what the laws are like here, but it feels wrong to barge into a teen's house?"

Big Aunt looms before me, and even though I'm at least an inch taller than her, somehow she's looking down on me and I'm gazing up, quaking with familiar fear. When she does speak, her voice carries with it the weight of gods. "They will thanking us for teaching this child good manner."

Abi, Ma, and the other aunties all nod solemnly. "Yes, this true," Second Aunt says with gravity. "They will all say, 'Wah, I fail to raise my child good, I so embarrass, thank you for teaching her manner.'"

"Okay . . ." I'm not sure if I'm truly convinced, but I know when I'm outnumbered, especially since it happens all the time. And anyway, we do need to get the title deed back, so it's not like we have a better option. As my insides churn with conflicting emotions, I follow my aunties out of the restaurant and into the huge minivan once more. I can't stop myself from picking at my fingernails as the minivan trundles down the roads toward Annabelle's house. This feels wrong. But we don't have a choice. And plus, I'm in Indonesia, not California, and the culture is vastly different here. My aunts would know better what is socially acceptable. Maybe they're right, maybe people would be grateful when complete strangers scold their kids.

When we arrive at Annabelle's house, Big Aunt reaches over the chauffeur's shoulder and smacks her palm down on the car horn. The honk blasts through the air, making me jump. "Jesus, Big Aunt, stop—"

She lifts her hand for just one second before slamming it back down. *Hooonk. Honk. Honk.*

I'm about to bodily yank her back into her seat when the gates open and poor Annabelle slips out, looking harried. It's an expression I've become very familiar with over the years, witnessing it often on the faces of people dealing with my mom and aunties. Annabelle waves at us with a half grimace, half smile as she rushes toward the minivan. Big Aunt gives a satisfied "harrumph" and leans back in her seat.

"Um, hi, everyone." Annabelle does a small bow as she climbs into the car. "Hi, Grandaunt Friya, Grandaunt Enjelin, Grandaunt Natasya, Grandaunt Mimi, and Auntie Meddy." She notices Abi and quickly adds, "Hi, Om." Everyone nods happily. Wow, I'm impressed. Annabelle is trained well, knowing enough to greet each auntie individually instead of the Westernized way of simply saying, "Hi, everyone."

I scoot to one side and she settles in next to me. "I'm so sorry for dragging you out like this," I say with a grimace.

Annabelle glances at Ma and the aunties before she swallows. "Of course, not a problem. I'm so sorry that my friend's being really weird about it all. I'm sure if we show up at her house, she'll feel bad and return the red packet. She's not normally like this." She tells the chauffeur Rochelle's address, and we start on our way. For a few moments, there's a painfully polite silence as Annabelle smiles with pursed lips and we smile back at her with equally tight lips. I scramble my mind to think of something to say to her, but Big Aunt beats me to it.

"So where you know such a rude girl from?" Big Aunt demands.

"Oh, um, school."

"Harrumph." Big Aunt narrows her eyes. "You go to Singapore school, right? This why I tell your mother, don't send you to Singapore school, they are too Westernized already. Better to send you to Taiwanese school."

"Um . . ." Annabelle nods hesitantly, her eyes wide, probably wondering if Big Aunt is actually about to bully her mother into taking her out of her current school. (The answer to this is yes, obviously.) "Well, uh, like I said, she's not normally like this." Then she quickly adds, "I'm not talking back, I'm not disagreeing with you, Grand-Aunt. You're totally right. But most of the kids at my school are very respectful."

Second Aunt narrows her eyes and leans forward. "So most of the kids there are good kids, but why you have to befriend this no-good one?" She stabs a very aggressive index finger at Annabelle's face. "You need to learn how to make better friends, otherwise aiya. You mix up with no-good crowd, then celaka deh."

Poor Annabelle shrinks back, nodding, her eyes pinned to Second Aunt's finger.

"Oh god, give the poor kid a break," Fourth Aunt says. "It's good of her to have friends who aren't all nerds." She winks at Annabelle, who only looks even more terrified, probably because she has no idea how she should react to this. My heart goes out to the poor girl. "Stick to this Rochelle kid, she sounds like she knows how to have fun," Fourth Aunt continues.

"Hah!" Ma snorts. "You see? You see what bad influence you are?"

Fourth Aunt rolls her eyes. "If by 'bad influence' you mean I'm trying to allow teens to live a little in an extremely restrictive environment, then sure."

I can practically see the cogs in Ma's brain whirring frantically as she tries to parse through what Fourth Aunt just said. After a moment, Ma grumbles, "Bad influence." She turns to Annabelle. "You don't listen to her, she is always like this, always disrespectfulling her elders, very bad."

Annabelle nods slowly, her wide eyes roaming everywhere. She looks like she's half considering jumping out of the moving vehicle.

Time for me to rescue her. "So tell me more about your interest in photography."

Annabelle's shoulders relax a little and her face breaks out into a smile. "Oh yeah. Well, my mom gave me a secondhand Canon 1D for my birthday last year, and I've been taking all sorts of photos with it." She takes out her phone and opens up her Gallery, and for the rest of the ride, we discuss photography with an intense determination, partly to make it clear to everyone else that we're done discussing manners, etc., but also, to my delight, Annabelle's a real photography buff, and it's refreshing to be able to talk about technique and lighting and different lenses.

Before we know it, the chauffeur announces that we have arrived. We all climb out of the minivan and geez, Rochelle's house is huge. Not as big as Julia Child's ridiculous estate, but it's definitely awe-inspiring.

"Yeah," Annabelle says, as though reading our minds, "Rochelle's family is loaded."

Big Aunt snorts again. "Harrumph. This probably why she so spoiled, and so sombong."

"Mm, yes, all this rich people, they are the most sombong ones in Indonesia," Ma agrees.

Annabelle texts Rochelle to let her know that we're outside

of her house, and a moment later, there is a buzz and the gates swing open. We trudge inside, and when we get to the towering front door, Annabelle knocks on it. Nothing happens. Annabelle gives us an apologetic look. "Might take a while because their house is so big, it takes some time to get to the front door."

Big Aunt reaches out and slams her fist into the door. *Bang. Bang. Bang.*

"Oh my god, Big Aunt, stop."

"Just let her knocking on the door," Ma mutters to me. "Nothing get her more angry than some kid making her wait like this."

As Big Aunt pulls her fist back for another round of aggressive knocking, the door clicks open and out comes Rochelle, wearing a half-bored, half-annoyed expression. She gives us all a deliberate once-over before saying, "Yeah?"

"Hey, Roche." Annabelle rushes forward. "This is—um, this is my family. They're visiting from LA. And they're here about the red packet."

Rochelle crosses her arms in front of her and leans against the door frame. A small, smug smile plays along her lips. Unlike Annabelle, who carries herself with that awkward gait that so many teenage girls have, Rochelle oozes confidence. She's pretty, and she knows it. She wears a plain white T-shirt and ripped jeans, but somehow, she looks like she would be completely fine strutting into a fancy restaurant. Her gaze is sharp as she takes us all in, obviously unimpressed by Ma's, the aunties', and even Abi's disapproving frowns. And in one hand, she holds a very official-looking document. I don't even need to see the words printed on it to know that it's the title deed.

When she sees us staring with open desperation at the deed,

she flips her hair over her shoulder and says lazily, "I told you I'm not giving it back."

I can practically feel the temperature among Abi, Ma, and the aunties rising. "It's really important—" I begin, but am interrupted by Second Aunt's pterodactyl screech.

"Aiya! You dare to go against your elder ah? Who raise you become so ngga bener? Hanh? We telling you now, you give us back red packet, or else."

Even though her rage isn't directed at me, I can't help but wince. Annabelle looks like she's ready to bolt. But Rochelle looks entirely unperturbed.

"Sorry, lady," she says, clearly not sorry at all, "but it's actually kind of rude of *you*."

"What?!" Ma and the aunties yelp in unison.

"Yeah, I mean, I was given the red packet. You can't just give a gift to someone and then demand it back. That's really rude. I mean, I would be embarrassed, if I were you."

My mind is blown. I blink at Rochelle, seeing her in an entirely new light, because this is the point where I realize that we're not dealing with a normal teen—we're dealing with an evil genius. Using the threat of embarrassment, and therefore losing face, against Ma and the aunties is like stealing their ultimate weapon and then pointing it back at them.

Sure enough, Ma and the aunties are standing there shell-shocked, mouths agape, looking like they're one step away from having aneurysms. They've wielded the threat of losing face so often to me and to others around them, but never, not that I can remember anyway, have they had someone— especially a younger person—use it against them. How are they going to deal with it?

Luckily, before they can explode, Abi snaps his fingers and

points excitedly at Rochelle. "I remember who you are now. I've been standing here trying to recall because you look so familiar, but I couldn't place it—" He takes a dramatic inhale, then says, "I recognize you from a wedding photo that was published in the Chinese-Indonesian newspaper last month. It was a photo of Kristofer Kolumbes Hermansah's family at the wedding of his youngest son."

Rochelle smirks, entirely unperturbed by this. "So you know who my grandfather is, old man. Now you know you shouldn't fuck with me."

Ma gasps. "Why you think we want to f—fudge with you? We don't want to f—fudge with you. Why your mind is so pervert?"

For the first time, Rochelle looks unsure. "Uh, I didn't mean it in a literal sense. It means like, to screw with someone."

Second Aunt narrows her eyes. "I hear this 'screw' quite a lot. I know it also means having the sex. Why you say that about us? We are not here to be having the sex with you."

"No," Rochelle groans. "It means like, don't fu—don't mess with me!"

"Ah." Ma, Big Aunt, and Second Aunt nod. Then they mutter to one another about how awful the younger generation is, to use such foul language so unnecessarily.

"Okay, they got distracted again," Fourth Aunt says. She turns to Rochelle. "Who's your granddaddy?"

Rochelle quirks a smug eyebrow. I don't actually know if eyebrows can technically be smug, but hers definitely are smug. They're the kind of brows you just want to take a razor to, because there's way too much smugness in them. "Why don't you tell them?" she says sweetly to Abi.

Abi frowns, his expression turning dark. "Julia, Kristofer,

and I are the top three conglomerates in Indonesia. We own the three largest corporations."

"So you're rivals?" I ask.

He nods. "Well, the thing is, it goes beyond professional rivalry. Something bad happened years ago. We got into a terrible disagreement. We'd been friendly before that, but after that, the three of us became enemies." He scoffs bitterly. "There have been plenty of times where we've gone out of our way to sabotage each other. We've each taken bad deals that we know we'd lose money on just to anger the others."

"Tch," Second Aunt tuts. "Why like that? Why you all so childish?"

Abi's chest puffs out with apparent indignation. "I'm not the one being childish. The number of times that Julia and Kristofer have stabbed me in the back—" He stops himself and takes a deep breath. "Anyway. It doesn't matter. What matters is . . ." He glowers at Rochelle. "You need to give us that title deed, child."

Rochelle's mouth twists into a sneer. "Child? Oh, you think I'm a child, do you? Would a child be able to steal your precious title deed?"

There's a collective gasp, and we all stare at her in shocked silence. Then Annabelle says, in a small voice, "Roche, what are you talking about, steal? You were given the red packet by mistake."

"Dude, seriously?" Rochelle laughs, an unpleasant sound. I'm finding that I really do not like this kid at all. "What are the chances that out of your humongous family, I would be the one who gets the red packet that contains the title deed?"

8

After her big reveal, Rochelle pauses, grinning, obviously savoring our astonished expressions.

"What?" I don't even know who says that, maybe all of us. Maybe just me. Maybe just Annabelle, who's staring at her friend like she doesn't know who she is.

Rochelle gives a dramatic sigh, something that it seems to me everyone in Indonesia has mastered, and rolls her eyes. "When I came to your family's celebration, I noticed the cavalcade out front. I mean, kind of hard not to notice that sort of thing, ya know? And so I knew that you had someone important there, and sure enough, once we were inside the house, I saw him." She nods at Abi. "Abraham Lincoln Irawan, one of my grandpa's archnemeses. Growing up, my grandpa was always telling us stories about how you and Julia Child Handoko can never be trusted, that you two are the dirtiest players in the entire business world."

Abi snorts. "Hah! That's *your* grandfather, not me."

"Mhmm." Rochelle shrugs, clearly unimpressed by his outburst. "So what's a good, filial granddaughter to do when presented with such an opportunity? Of course I decided to hang around, see if I could learn any useful information. You think your family's huge? Mine's even bigger, and my cousins are so competitive. I need some way to prove to my grandpa that he should pass down his business to me, and I got it. I saw the gift baskets you had your people bring in to impress everyone. I noticed that one of the red packets was different from the others." She taps her temple and winks at us. "Shows that I have amazing observational skills, right? I positioned myself to accept a red packet from you." She nods at me. "You gave me one of the normal ones, which is fine. I just looked out for that special one and found the kid you gave it to and traded a couple of red packets for it, and voilà!"

"What?" we all cry out. My mind is swimming, caught in a storm of confusion. "But why?"

She shrugs. "It was obvious that whatever was in the red packet was special. I originally thought it would just contain more money, so no harm in getting it, right? But then it turned out it contained a title deed. I looked up the plot of land, by the way." Her grin widens. "Nice spot. Right in the middle of the business district, within walking distance to the Agung Tower and the Fortnum Tower. I see now why it's such a strategic plot of land."

"You give that back to me now," Abi hisses.

Rochelle lifts her chin. "You can't bully me, old man. Especially not when you're on my property. I'll have you arrested."

Abi's hands tighten into fists. "You stole from me. That's theft."

"Uh, how is it theft when you guys gave it away? You literally gave it to some kid, and then I exchanged my red packet for his. There's a business term for it? I think it's called . . ." She knits her eyebrows and taps her chin. "Oh yeah, I think it's called trading," she says with a smirk.

Was I ever this insufferable as a teen? God, if I was, I owe Ma a world of apologies. My stomach roils with frustration as I take in Rochelle's smarmy, victorious expression. I want to reach out and shake her, scream at her until she succumbs. Instead, I remind myself to calm the hell down. Clearly, trying to intimidate her isn't working. So I need to try a different tack. As much as I hate this kid, I have to admit that she is smart. So maybe reasoning to her sense of logic would work better.

"That is really resourceful," I say, trying to keep my voice even. "If I were your grandfather, I would be very impressed."

"Thank you." She does a little curtsy.

"Um, but you see, the thing is, I'm kind of in a difficult situation because of it. That title deed was arranged to be given to someone very important and very powerful—"

"Duh." She rolls her eyes, and I resist the urge to kick her in the neck. "I figured it was meant for Julia Child Handoko. Who else would be given to? This is not rocket science, you guys. Which, by the way, I'm studying."

Do I hate this kid or do I admire her? Is there a difference anymore? Does it matter? God, the situation and everyone involved is just so out there that I'm having a hard time putting together a single coherent thought. "Anyway, the problem is, you see, we went to Julia's house to explain to her that the title deed went missing, and she, ah, she kind of kept my husband behind as a . . ." The word is so alien, so wrong, that it resists being said. I have to spit it out. "Hostage." Tears rush into my eyes because saying it makes it so real. "My husband is innocent, he has nothing to do with any of this. We're just visiting from California. We don't even live here, we've never heard of any of these companies, we have nothing to do with your rivalries. He was trying to do the right thing, and now he's literally locked in her house, and I need to get the title deed to her so she'll set him free."

By the time I finish talking, I'm breathing hard, feeling like I've just scooped out the innermost fears in my heart and displayed them to her. Would it be enough? Would it sway her? Unlike Ma and the aunties and Abi, I haven't threatened or cajoled or tried to trick her into giving the title deed back. I've just used honesty, and sincerity, and I was vulnerable and—

"Wow, sucks to be you. I wish I could help, but . . ." She throws up her hands and shrugs her shoulders. "Sorry."

It's the least sorry of all sorries. Something inside me breaks. The cruelty of her. I can't believe it. I take a step forward, unsure what I'm about to do, when there's a bloodcurdling wail and Ma charges past me. "Ma, wha—"

The aunties follow her a split second later, rushing at Rochelle like a hurricane. Rochelle's eyes widen, and she has time to say, "What the f—" before they slam into her.

"Hold her arms!" Fourth Aunt yells.

"Oh my god, oh my god—" Again, I have no idea if it's me or Annabelle or Abi saying this. The three of us stare in horror as my mother and aunts physically accost Rochelle in the most awkward, arm-flailing struggle imaginable.

"Ah!" Second Aunt yelps as Rochelle knocks her hair askew. "This girl. So rude!"

Noises come from inside the house. I hear a man saying, "What's going on?"

"We gotta go!" I cry.

Somehow, in the confusion, Big Aunt jumps up and rips the title deed out of Rochelle's hand.

"Hey, give it back!" Rochelle shouts, but Ma and the aunties dash away. I grab Annabelle's wrist and tug, and we all run away from the house and clamber into Abi's waiting minivan.

"Drive," Abi barks at the chauffeur before we can even close the doors. It disturbs me that the chauffeur doesn't even seem shocked. He even—I notice belatedly—turned the car around while we were talking to Rochelle so he didn't have to back out of the driveway. The car zooms forward and I fall into Fourth Aunt's lap. I scramble to an empty seat and clutch fearfully at the handhold as the car speeds onto the road. I twist in my seat and look out the rear window to see Rochelle and a group of people running after us, shouting.

Never mind my heart racing, it feels as though my entire body is vibrating with electricity. I stare, wide-eyed, at my family, all of whom are looking somewhat shaken. Poor Annabelle is going, "Holy crap, holy crap, hoooly crap!" like she's stuck in a loop. My heart goes out to her. This is her first encounter with my mother and aunts.

Speaking of which, Ma and the aunties are quickly regaining their composure. As soon as we're out on the main road, they lean back in their seats and each and every one of them focuses on smoothing down her hair. Well, I say smoothing down, but really they're puffing it back up, because god forbid their exertions put a dent in their big, poofy hairstyles. Meanwhile, Abi is sitting up front and furiously typing on his phone. Okay, so I guess I'm going to have to be the one who brings up the obvious.

"What the hell was that?"

Ma and the aunties look up. Annabelle stops muttering "Holy crap."

"What you talking, Meddy?" Ma says.

I flail my arms, the words refusing to come out for a moment because of the sheer ridiculousness. "You guys just—you assaulted a teenager!"

They all gape at me like I've just told them that they've each grown an extra head on their necks. After a beat, Big Aunt says, "What is this, assaulted? Like, salting something? Pouring salt on wound, that kind of saying?"

"No. Like, uh . . ." Damn it, what's the proper definition of "assault"? "Like, attacked. Physically. You physically attacked a kid!"

There's another shocked silence, then they all, as one, start cackling. Poor Annabelle shrinks away from them, terror written across her face. I do not blame her one bit.

"It's not funny," I call out, raising my voice to be heard over their laughter. "If we were in the States, she could press charges. I mean, I'm pretty sure we'd be arrested. I don't know what the laws are here, but—"

"She's not going to report it to the police," Abi says from the front.

"How are you so sure?"

"Because of who she is."

Ice prickles down my arms, making my skin break out in

gooseflesh. "Right, because she's the granddaughter of a mafia family who happens to be your bitter rival."

"No, I told you before, there is no such thing as mafias or crime syndicates here," Abi snorts. "We're all law—"

"Law-abiding citizens, right," I mutter. "Law-abiding citizens who don't report anything to the police. Okay. I see." I glare at Ma and the aunties. "Great, so you got lucky because the person you assaulted happened to be the grandchild of totally-not-mafia, so she won't be reporting you to the police. But still, that was crazy, what you did. You could've hurt her."

"Hah!" Big Aunt barks, slamming her palm down on the armrest, suddenly looking furious. "Then maybe it make her think twice next time about being so rude to her elders."

Second Aunt, Ma, and Fourth Aunt all nod vehemently.

"She was bad egg, so bad," Second Aunt agrees. Great, of course the one time Second Aunt agrees with Big Aunt, it's over this. "She need to be taught lesson."

"Yes, her parents do bad job raising her, you know," Ma adds. "I always raise you to respect your elder, ya kan? Ya?" She glares at me.

"Um, well, yeah, but—"

"Let's face it, she was a smug little shit who deserved taking down a peg or two," Fourth Aunt says, with zero remorse.

"Fourth Aunt!"

Ma nods, because of course they are all in agreement right now. She turns to Annabelle, who looks like she's wishing she could melt into the leather seats. "You listen, ya. Annabelle, you better not be friend with that girl. She is anak ngga benar."

"Yes." Big Aunt nods. "Not-right kid."

"Not-right kid, exactly," Second Aunt chimes in.

Annabelle nods quickly. "Yes, okay, Grandaunts. I won't hang out with her anymore."

They all glare at her a few moments more before Big Aunt sniffs and nods. Annabelle sags back into her seat. The poor, poor kid. When Ma and the aunties are sufficiently distracted by something else, I reach out and pat Annabelle's arm. She gives me a terrified look, like: What the hell did you just get me involved in?!

"We need to drop Annabelle home first before going to Julia's," I call out to Abi. There is no way I'm letting us drag her into the dangers of Julia Child's clutches. Ma and the aunties all nod in agreement.

Minutes later, we arrive at Annabelle's house. I have never seen anyone climb out of a car so fast; she basically jumps out before the car's even stopped moving, and dashes away while shouting, "Thank you, *bye*." My heart goes out to her. She reminds me of myself when I was her age. Or maybe by the time I was her age, I was used to my mom and aunts and knew it was futile to try to fight them?

I turn my attention back to our task at hand as we roll back onto the road. What happened today was awful, no doubt about that, but I can't undo it, and to be honest, Ma and the aunties do have a point: Rochelle was an immensely horrible kid, and though she didn't deserve to be attacked by them like that, I can't see any other way we could have gotten the title deed from her. And now, we have it in our hands and we're on our way to Julia Child's house to rescue Nathan. The knot around my stomach eases a little at the thought. Despite all of the mishaps, we have made actual progress. In just minutes, an hour max, I would be reunited with my sweet, long-suffering, loving husband.

Julia Child's estate is just as imposing in the daytime as it was last night. Maybe even more so, because in daylight, it becomes clear just how awe-inspiring it is, so expansive, and the walls around it so impossibly high that it looks like the embassy of a country that's invested all of its GDP into the defense sector. My eyes are riveted to the walls as we drive through the front gates. Truly, I have never seen such high walls around a private residence. They look about fifty feet tall and at least three feet thick, and at the very top of the walls are coils of literal barbed wire. Law-abiding businesswoman, my ass.

The car creeps forward up the driveway and we alight at the front door. We climb out warily. For once my mom and aunts are quiet, their usual confidence muted by the imposing mansion that looms before us. Abi smooths down his shirt and hair as he strides to the front door. It clicks open and we all jump a little. A man dressed in an impeccable suit stands before us.

"Welcome back, we've been expecting you."

Abi nods, and we all follow the man as he leads us through the beautiful foyer and into the living room, where Julia Child awaits in all her glory. Today, she is dressed in an expensive-looking pantsuit, and her makeup is 100 percent on point, down to the perfectly painted lips. Next to her are two men dressed in black suits, and next to them is Nathan.

"Nathan," I cry out, taking a step toward him. The two men stand up. They are very, very tall. I stop in my tracks, all of my instincts suddenly screaming.

"Oh, for goodness' sake," Julia Child mutters, rolling her eyes. "Boys, just—calm down, will you? You know what? Actually, just leave us, please." She waves the two men away.

They hesitate. One of them leans down and murmurs, "Ma'am, are you sure? This is a sensitive situation, and—"

"Do I need to repeat myself?" The casual tone that had graced her voice just a moment ago is gone, replaced by icy sharpness. The man straightens up immediately, gives a short shake of the head, and strides out with his companion. Julia Child turns back to face us and smiles. "I'm sorry about that. It's so hard to get good help nowadays, don't you think?"

"I wouldn't know, I've never had to hire bodyguards," I blurt out.

"Oh, they're not bodyguards," she laughs. "They're my personal assistants."

"Uh huh . . ." I nod, not at all buying it, not even for a second. I shift my attention back to Nathan. My heart swells at the sight of him. "Uh, can I . . . go to my husband?"

"Of course. Goodness me, why would you ever think that you can't?"

Because your bodyguards literally almost jumped me when I tried to? But I don't bother replying before Nathan and I cross the distance between us. I fall into his arms, and he embraces me so tight that he lifts me off my feet.

"Are you okay?" we say to each other at the same time. I pause, laughing, and we say it again. "I'm okay, are you okay?"

"Oh, isn't this touching?" Julia Child smiles at everyone, putting her palms together under her chin. "There is truly nothing I love seeing more than young love. It's just so inspiring, don't you think? Is there anything you wouldn't do for your husband, my dear girl?"

I turn to her, my fingers weaving through Nathan's, and I say, without a single doubt, "No."

Nathan and I gaze into each other's eyes and he gives me a

small nod. It's a tiny gesture, but behind it is all our history, and the knowledge that despite everything—all of the crap that I've put him through—we are okay.

"Ah, I knew it." She sighs happily, before turning back to face the rest of the group. "So." With that single word, she has suddenly morphed back into business mode, all the motherly warmth replaced in a snap with cold efficiency. She levels a serious gaze at them. "I assume that since you have returned here, you have the title deed with you?"

Abi comes forward and takes the title deed from his inner jacket pocket but doesn't hand it to her. He pauses very dramatically, knowing that all of our eyes are drawn to the piece of paper in his hand. He doesn't take his eyes off Julia Child's. "Before I give this to you, I need your reassurance that our agreement is still intact. Despite all of the mishaps that have occurred, it was never my intention to cause offense or mistrust. Are we still okay going forward with our business arrangements?"

Not a single breath is drawn in the time it takes Julia Child to respond. Then she sniffs. "Yes, it's obvious that this has all stemmed from incompetence rather than malice."

Abi's shoulders stiffen, and fear shoots down my spine. I take a step forward, my thoughts racing to say something, anything, that would break the tension before Abi's temper gets the better of him. But before I can think of anything, Nathan says, "You must forgive us, Tante Julia, it really was my fault, because I'm not accustomed to the traditions here. I was the one who made the mistake. It was my incompetence and no one else's."

Julia Child spares him a small smile. "He's a very charming young man, isn't he, your husband? I can see why you like him so much." She turns her attention back to Abi, and her gaze flattens as she holds out her hand. "Yes, Abraham, our agreement is still in effect. I shall forget all of this debacle."

Abi cracks a smile. "You forget nothing."

They share a laugh and the title deed is passed into Julia Child's hands. The moment the piece of paper lands on her upturned palm, the grip that was caught around my chest releases and I exhale, all of the breath deflating out of me. So. Much. Relief! I sag against Nathan. Ma and the aunties are grinning at one another.

Julia Child scans the piece of paper and nods, satisfied. As she struts behind her desk and slides the title deed into a drawer, she says, "Well, I hope you gave the poor kid you took this from a sizable red packet in exchange."

The uncomfortable silence that greets her words makes her glance up. She frowns, straightening up and locking the drawer. "What is it?"

Images of my mother and aunts slamming into Rochelle like a group of overeager linebackers crash through my mind.

"What's wrong?" Nathan whispers.

"Nothing." I punctuate it with a grin, but it's obvious it's not sincere.

Julia Child narrows her eyes at us and stalks to the front of her desk before leaning back against it. She crosses her arms in front of her chest and cocks her head to one side. "Out with it. You're in my house. Do not even think you could lie to me."

Ma and the aunts exchange a quick glance. This is completely new territory for them, and I can see the conflicting emotions warring inside. They're not used to being in the presence of such a formidable figure. I'm used to it because I grew up with four of them. I'm used to cowering in the presence of greatness, but not so for Ma and the aunties, especially for Big Aunt, who looks like she's torn between treating Julia Child with deference and telling her off.

Abi is the first to speak. "Ah, well, the red packet wasn't with any of their family members. It had been taken by some-one else."

An eyebrow quirks up. "Oh?"

"It was a teen. She just happened to be dropping by to see her friend, and—"

"Oh, for goodness' sake, out with it. What happened? Did you harm a random teenage girl?"

Should I be worried by the fact that Julia Child doesn't seem at all surprised, merely irritated?

"No, I—well, ah—I didn't lay a finger on her—"

"Aiya," Big Aunt snaps. "Why you must say like that? Like, so omnipotent."

We all turn to stare at her. "Omnipotent?" Julia Child says.

I raise my hand. "I think she meant 'ominous.'" I give Big Aunt a smile and she nods gratefully.

"Yes, so omni-nous. Like something so bad happen. Actu-ally, nothing bad happen. We just teach her a lesson, be re-specting to your elders!"

Ma and the other aunties all nod, even Second Aunt. "Yes." Second Aunt wags a finger at the world in general. "Waduh, she was so rude, very talking back. What kind of parent rais-ing her to be so rude to her elders?"

Julia Child's top lip curls into a sneer. "Nothing worse than people who have no respect for their elders."

Ma and the aunties nod vigorously. "Yes, exactly," Ma cries. "Good thing, you agree. I know you will agree because you are proper person."

A thin smile appears on Julia Child's face. "So you got the title deed back and you taught a disrespectful teen a lesson. I don't see any downsides here. You may go."

"Er—" Abi says, his face seemingly stuck in a permanent grimace. "Yes, about that. The teen—who was very disrespectful, this is true—ah, the tricky part is about who she was."

Julia Child stares at him. After about two seconds, or maybe it was three hours, Abi finally spits it out. "She's Kristofer's granddaughter."

There is a shocked silence. Even though I'm still unclear on what this means to Julia Child and Abi, I get the feeling that this isn't good news. Not good news at all. In fact, it might even be catastrophic news.

In a low voice, as though she's afraid someone might overhear, Julia Child whispers, "Kristofer Kolumbes?"

Abi nods. The silence that follows is as thick as Big Aunt's buttercream. Then, just as I can no longer stomach the tension, Julia Child opens her mouth and . . . cackles. She literally cackles, like a witch, throwing her head back, clutching her stomach, and letting the maniacal laughter rip out of her. It's the first time I've seen someone do that whole "*Mwahaha!*" laughter, and it's disconcerting as hell. I have no idea how to react, and neither does anyone else in the room. We all glance at one another like, uh, what should we do? The hell if I know.

"Kristofer—Kris—" Julia Child gasps in between cackles.

Ma and the aunties give Abi a look, and he shrugs helplessly. The laughter goes on another few minutes before Julia Child finally catches her breath. She wipes away her tears and, still huffing with laughter, says, "Seriously? Wait, so you told off his grandchild?" She snorts again.

"I would say she was more than just told off." Abi looks down at his shoes.

"She didn't want to let go of the title deed, that little brat," Fourth Aunt snorts.

Julia Child gapes at them. "Did you—did you accost her? Physically?"

There's another thick silence as Ma and the aunties are suddenly very interested in the walls and the ceiling of the room.

"Yes," I finally choke out. "There was—ah—a physical struggle. She wasn't hurt though," I add quickly.

This is greeted by another round of cackling. Julia Child smacks the table and laughs and laughs. "Oh my god. This is the best thing I've ever heard. So the lot of you went to Kristofer Kolumbes's grandchild's house, physically wrestled the poor girl, and snatched the title deed from her. Oh, this is—this is wonderful." Her eyes glitter with gleeful triumph. "To be a fly on the wall when she tells him about it . . ."

Dread gnaws at my stomach. "Is that—are we in trouble? Who exactly is this Kristofer Kolumbes?"

Julia Child sniffs, her expression turning sour. "Kristofer Kolumbes Hermansah. A small man, petty and childish and insecure."

There's clearly a whole history between Julia Child and Kristofer Kolumbes. A dangerous story, probably pockmarked with land mines. I'm not about to go traipsing in there, but before I can say anything, Ma pipes up. "Hmm, sound just like my ex-husband."

Second Aunt and Big Aunt nod, both of them frowning at the thoughts of their respective ex-husbands. Julia Child's expression softens. "Well, I wouldn't know. I've never married. I think it was the right decision, don't you?"

We all nod vehemently. Well, at least I do. Ma sighs and says, "I don't know, without Meddy papa I won't have my Meddy, and without Meddy I won't have my Nathan, and without—"

"I think we get the point, Ma," I say loudly.

Julia Child smiles. "I was never fond of children myself, but I understand. And maybe in another life, I would've liked to . . ." She gets this faraway look on her face. "But anyway. So you got into it with his grandchild, huh? Ah, he's not going to be happy about that."

That same fear coils itself around my spine. "Um, so as I was asking before, are we in trouble with him?"

Julia Child shrugs. "Who knows?"

Very reassuring. Not.

"That's the thing with these childish, petty people, isn't it?" she goes on. "But what right does he have to be angry about anything? It's not his title deed. His grandchild simply stole it and then disrespected these fine women here." She gestures to Ma and the aunties, who straighten and lift their chins with pride. "Sounds like the kid only has herself to blame. Just like Kristofer," she adds in a poisonous hiss. "If he knows what's good for him, he'll wash his hands of the whole thing and stay the hell away."

It's not really a no, but I get the feeling that this is all we're getting out of her. Just as I think that, Julia Child says, quite simply, "Well, thank you for coming. Our business is done."

It's our cue to leave, and I'm not about to miss it. I jump to attention and say, loudly, "Yes, thank you. Goodbye!" I link my arm through Ma's and pull her along while pushing Big Aunt along with my other hand in a gentle but firm way. They take the hint and say their goodbyes to Julia Child. Outside of the room, her burly bodyguards stand to attention when they see us. They look at Julia Child, who nods at them, and with that, they escort us through the mansion and out into the blinding sunlight. I dare not think what would have happened if Julia Child had shaken her head instead of nodding. Would it have been the last time that I saw the world outside these walls?

No, don't think like that, I chide myself. It's done now. It's over. We've had our entanglement with whatever Julia Child is—mafia lady, scary CEO, cartel leader—and we've managed to resolve it peacefully. Despite everything, we're going to be okay.

9

The first thing I do when I get back to the house is try to book an earlier flight out of Jakarta. We're supposed to fly to Bali in two days' time, but I look for flights going out of the city that night. Because even though we've managed to claw our way out of trouble this time, there's still a strand of fear twined around my stomach, knotted up tight. I have a bad feeling about all of this. I'm still scrolling through flight options when Nathan comes out of the shower, a towel tied around his abs.

"Man, that shower is amazing. I'm surprised you didn't want to go first." When I don't reply, he comes over, still toweling his hair dry. "You okay?"

"Ah, yeah. I'm just busy looking up flights."

"Oh? What for?"

"To go to Bali earlier. I don't wanna stay in Jakarta."

Nathan sits down on the bed next to me and puts his arm around my shoulders. "Hey. Look at me for a moment."

I do so, and the sight of him cracks my heart a little because only a few hours ago, this man had been in the clutches of a possibly unhinged, extremely powerful woman who was clearly dangerous, and it had all been my and my family's fault. As usual. How many times can I put him in danger before he finally has enough of me? I open my mouth and take a breath that feels like it's crushing my lungs before realizing I don't really know what to say.

Nathan must have seen something in my expression because his gaze softens. "It's okay. I'm here. You got me out safely." He tucks a stray lock of hair behind my ear and smirks at me. "You're my hero."

That gets a laugh out of me. Damn it, how does he manage to make me smile, even now? "But—" I half laugh, half groan, "Nathan, you were literally in the clutches of the mafia."

He gives me a deadpan look. "They're law-abiding citizens, Meddy."

My laughter takes over my entire body, shaking out from deep in my belly. How ridiculous is the whole thing? "They're clearly not."

"I know." Nathan grins. "I've never seen anyone look more uncomfortable in a formal business suit than Abi does."

"Oh god," I moan, "he looks like he's dying to rip the suit off so he can go around in a undershirt and a machete slung over his shoulder." I pause. "But you know what's even weirder than that?"

"What's weirder than meeting a guy who looks like he stepped out of a movie about Hong Kong triad members?"

"How terrified he is of Big Aunt."

This time, we both dissolve into peals of wild laughter. "I

don't blame him. I'm terrified of Big Aunt. I mean, I admire her, of course, but I wouldn't dare cross her. Ever."

"Wise." I sigh and sag against Nathan, putting my head on his muscular shoulder. I close my eyes and inhale the freshly soaped scent of him, and it feels as though every muscle in my body is finally unknotting. "I was so worried," I murmur.

"I know." He puts an arm around me and strokes my hair with heartbreaking gentleness. "But for what it's worth, I was never afraid, not even for a moment."

"Really?" I lift my head so I can look him in the eyes.

"Yeah." He puts a hand under my chin and gazes down at me. "Because I knew you'd do whatever it took to come get me."

Even now, even after we've been together for over a year, and are married, he still manages to make me blush. Warmth oozes from the pit of my belly and into every part of me. "Aww, that's so s—"

Then he adds, "Well, and your mom and your aunts. I knew they'd rain hellfire down on the world to save me."

I narrow my eyes at him. "So when you said I was your hero, you really meant Ma and the aunties?"

"Well, I mean, am I wrong? You said they literally wrestled the title deed off some poor teen. I'm guessing you didn't join in the fray."

"And assault a teenage girl? No, of course I didn't."

Nathan holds up his hands and shrugs. "Okay, so I stand corrected; the only knights in shining armor here are Ma and the aunties."

I turn away so he doesn't see the little twitch of a smile on my face. Every time I hear him referring to Ma as "Ma" instead of "your mom" or even "your ma," it sends a jolt of affection straight into my heart. Honestly, could I love this guy any more than I already do?

But I shouldn't let myself get carried away. There are important things to take care of now. Like getting the hell out of here. With a sigh, I turn back to Nathan. "Anyway, I don't like the mess we've gotten caught up in. I don't like that we had people like Abi and Julia Child and this Kristofer guy involved."

"Can I just take a moment to revel in the glory of their names?" Nathan grins. "Although, hang on, why aren't any of them named after great Indonesian or Chinese people?"

"Oh, they'll have Chinese names honoring great Chinese heroes too. But yeah, when it comes to Anglicized names, people here tend to go for famous white people. It's a whole thing. Can we focus? As much as I'd love to discuss the deep and complicated ways that colonization has affected Indonesia, I think we should concentrate on getting out of here. These people—they're not people we should be involved with."

"Yes, but technically, we're no longer involved with them. The matter has been resolved, and we can all move on—" His voice trails off and he looks up at the ceiling. Then he sighs. "Never mind, even as I say that, I realize how naive I sound." He squeezes my hand. "You're right. It's definitely not great that we've crossed paths with people this powerful. When I was at Julia Child's house, she and I chatted a bit, and I definitely got the feeling that she's not someone to be crossed."

I can't stop the shiver that runs up my spine. "What do you mean by that? Did she tell you things? What does she do when someone crosses her? Gunshot to the head? Dismemberment? Acid bath?"

"Uh. None of the above. Jesus, Meddy, you've been watching too much *Squid Game*."

I flap my arms up and down, like an angry chicken. "You just said in this really ominous tone that she's not someone to be crossed. What in the world am I supposed to take from that? Obviously it's something sinister."

"No, I just meant like, she'd go out of her way to take down her business rivals."

"Yeah, by killing them."

"No! Just—you know, by buying their businesses and then taking them apart, that sort of thing." He hesitates, thinking. "I guess some people might argue that it's a kind of death. But a business death, not the kind that comes about from a machete to the head."

"Oh. Well, why didn't you just say so?"

"Because I thought you were a normal person and would jump to the normal conclusion?" Nathan shakes his head, smiling at me, but the smile doesn't stay long on his face. "You're really worried, huh?"

"You don't get it, do you? When you were held up in her house—that was one of the worst moments of my life. I know this sounds really cliché, but I wouldn't know what to do if something had happened to you."

"Meddy." Nathan pulls me close, his fingers tangling in my hair. He sighs and kisses my forehead. "Okay, let's do this. Let's catch an earlier flight."

My rib cage seems to loosen and I take a deep breath. "Thank you." I can't believe it was this easy to convince Nathan. I guess I'm just used to Ma, who would argue with me endlessly before telling me to wait while she consulted with the aunties, and each auntie would undoubtedly have conflicting opinions that they would need to thrash out with one another in the loudest possible way. The thought of Ma and the aunties makes my chest tighten again. "Now we just need to convince Ma and the aunties."

Nathan winces. "Oof, yeah, I'm gonna let you handle that—" He laughs when I punch his arm. "Just kidding! Come on, let's go talk to them together."

"Hanh?" Ma squawks. "What you say?"

I grimace. That was a definitely unhappy squawk from Ma. Next to me, Nathan rallies valiantly. "We think it would be wise to leave Jakarta as soon as we can."

Fourth Aunt looks up from her handheld mirror, her other hand, holding a pair of tweezers, poised above her upper lip. "Why?" she says, before plucking a stray strand of mustache and wincing.

"Because we got involved with the triad?" I say loudly, gesturing for effect.

"Not triad," Second Aunt sighs. "I tell you, Abi is good man, he is good businessman. Why you have to say 'triad' like that? Make him sound so bad."

I grit my teeth so hard that I can practically feel them cracking. But I still need to bring Second Aunt on to our side if I'm to have any hope of convincing them, so I must be patient. "Yeah, maybe Abi is a good man, like you say, but Julia Child and the guy they crossed—the guy *we* crossed, actually—Kristofer Kolumbes, sound like bad news. I just don't think we should be sticking around after the huge mess today."

"Aduh, Meddy," Ma says, shaking her head. "Why you must be so mellow dramatic? I tell you all the time, please, just relax, okay?"

Oh my god. My mother, of all people, telling me I'm melodramatic? I'm in some kind of hell, I know it. Still, I make myself take a deep breath and release it through my teeth. I turn to Big Aunt, who is surely my best chance of getting some sense into my mother. "Big Aunt, you saw what happened. You were there. Julia Child literally kept Nathan hostage."

Big Aunt frowns. She's been sitting there quietly, calmly pondering what Nathan and I just brought up with them, and now all eyes are on her as she prepares to deliver her verdict. "Mm. This is hard decision, Meddy. On one hen, I also not like these people we tangle with. On the other hen, if we leave so suddenly, all of us, maybe people will think: Why? Why they go so fast?"

"Aiya, we will lose face for sure!" Ma gasps. "Yes, you are right, Dajie. Everyone will asking this and that. Why you must go so sudden? Suddenly you leaving, must be something wrong, maybe business in California fail."

All of the aunties' faces pale at this. Even Fourth Aunt lowers her handheld mirror to gape at the others in dismay.

Poor, unsuspecting, sweet Nathan clears his throat. "Um, I'm sure the rest of the family wouldn't jump to that conclusion," he says before I can stop him.

Oh no. He's done it now.

All four women descend on him like shrieking harpies.

Second Aunt: "*Hah.* That is exactly the first conclusion they jumping to."

Ma: "Oh, they will be so smug, you can just see that Marilin face, she will smile like this and say, 'Oh, such shame that your business got trouble. I tell you all those years ago, don't move to California, but you never listen to me.'"

Fourth Aunt: "You have no idea what these bitches will say about us."

Nathan now has his palms up in front of his face, shielding

himself from them. "But—wait—I don't get it—we just had a lovely celebration with these people. They're so close to you. They're so friendly. Why—"

"Tch," Big Aunt tuts, and everyone else quiets down. She narrows her eyes at Nathan. "Nathan, you are half-Asian, how you cannot understand this?" When he opens his mouth to reply, Big Aunt holds up her palm and shakes her head. "Never mind. Is because you growing up in small family, I know. But with big family, everything is complicated. Yes, of course we love one another. But we all have our own argument with one another. And when we leave Indonesia for America so many years ago, there are many—what you call it—"

"Petty bitches," Fourth Aunt pipes up.

Big Aunt nods somberly. "Yes, petty bitches." I have no idea if she even knows what the words mean. I hope she doesn't. "They get angry. Why we leave? Maybe some of them want to leave, too, but they cannot because this reason, that reason. So yes, they are happy for us, wah, we make it in America. But they also not that happy because maybe they are a bit jealous."

"But they've made it here," Nathan mutters. "I mean, look at this house. It's massive."

"Yeah, we're petty bitches about it too," Fourth Aunt says. "Have you not heard the number of backhanded compliments we've given them? Do I regret leaving Indonesia? Sometimes. Am I ever going to admit that to them? Over my dead body."

Big Aunt nods. "But is like, how you say, the grass got early worms on the other side."

"The grass is greener on the other side," I say.

Big Aunt frowns. "Why it would be greener on other side? It will be the same green. But got more worms, so the soil more fertile, then you can grow more veggie-tibbles."

"Uh . . ." I give up. "Yeah, that's true."

Nathan nods slowly, looking dazed. "Right . . . I think I get it?" He glances at me, and I shrug. I don't even really get it, and I've grown up with this. But no world politics is more complicated than the aunties network. He turns back to Ma and the aunts. "So even though you've all done well, half of you by moving to America, and the other half by staying behind, you secretly wish you'd done a lot better than them."

Ma nods happily. "Yes, exactly. Aduh, you very smart deh, Nathan. Surely your babies all be genius, go to Mensa."

Nathan gives a weak laugh. "Maybe we can make up some urgent reason for us all to leave Jakarta?"

Ma harrumphs. "No, is been so long since we see everybody. I want to spend more time with my family."

"You all just talked about how much you can't stand each other!" Nathan's voice has reached a pitch I'm very familiar with myself, because that's the pitch I always hit when I'm trying to convince Ma and the aunts to do something they don't want to do.

"Yes, but they still family," Big Aunt says sternly.

"We might all be in danger," I point out.

"Tch." Second Aunt flaps her hand at me dismissively. "You just being drama queen again, Meddy. Of course we not in danger. Got Abi to protect us." She simpers, and I decide I don't like Second Aunt in love.

"He seemed really scared of Julia Child." I have to admit that I take a bit of pleasure in reminding her of this.

Second Aunt glowers at me. "He not afraid. He just being diplomatic. Nathan, you know all about that, you are also businessman." Her laser gaze drills into Nathan, who stares back with naked panic.

"Uh. To be fair . . ." Nathan swallows and proceeds with the care that one takes approaching a live bomb. "He did seem slightly more nervous than one would expect. Perhaps there might be more danger than we're all privy to?"

Ma shakes her head. "You kids are too Westernized. You just not used to how Asian business go. We always have to show respect. But you think showing respect is being scared."

I think back to the expression on Abi's face. It was very definitely fearful, and not just fear of losing a good business deal but a primal sort of fear of the possibility of losing one's life. "Look, I know what I saw on Abi's face, and I'm telling you, we're playing with fire."

"Who play with fire?" Big Aunt snaps, looking around.

"No, not literally, Big Aunt. I just mean we're involved in something really dangerous, and I think it's best to put some distance between us and these people."

"You can go," Second Aunt says. "You and Nathan go sana, if you so worry. But I am staying here." Her expression is so determined that I know there is no hope in hell of convincing her otherwise. And can I blame her? I of all people know exactly how it feels to finally be reunited with the love of my life. I look at Nathan and think back to that fateful day when I saw him again on the island after years of pining after him. We lock eyes, and I know he's thinking the exact same thing. And for Second Aunt, it's been even longer. An entire lifetime away from Abi before finally meeting him again. Of course she's not going to let that chance slip from her fingers. What would make anyone give up a chance at true love?

I reach out and put a hand on Second Aunt's arm. "Okay, Second Aunt. You get your man." She giggles—actually giggles —and my heart twists because in a crazy way, this is really kind of romantic. I truly hope things work out for her and Abi this time around.

"So you two going to leave me here?" Ma says plaintively.

My insides explode in the world's biggest groan, but I manage not to say it out loud. Trust Ma to pull the parental guilt on me. I meet Nathan's eye and a whole unspoken conversation ping-pongs between us. *What do we do? Stay? Go?*

How long of a grudge will your mom have for us?

Oh, this is a forever thing. When she is old and bent over a walking stick, she'll still be telling everyone about how we abandoned her and her sisters in Jakarta that one time.

Are we in actual danger? Because if we are, then we should still go even with the threat of a forever-grudge.

And that's the million-dollar question: Are we in actual danger? Who knows? The point is that we're trying to mitigate any possible threat to our safety.

A look around the room confirms that there are no answers to be found here, and despite myself, I feel my resolve crumbling. "We'll sleep on it," I say finally, not wanting to completely give in to them. "We won't leave tonight, but I'm leaning on leaving tomorrow, if that's okay with you, Ma?"

Ma sighs. "Of course is okay with me. Why not okay with me? Is okay you want to leave me behind, forget all about your mother."

"We're not leaving you behind," I say through gritted teeth. "We're literally asking you to come with us."

"And lose face," Ma snaps. "What we will say to everyone? They will ask so many questions."

"We'll sleep on it," Nathan says in his usual firm but gentle way.

Glares zap through the room as we all agree on this uneasy

truce. I know Ma is rattled because I don't usually stand up for myself like this. The old me would've broken under their usual guilt trip and agreed to stay for as long as they want, but I can't be like the old me anymore. I have to be firm, I have to draw the line somewhere and make the best decisions I can think of, and sometimes, those decisions are going to be diametrically opposed to what Ma and the aunties think is best. I remind myself of this as Nathan and I trudge out of the room, the atmosphere heavy on our shoulders. I remind myself of this throughout the rest of the day, when we spend time with the extended family and we all have to laugh and act normal around them, and I remind myself of this at night, when Nathan and I lie down in bed, our eyes wide open in the darkness, our thoughts rushing everywhere like frightened horses.

His hand finds mine under the covers. "You okay?" he whispers.

"Were they right? Was I just overreacting?"

"I don't know. I mean, all that stuff they said about this being down to cultural differences . . . who knows, right?"

An awful thought sinks in. "Nathan, am I like my mom and aunts?"

In the silence, I can hear that Nathan's breathing has paused. An eternity passes before he says, "In what way?"

"Oh my god, you think I'm like them."

"What? No. Well, only the best parts."

I frown. I'm about to press him, find out exactly in what way he thinks I'm like Ma, when I realize that's exactly what Ma would do. Damn it. Okay, what would Ma not do? She wouldn't let it go. She would spend the rest of the night ruminating, and then confront him for answers the following morning. And I am not going to be like that, because I am not Ma.

I take a deep breath and force my muscles to relax. I think of happy sheep trundling down a meadow and jumping over a fence—no, that's stressful. Why would they jump over a fence that's clearly there to protect them? Nothing good's on the other side, sheep. Okay. I take another deep breath and imagine myself in a beautiful forest, surrounded by leafy trees. Cool, this is working. As I slowly drift to sleep, I congratulate myself on successfully not turning into Ma.

But when we are shaken awake in the morning by Ma and find ourselves blinking, confused, at Ma, Big Aunt, and Fourth Aunt, all of them wearing terrified frowns, I realize that I've made a horrible mistake. I should have pushed them harder. I should've morphed into a forceful auntie myself and insisted on getting my own way. I should've nagged and guilted and prodded until they all packed their bags and drove to the airport. Because the first thing Ma says is: "You have to get up. Second Aunt is kidnapped."

10

Nathan is the first to speak. "What do you mean 'kidnapped'?" I have no idea how he manages to sound so lucid and alert when I'm still sitting there blinking stupidly. The world has a murky quality to it that makes me feel as though I'm underwater, my thoughts swimming slowly. I squeeze my eyes shut and open them again, hoping it will wake me up.

"Aduh, what you mean, what I mean, kidnapped?" Ma cries. "Kidnap itu ya kidnap. Is there other meaning to kidnap?"

"I think he's asking how it happened and who did it," Fourth Aunt snaps. She turns to Nathan. "Second Aunt likes to do Tai Chi every morning—"

Big Aunt snorts. "He know. Everybody know. She always telling everybody how she like to do the Tai Chi every morning, always boasting about it." Her words are callous, but I catch the slight crack in Big Aunt's voice, and this is what wakes me up. Big Aunt is worried. Sure enough, when I look at her closely, I see the telltale signs of anxiety; the way her mouth is pinched, the way she's woven her fingers through each other and is grasping so tightly that her knuckles have turned white. My breath catches in my throat. Big Aunt is worried about Second Aunt, her nemesis. Things are serious.

"Right," Fourth Aunt continues, "so this morning, she went out to the front yard to do Tai Chi—"

"Aiya, how you know what happen?" Ma interrupts. "You were sleeping, you lazy bum. I was awake, I was in the kitchen making tea for me and Second Aunt—"

"Right, so you were making your weed tea as usual—"

"Not weed tea. Jasmine tea!" Ma snaps. "Anyway, then I hear cars screech. I look up and I see this big black car stopping outside the gate, then these men come out—aduh, they so scary deh—they force gate open like this—" She mimes wrenching open the gate. "And they—they—" Her voice breaks. "They just take her! She doing the Tai Chi and they just grab her. I run outside but they gone already."

Horrified doesn't even begin to describe what I'm feeling. Whatever is going through me right now, it actually feels physical, like someone's punched me directly in the stomach, knocking all of the wind out of me. Nausea pulses through me in sickening waves. Next to me, Nathan looks just as shellshocked as I feel. I don't know how to process this. Maybe I should, after all that we've been through—accidental murder, overpowering a bunch of fake mafia members at our wedding— this shouldn't come as such a blow, but it does.

It's the thought of poor Second Aunt, grabbed by unknown men while she was doing something as innocuous and mundane as Tai Chi. This isn't supposed to happen. Not to normal people like us. But then again, after everything we've done, maybe we're not normal people. Maybe it's exactly the kind of thing that happens to people like us.

Tears flood my eyes. My head feels hot, like my skin is about to melt right off my skull. *I told you we should've left!* I want to shriek at them. But Ma and the aunties look so wretched, their faces twisted with anxiety and sorrow, that I can't possibly allow myself to play the blame game right now. No, what's most important right now is getting Second Aunt back.

"They leave this on front lawn." Ma produces an envelope, and Nathan takes it.

For kidnappers, they have strangely good taste. The envelope is made of thick, creamy paper with a letterpress logo on it that says: KKH. My stomach sinks so low it threatens to fall right out of me. That can only be Kristofer Kolumbes Hermansah.

Sure enough, when Nathan takes out the card inside and reads it out loud, my fears are confirmed.

"You stole something from my granddaughter."

"This is preposterous!" Abi roars. He starts pacing about the room like a caged tiger, his teeth gritted, his hands squeezed into fists. His rage emanates from him in a blinding aura, and I find myself leaning away from him without even realizing it.

Julia Child, who has made herself comfortable despite just arriving moments ago, rolls her eyes, seemingly unperturbed by this outburst. "It's somewhat unfortunate, yes."

"Unfortunate?" Abi swings around to face her. What happened to all of that deference and fearful respect he had toward her just a day ago? Even as I think that, I realize that it's all gone, burned away by his love for Second Aunt. It's touching in a really horrible, awful way. I want to weep for him and everyone involved, but most of all, I want to sob out of anxiety and concern for Second Aunt. I hope she's safe. "This isn't what I'd call unfortunate. It's unacceptable. This is a slap in the face. It's a challenge. We have to meet it."

Something cold tingles across my skin. Hang on, this sounds like an escalation, not a resolution. I've spent enough time with my own ma and aunties to know that when they go into escalation mode, I really need to step in before they cause World War III. "Can we maybe try to speak with Kristofer peacefully and come to some sort of compromise?"

"What?" Abi roars. "Speak with Kristofer peacefully? You might as well try to reason with a snake."

Julia Child snorts. "Unfortunately, in this instance, I agree with Abraham. Kristofer is not someone who is receptive to reason and logic."

Abi nods. "The only way we can get Enjelin back is by going head-to-head against him." He pauses and stands up straight, his chest swelling with incandescent anger. "War," he whispers.

Julia Child clicks her tongue, still looking unimpressed. "Hmm."

"War?" Nathan says. He breaks his stare from Abi to give me a look that says: *Is he serious?*

Oh god. I raise my hand meekly. "What do you mean by war?"

"Tch, Meddy, you don't malu-maluin Mama dong," Ma says. "Is obvious, war is mean fight. We fight them." She gets that glint in her eyes again, like Gordon Ramsay when he's just cut into an overcooked piece of steak.

"Fight them?" I wish my voice didn't come out so squeaky.

"Yes," Big Aunt intones in the Voice of God, crossing her thick arms in front of her massive chest. "We fight. We cannot allow our sister to be kidnap like this. We teach them lesson."

"What the—whoa, whoa," I cry. "What the hell happened to 'law-abiding businesspeople'?" I'm stuck in a nightmare. I know it. Maybe I should smack myself to wake myself up. "Why don't we just go to the police?"

At this, Abi and Julia Child both jump up as though I've just tapped them with an electric prod. "*No police!*" they both shout.

I gape at them. They exchange glances with each other, as though surprised that they've reacted so quickly and decisively.

"Let me explain," Julia Child says with a practiced smile. "Indonesia is very different from America. Here, we try not to get the police involved as much as we can. We prefer to . . . solve our own problems."

"Yes, yes," Abi says, nodding vigorously. "Solve our own problems."

"Wha—" I close my mouth. Open it again. "But this involves literal kidnapping. Surely that's gone well beyond the scope of peaceful conflict resolution. It's an actual *crime*. That should be handled by the police."

Neither one speaks. Their faces are both painfully resolute, cold and unmoving as stones.

"This is because you two *are* triad leaders, aren't you? All that stuff you said about being legit businesspeople, that was all bullshit." Next to me, Nathan shifts warily and Ma and the aunties wince at how harshly I'm speaking to my elders, but I can't help it. There have been so many lies, and they've all culminated in this. In Second Aunt being literally kidnapped. There's a shocking protective instinct that's caught me by surprise,

rearing up from deep inside me and striking with claws un-
sheathed, teeth out. I don't care whom I offend, I need my
family intact.

"You don't understand what the police are like in countries
outside of America," Julia Child says simply. "You're looking
at this through an American lens. Did you never read that
god-awful story about Amanda Knox?"

Ma shakes her head while Fourth Aunt's head bobs back
and forth. "Foxy Knoxy," Fourth Aunt says.

"Hanh?" Ma says.

"That was the unfortunate name that the Italian police
came up with for Amanda Knox after her roommate was
found murdered in Italy," Julia Child says. "The Italian police
immediately pinned Amanda as a suspect, and all of their in-
vestigation seemed geared to proving she was guilty instead of
finding out the actual truth. And you know what? Her case
wasn't at all unique. It only went viral because she's a beautiful
Caucasian woman, but every day, all over the world, tourists
find themselves in bad situations, and when the local cops get
involved, guess who they're going to blame?"

My stomach sours. This is completely not the way I saw this
conversation going, but as much as I want to refute Julia
Child's logic, it makes perfect sense. Tourists make for a con-
venient scapegoat.

"You are visitors in this country," Julia Child continues.
"Your aunts renounced their Indonesian citizenship, didn't
they?"

Ma and the aunties nod hesitantly, and Julia Child sniffs.
"Right, so you're American citizens. You're tourists. You're in
a foreign country, and you're suggesting we go to the police
and tell them that the most powerful and respected business-

man in Indonesia has had your auntie kidnapped while she's doing Tai Chi?"

I gape at her for a second, realizing how utterly ridiculous it all sounds. But I forge ahead. "Well, *yes!*" I sputter. "I mean, that is literally what happened. Or maybe we could go to the US Embassy—"

"They will only make things worse. Americans, always marching everywhere, claiming power where they have no right to. If you get the US Embassy involved, it'll likely make the local authorities more defensive and less likely to help you."

I grit my teeth, and Nathan squeezes my hand. "She's right," he murmurs. "I travel a lot for business and I hear a lot of things—incidents that involve tourists in foreign countries. Ninety-nine percent of the time, the local authorities would take advantage of the fact that tourists rarely know the laws of the country and they'll pin the blame on the tourist. Before they know it, they're imprisoned for years for breaking a law that they didn't even know existed."

"But we haven't broken any laws!" I cry. Then I stop myself. Because that's not strictly true, is it? We've broken plenty of laws, including the biggest of them all: murder. And maybe if the Indonesian police were to look into our backgrounds, they might discover incriminating evidence about our old crimes. It's a horrible realization, slamming down with the force of an anvil. I feel as though my very bones have been crushed and flattened. I can barely keep myself on my feet. I just want to lie down and weep.

"Okay, so no polisi," Big Aunt says. Her face is still sickly pale with worry, but she looks resolute, far stronger than I'm feeling. Shame burns in my veins. Big Aunt, who is in her sixties, is holding up better than I am even though it's her sister who's gone missing. I need to be stronger. I take a deep breath, willing the air to fortify me. "What we do now to get Enjelin back?"

"War!" Abi roars again. Now that the discussion about calling the cops has been thoroughly dismissed, he's fully embraced his rage once again. "Julia Child, you need to round up all of your men. We need to gather our forces and storm his house and—"

Julia Child scoffs at the same time as my mouth drops open. "I think not," she says with finality.

"What?" Abi shouts.

"I want nothing to do with Kristofer." Her nose wrinkles with obvious distaste. "No, if I never speak to the man again, it's too soon."

I want to scream. I can't believe that even someone as powerful as Julia Child is still concerned with "What might people say?" And we're in such dire straits that it's ridiculous that anyone could be hung up on something so trivial. We're talking about literally saving someone from a kidnapper. But then again, I'm not convinced by Abi's idea of "war," whatever that means. Surely it can't mean a literal battle, but I have no idea what passes for normal with these people anymore.

Ma and the aunties are gaping at her. "Are you saying you won't help get my sister back because you're scared it'll make you look bad?" Fourth Aunt says.

Julia Child's gaze flattens. "I wouldn't put it that way."

"I don't care what way you put it," Fourth Aunt snaps. "You had a hand in this, you'd better step up, lady."

Julia Child's chin lifts ever so slightly. "Oh?"

Suddenly, the atmosphere in the room drops, turning icy. If Fourth Aunt is a scrappy warrior, Julia Child is a ruthless empress. Big Aunt must have felt the shift, too, because she places a hand on Fourth Aunt's shoulder, as if to say: *Back off and let me handle this.* She nods at Julia Child. "What your suggestion?" Her voice comes out very measured. Calm, but with just a touch of accusatory note that makes it clear that she hasn't let Julia Child off the hook. "We appreciate your help to get our sister out."

Julia Child sighs and turns away, crossing her arms and tapping her chin with an immaculately manicured fingernail. "I really don't want to get involved in this. It's your mess, Abraham." At the rushed intake of breath from all of us, she holds up a palm. "But let me think." She gazes out of the window for what seems like an entire year before finally speaking again. "Ah, I think I have an idea. Kristofer always throws a lavish feast for every holiday. Chinese New Year, the Full Moon Festival, even Christmas."

"Isn't Chinese New Year over?" I say. "We had our big celebration two nights ago."

"You would think. But not for Kristofer," she says dryly. "He holds a celebration for his family on the night of Chinese New Year, and then another two days later for everyone else— his business partners, his friends, everyone. It's a huge feast with hundreds of guests, and it's happening tonight. The perfect chance for you all to get in, get your aunt back, and get out without Kristofer knowing."

"What? How are we going to do that?" I blurt out.

Julia Child levels a serious gaze at me. It feels as though she's looking directly through my skin and flesh and straight into my soul. Then she nods toward Big Aunt. "I'm sure you'll all figure something out."

"We'll get it done," Fourth Aunt says flippantly, as though she's talking about a trip to Target.

"How we going to steal into someone's house?" Ma gnaws at a fingernail. Big Aunt frowns at Ma, and Ma quickly puts her hand back down on her lap.

With a sniff, Big Aunt turns to Julia Child. "We handle it."

The question of how is almost out of my mouth before I manage to swallow it down. If I asked Big Aunt that right now, she'd probably see it as me talking back, and worse, doing so in front of outsiders, which would bring extra shame. But really, what in the world can we possibly come up with that could get us into some mafia lord's house? And, don't forget, out of said mafia lord's house, preferably in one piece? Still, my mouth refuses to open and betray Big Aunt's confident facade.

Julia Child nods at Big Aunt. "Once you get her out, go to the private airstrip. I'll have my jet fly all of you out of here so you can leave all this mess behind. That's my best offer of help."

My heart is racing. With fear? With anticipation? With excitement at the chance to get Second Aunt back? Who knows. I feel like vomiting. Nathan looks just as conflicted as I feel, but Ma and the aunties' eyes are glittering. There's even a small smile playing on Fourth Aunt's lips. Of course they would be excited by the prospect of breaking into a triad leader's house.

"And you—" Julia Child turns to Abi. "You'd better wait at your house. You can't show your face there, otherwise the whole operation would be discovered."

Abi's hands clench and unclench as he grits his teeth. It's obvious he's dying to come with us, but Julia Child is right. He would be recognized immediately.

"I—I don't know . . ." I mumble. I keep my hands together to stop them from trembling.

"Okay," Big Aunt says. "We do this. And you will fly us away right after?"

"Tch." Abi waves a hand flippantly. "I'll fly you all in my private jet. That's not a problem."

Julia Child shrugs. "If you wish. But my jet is also at your service. As my thanks for helping to get the title deed back."

I look at Nathan, then at Ma and my aunties, and I see the answer written plainly on their faces. There's never been any question about it, because of course we would go to the deepest reaches of hell to save one of us. We're going into Kristofer Kolumbes's estate, and we're going to get Second Aunt back, even if it kills us.

11

The plan is very straightforward. Well, as straightforward as rescue missions can go, which is to say not at all straightforward. First of all, we need to come up with a way of getting inside Kristofer's house. Julia Child allows us to use her office as a strategy room, and after Googling Kristofer and reading a few articles on him, Nathan and I spend some time scouting Kristofer's estate using Google Earth, a technology that mystifies Ma and Big Aunt.

"You mean, every house is on this Earth thing?" Big Aunt says, as we zoom closer in on Kristofer's house.

"Yes," Nathan says. He double clicks, and the satellite image goes to ground level, giving us a sharp view of the front facade of Kristofer's mansion.

"Aiya, definitely not in America," Ma says confidently. "America won't let such peeping Tom thing to happen."

Nathan and I exchange a glance. Which one of us is going to break her pure heart?

"You do realize Google is an American company?" Julia Child says.

Ma's mouth snaps shut into a thin line. A deep crease appears between her eyebrows as the weight of Julia Child's words sinks in. "But—" she says after a while. "Our house— it's not on this thing, ya kan?"

"It is, Ma," I say gently.

"What?" Ma cries. "So this whole time, there are all this people peeping at our house like—like—" She flaps her arms like an angry chicken. "Like we some peeping show for pervert to look at?"

"Who would want to do that?" Fourth Aunt says with a roll of her eyes. "You think people don't have anything better to do than watch your boring old house?"

"Not boring," Ma snaps. "Is only two years ago when—ah—"

I close my eyes. I can't believe she was about to bring up that whole thing with Ah Guan just to win an argument against Fourth Aunt. Well, who am I kidding? Of course she would. "It's fine, Ma," I say loudly. "Nobody's looking at our house from space. We're just normal people."

"From space?" Ma cries.

"Never mind, forget I said anything. Let's focus on this." I pat her hand and turn her attention back to the screen, where Nathan is expertly studying the house from every possible angle.

"Those are some serious walls," Fourth Aunt muses. She's right. The walls surrounding Kristofer's house are definitely unscalable by the likes of us. And even if we did manage to somehow scale them, there are coils of barbed wire on top that would tear us to shreds.

"You'll have to go in as his guests," Julia Child says.

"Tch, he'll know they're strangers," Abi sighs. "I'm loathe to say anything nice about Kristofer, but he's a devil for details. You and I might not notice a handful of extra guests not on the list, but he would."

Julia Child's top lip curls into a sneer. "You're right. He is a stickler for details."

I chew on my bottom lip. "Um, we could go in as service staff. For a party this big, he'll definitely have helpers, right? And probably caterers, maybe even photographers?"

They both look at me as though seeing me for the first time. "Good idea, girl," Julia Child says.

Ma beams with unabashed pride. "Aduh, of course my Meddy coming up with good idea. She is best photographer, you know? Back in LA, she win this very prestigious photography award, and—"

Oh god. If I don't stop her, she'll talk their ears off about all of my achievements, which is sweet in a completely mortifying way. "Anyway," I say loudly. "Maybe we can get in as caterers."

Nathan nods at me. "Great idea. That way, we won't even have to show our faces at the main party. We'd be inside the kitchen."

"But how would we get in as caterers?" Fourth Aunt says with a frown. "We'd need a van, and not to mention food, and . . ." She trails off at the sight of our forlorn faces.

This is the thing about plotting something illicit. Even though I've been through it with Ah Guan's death, and then again at our wedding with Staphanie's family, I'm still taken aback by the sheer amount of planning that one has to do every step of the way. Committing a crime is never as easy as the movies make it seem. Obstacles sprout like weeds, and each one requires meticulous planning, otherwise the whole thing falls apart.

"Do you know who he might have hired as caterers?" I say to Julia Child. Despite her vehemence about loathing Kristofer, she seems to know a lot about what he's up to.

Sure enough, Julia Child sniffs and says, "Oh, that unimaginative man? Every year he hires the same people. The Ritz. How boring does one have to be? I've hired them a couple of times myself. They're good, but there's something to be said for variety, you know."

Big Aunt's eyes widen. "The Ritz? I use to work there. I was head baker. They use to call me Mami." Her face softens at fond memories of her years at the Ritz.

"Oh yes," Ma laughs. "We use to call your chefs 'the ducklings,' because they always following you around like little ducklings. Aduh, those were good years." For a moment, Ma and Big Aunt smile into the distance, lost in their memories.

"I will call them," Big Aunt says. "Maybe they allow us to come along with them."

We're all silent as Big Aunt goes through her contact list on her phone, muttering to herself. After a minute, she goes, "Okay. I know who best to call." I swear none of us even dares to breathe as she hits Call. She puts the phone on speaker for our benefit. It takes three rings before it's answered.

"Mami Friya?" the man on the other side booms in Indonesian, the joy in his voice palpable. "Can it really be you? It's been so long!"

A smile spreads across Big Aunt's face, rearranging the

wrinkles on it into a picture of sheer happiness. "How are you, my dear Wito? Aduh, it's been too, too long."

"Take the carrots out now," Wito calls out to somebody in the background. "Fork tender, not mushy, okay?" He directs his attention back to the phone. "Mami, it's good to hear from you. Are you in town? You must come and visit the kitchen. Everyone will be so happy to see you."

Big Aunt nods as though he could see her right now. "Ah, I would love to, Wito. I hear you have been promoted to sous chef. How wonderful. Congratulations!"

"Well, yes, after that glowing recommendation letter you wrote, there was no way I wasn't going to get the promotion. Aduh, Mami, I owe it all to you."

Tears form in Big Aunt's eyes and she blinks them away rapidly. It's only then that I realize I'm beaming too. Seeing Big Aunt in her element, adored and admired by her ex-colleague, is wonderful. It reminds me just what a rich and fulfilling life she had back here.

"So is there anything I can do for you?" Wito says.

The smile fades from Big Aunt's face. "Yes, actually. I heard that you're catering to Mr. Hermansah's feast tonight?"

"Oh yes. We're prepping for it right now, in fact."

"Would it be possible if I—ah, if I tagged along?"

There's a short pause. When Wito next speaks, his words ring with confusion. "Tagged along to the event?"

"Yes." Big Aunt's eyes roam the room for a second, moving in rapid panic, then she quickly adds, "I heard that his mansion is amazing, and I've always wanted to see what it's like. I will help out with the catering, of course. For free! I can make my famous mocha velvet cake with brandy frosting?"

"Waduh, Mami, this is . . ." It's obvious that Wito is torn

between enthusiasm and concern. "Wah, gimana, ya? Hmm. I—" He's interrupted by someone talking to him in the background. "It's Mami Friya," he says to the person on his end.

"Mami Friya?" she cries with unabashed excitement. Her voice comes out loud through the phone. "It's Nana!"

"Oh, Nana, hello," Big Aunt calls out, smiling again.

"Mami, it's been too long. How are you? I follow your Insta and your cakes are even more beautiful than I remember. Hey guys, it's Mami Friya!"

A chorus of happy greetings pour out of the phone, and by now, we're all beaming at Big Aunt, loving every moment of her being worshipped like the goddess she is.

"Mami Friya is asking if she could help us cater to the Hermansah event tonight," Wito says to the other chefs.

Immediately, there is a loud chorus of yeses. "That will be amazing, Mami!" Nana shouts.

"Great, wonderful," Big Aunt says, somewhat less enthusiastically. "I will meet you all at the kitchen."

"Be here at four. We'll start loading up then."

They say their goodbyes and hang up. As soon as the call ends, Big Aunt's shoulders droop like a deflated balloon.

Julia Child claps politely. "That was beautiful to watch. They did not suspect a thing." She considers Big Aunt. "I could use someone like you."

A scowl takes over Big Aunt's face. "I hated lying to them. They're as good as family to me."

Julia Child shrugs. "In this line of business, you'll have to get used to this kind of thing. Sons will stab their fathers in the back."

I hate seeing Big Aunt looking so conflicted, so I quickly

say, "Well, we have no other choice. We need to save Second Aunt."

"Yes, Dajie, you did good," Fourth Aunt pipes up.

Big Aunt manages a small, sad nod and reverts to English for Nathan's and my sake. "But now how? I have a way inside the mansion, but you all still don't have a way inside. I don't think they will let all of you to join the catering, you know? Will look very strange."

For a moment, we're all silent. Then Fourth Aunt steps up. "Don't worry about it, Dajie. Sanjie and I will take care of it."

Ma gapes openly at her. So do I. "What you mean, you and I taking care of it?" Ma says, obviously aghast at the thought of having to cooperate with Fourth Aunt.

Fourth Aunt looks at her with all the innocence in the world, which is when I know she's plotting something nefarious, because Fourth Aunt is a lot of things, but innocent isn't one of them. "Oh, you'll see. Don't worry, I have a fabulous idea."

"That's when we should worry, when you say you got fabulous idea," Ma mutters.

Fourth Aunt grins and wiggles her eyebrows. I swallow the lump in my throat and wonder just what in the world we're all about to get ourselves into.

Big Aunt spends the rest of the late morning and early afternoon baking her famous mocha velvet cake in Julia Child's enormous, state-of-the-art kitchen. Hah, it's only after thinking of the words "Julia Child's enormous, state-of-the-art kitchen" that it hits me how ironic it is that I'm not even referring to the original Julia Child, who also probably had an enormous, state-of-the-art kitchen. But no, we're referring to the knockoff Julia Child, the one who is totally-not-a-triad-leader but also happens to have a kitchen that the original Julia Child would've approved of. God, I'm even rambling in my own head. This is a sure sign that I'm losing it.

The rest of us pore over the dining table, working on making our plan as watertight as we can. Nathan writes the plan into a list. A to-do list on How to Break into a Not-Triad Leader's House.

1. Convince caterers to let the rest of us join their catering group somehow. (Key person: Fourth Aunt. Method: TBA.)

2. Go into the house. (Method: TBA.)

3. Locate Second Aunt. (Method: TBA.)

4. Dress Second Aunt in caterer's uniform. (Note: Must have extra caterer's uniform handy.)

5. Steal out of the house without anyone noticing. (Method: TBA.)

6. Drive straight to airstrip. Fly off on ~~Abi's Julia's~~ Abi's plane to Dubai, refuel. (Julia Child: "Hah! My plane has the capacity to fly all the way to LA without having to refuel in Dubai.") Fly off in Julia's plane. (Abi: "Too obvious. They'll be looking for you in LA. A layover in Dubai would throw them off the scent.") Fly off on a plane.

Despair threatens to overwhelm me as I stare at the list. There are so many ways that it could go wrong. But apparently, Ma and Fourth Aunt must be looking at a different list, because they both straighten up with gusto, their faces shining with triumph.

"Good plan," Ma announces. "Very simple. So easy."

"In and out," Fourth Aunt agrees. "So straightforward."

Really? For once they're agreeing, and this is what they choose to agree on?

"I don't know that it's as straightforward as you guys think," I mutter. "Each step has a lot more to it than it seems. I mean, the first step, convincing the caterers—"

"Don't worry about it." Fourth Aunt flaps her hand at me, her bejeweled nails very nearly taking out an eye. "I've got it all under control."

I let the silence hang for a second before I go to the next foreseeable obstacle. "Then there's locating Second Aunt. The house looks humongous. How are we going to—"

Abi holds up a finger. "Ah, I might be of some help there. I think there are a few likely options: a guest bedroom . . ."

Nathan dutifully jots this down on the list.

"The helpers' quarters, away from the main party . . ."

We all nod thoughtfully.

Abi's face darkens as he says, "Or a dungeon."

"I'm sorry, what?" I blurt out.

Abi and Julia Child glance at each other and sigh. "Well, there is a high chance that Kristofer has a specific room made for—"

"For what?" I cry out. "For imprisoning people? Torturing them? Oh god. How can you still maintain that he's a legit businessman?"

Abi frowns. "Not to torture them. God, I'm telling you, we're not triad leaders. We don't do such things."

"No, you just kidnap people and lock them up in a literal cell in your mansions. Oh god," I moan.

"Tch." Julia Child shakes her head. "I wouldn't call it a dungeon. How silly. It's more like a wine cellar. We all have one, we're not animals. Where else would we keep our vintage wines, so carefully imported from France, if not the cellar?"

So this is what being gaslit feels like. I honestly have no idea who's telling the truth. But I guess it doesn't matter. Either way, whatever they are, legit businesspeople or triad leaders, there is no question about it. We're still going to get Second Aunt out.

"You can do this," Abi says to all of us. "Julia Child and I will be waiting right outside. As soon as you get out, we'll drive you straight to the airstrip. Before the day is over, we'll all be on a flight out of Jakarta."

Hope flutters frantically, tangled with fear and anxiety. My hand finds Nathan's, and our fingers weave through each other's before squeezing tight. I breathe a little easier, knowing that Nathan is going to be with me every step of the way. And this time, we're going in with a plan. We're going to be okay.

12

The minivan is unnaturally quiet as it travels along the highway to Kuningan, where the Ritz is located. I've always loved South Jakarta, with the Sudirman Central Business District and Kuningan areas—they are easily two of the most beautiful and modern parts of the city. Growing up in LA, friends have often asked me what Indonesia is like. Most of them see it as this *National Geographic*–esque place where the people live in shacks made of corrugated metal or bamboo huts. A place without electricity or running water. I always wished I could whisk them to Kuningan, or the SCBD, because then they'd see that Jakarta is even more modernized than LA is. Every time I visit Jakarta, there's a handful of newly built skyscrapers, all of them shiny structures of steel and glass. The skyline never stays still in Jakarta. There is so much development going on all the time.

But now I'm unable to enjoy any of the scenery. As I gaze out of the window, all I can think of is how much danger we're in, and how we're about to willingly go into yet more danger. The skyscrapers around us cease to be beautiful. Now they just look menacing. We're entangled with such powerful people. These people probably own many of the towering buildings we're passing by. I feel miniscule, a tiny ant going up against Goliath.

As though reading my mind, Nathan puts his hand over mine, reassuringly big and warm, and gives me a small smile. For his sake, I try to smile back, though I can feel that it doesn't reach my eyes. My cheeks tremble at the effort it's taking for me to hold the smile.

Ma and the aunts aren't talking either, and for once in my life, I wish that they were. Their nagging and constant bickering always gets on my nerves, but their anxious silence is so much worse. Big Aunt looks small and deflated. Her face looks so worn, like she's aged ten years in the course of a single day. My heart twists painfully at the sight of her looking so vulnerable.

"Hey, Big Aunt." I reach out and pat her arm. What I really want to do is give her hand a reassuring squeeze, but our family isn't really into hand-holding and hugs. We're more into subtle arm and shoulder pats. "You okay?"

Immediately, she stiffens, her chin hardening as she sits up straight. "Yes, of course, Meddy. Why you ask such silly question?"

"Uh." I should've known better than to show concern. Now I'm in trouble with Big Aunt.

"Of course I okay. Why I not okay?" she continues. "Enjelin know how to looking after herself, she be okay. Hah," she snorts. "She probably nagging everyone to do the Tai Chi right now, ya kan?"

It strikes me then that despite all of the friction between her and Second Aunt, Big Aunt is scared to death for Second Aunt's safety. My breath hitches and tears fill my eyes because I really need Second Aunt to be okay too. I force a small smile and nod at her. "Yeah, I can totally see Second Aunt convincing them to do Tai Chi." This time, I do reach out for Big Aunt's hand. She starts a little, but I give her hand a firm squeeze before letting go.

Meanwhile, Ma and Fourth Aunt keep their eyes firmly on their hands, though once in a while, they exchange furtive glances with each other. The back of my neck prickles. Something's going on between the two of them. I frown as I try to work out what it could possibly be, but my mind comes up blank. I can't think of anything the two of them could want to hide from Big Aunt. And maybe it doesn't matter. Maybe I'm just being paranoid.

"Here we are," Abi announces as the car pulls up at the lobby of the Ritz. In keeping with the modern skyscrapers around it, the hotel looks like it's been built entirely out of glass, like a giant greenhouse filled with humongous towers of tropical flowers, complete with a waterfall that's visible from out here. Despite myself, I'm impressed.

But before we can get out, Big Aunt shakes her head. "No, you need to go to back of hotel. Service entrance."

"Oh." Abi nods. "Yes, of course. Sorry, I didn't even think of that."

The car starts up again, going around to the back of the hotel, where it's markedly less impressive. There's an empty lot with a sign that says: "Reserved for Delivery. Do NOT loiter. Do NOT park here. Drop-offs only."

There's a van waiting outside the back door and a handful

of people walking in and out, carting huge boxes from the hotel into their van. The van is shiny black with the words "Ritz Catering" painted on the sides. Abi instructs the driver to park next to the black van. Big Aunt takes a deep breath, and before us, her whole demeanor changes from somber to elated, her body inflating once more. It's quite the transformation. She climbs out of the minivan crying out, "Rahman. Tommy. Hallo!"

The caterers pause and look up, and all of their faces break into joyful grins. "Mami Friya!" they shout, hurriedly loading up the boxes before rushing over and enveloping Big Aunt in a tight group hug.

It's wonderfully heartwarming to see such a beautiful reception for Big Aunt, who is no doubt deserving of all this affection. We're all smiling as we climb out of the minivan. Abi mutters something about staying in the car so as not to bring any attention to himself, which is probably for the best.

We stand aside, wanting to give them space for their emotional reunion. The caterers call out into the doorway, and more caterers run out, their eyes widening, their mouths splitting into laughter as they see Big Aunt. Without hesitation, they all run up and hug her. Watching Big Aunt in her element, like a mother hen surrounded by clucking, loving chicks, is like chicken soup for my withered soul.

"I can't believe it," I say. "It's been decades since Big Aunt lived and worked here, right? And they all still remember her."

"Oh, they will have pass down the legend of the Big Aunt," Ma says, with a confident smile. "And she still Zoom call them from time to time."

And when Nathan retrieves the cakes that Big Aunt has

made from the trunk of our minivan, the caterers break out into an excited cheer.

"Ah, Mami Friya, there is truly nothing better than your mocha velvet cake," one of them says.

"I've made enough for one hundred people," Big Aunt says with false modesty, "and also for all of you, of course. Here, help yourselves. I set some aside in a Tupperware for you kids. You work so hard, you have to eat more."

The caterers cheer and crowd around the Tupperware, all of them reaching for a piece of cake with enthusiasm. As they eat, one of them asks, "What brings you here, Mami? Not that we're not overjoyed to see you, of course, but it's a surprise to hear that you want to join this catering event."

"Oh, I've missed the hustle and bustle of catering to an Indonesian event." Big Aunt's eyes sparkle. "We do plenty of events in LA, but there's nothing quite like an Indonesian event, is there?"

They laugh and nod. "Well, it's a treat to have you on board, that's for sure."

Big Aunt's smile wavers as she prepares for what is no doubt the big ask. "Ah, and this is my family. Natasya and Mimi, my sisters. Meddy, my niece, and Nathan, my nephew-in-law."

We all smile and try our best to look as unthreatening as we can. I'm glad Abi decided to stay in the minivan, because I have no idea how he would have come across to this wholesome group of people, especially with his full-body tattoo and his fearsome expression. The caterers wave and beam at us, and for a minute, we all exchange pleasantries with one another before it becomes obvious that they're confused as to why we're here.

"It's been so nice getting to know your family, Mami," one of them says, apparently the new head caterer now that Big Aunt is no longer working there. "We do need to get going . . ."

"Oh, ah—" Big Aunt clears her throat before barreling ahead. "I was wondering if it would be possible for my family to tag along? We run a catering business ourselves back in LA, and I've been really looking forward to showing them how things are done in Indonesia. We want to learn from all of you."

The head caterer cackles like this is the funniest thing she's ever heard. "Aduh, Mami. No way! Learn from us? Why would they want to do that when they can learn from the best? Everything we know how to do here, we learned from you, Mami."

Big Aunt laughs weakly, clearly trying to find some other way of pushing us into the catering group. "That's very kind of you, but I'm getting old, and I'm forgetting a lot of what I had learned from my years here. I would really appreciate it if you could fit us all in."

"We won't get in your way, I promise," I pipe up. "We're really good at staying unnoticed in the background."

The mood shifts, turning uneasy. The smiles have mostly melted away, replaced with uneasy grimaces. "Oh, I . . . I don't know, it's against our safety and hygiene protocols," the head caterer says. "You know how it is. Even taking just you along is technically a breach of our protocol, but I was okay with it since it's—you know—you. But taking on more people . . ."

"Forget it!" Fourth Aunt shouts all of a sudden. Heads whip around to stare at her, and she waves a casual hand at them. "Don't worry about it. We knew it was a big ask. Hey, it's just really awesome to be able to meet all of you. My big sis, she talks so much about you. You're all like family to us."

She gives them a wide grin, eyes shining, and throws her arms around two unsuspecting caterers, who smile back hesitantly. "In fact, I'm so happy to finally see you guys that I propose a toast!"

"A toast?" someone says.

"Yes. I've prepared a special drink—lots of herbs and such—here we go." She takes out a large bottle from her handbag, along with plastic cups, and hands one to each caterer. Before they can protest, she goes around and pours each one a generous serving, tittering smoothly as she goes, like a hostess at a karaoke lounge whose job is to get patrons drunk so they spend more money on food and drinks. She does this with such panache, her movements bewitchingly smooth, her voice modulated into a perfect, bubbly pitch, that no one thinks to resist her charms.

No one but me, that is. Because my senses have stood up and are ringing all of the alarm bells inside me. Oh no, please don't let it be what I think it might be. They wouldn't do that. They wouldn't—oh, who am I kidding? Ma and Fourth Aunt would 100 percent do what I think they've done.

Right then, the caterers raise their glasses and say, "To Mami Friya's health!"

I move forward, my mouth already forming the word "No," but I might as well be moving in slow motion. And before I can say anything, Ma's hand shoots out, quick as a hunting octopus, and grabs my arm. She gives a small shake of the head. My mouth drops open, my face frozen in horror, as the caterers down their drinks.

They wince like people do when they've just taken a shot of fiery tequila. "Whoo whee," the head caterer says. "That's quite . . . something."

"Wow, yeah, that tasted really sharp," one of the other caterers says.

"You'll get used to it after a while," Fourth Aunt says.

I stand there, frozen, my mouth half-open in horror. What do I do? It's too late to do anything. But it also feels so wrong to not say anything. My mouth is opening and closing and opening again, like a fish stranded on land. Ma is staring hard at the caterers, a myriad of expressions warring on her face— worry, guilt, hope. We stand there, not saying anything as Fourth Aunt engages the caterers in some banal conversation about the weather. How does Fourth Aunt remain so cool after—after roofie-ing these poor people?

Minutes pass, and the head caterer suddenly falters mid-sentence. She takes a step forward, blinking hard.

Big Aunt is still standing there, looking confused, when the head caterer's eyes droop ever so slightly and her face goes slack. I hold my breath. Next to her, the other caterers are having similar reactions, as though the lights inside them have dimmed. Are they all going to pass out? Oh god. This is so wrong. I pull my arm out of Ma's grip and rush to the nearest caterer, a young man in his twenties.

"Hey, you okay?" I say, shaking his arm.

He slowly turns to face me and blinks. His eyes blink at different times. Slowly, his mouth stretches into a joyous expression. "Whoa, dude. I feel gooooood."

I whip round to face Ma, incandescent with rage. "I can't believe you did this, Ma."

Ma wrings her hands. "I just—I don't—"

"Calm down, Meddy, we're just showing them a good time," Fourth Aunt says smartly. Already, she's put one arm around a caterer and is leading him into Abi's minivan. "Come on, let's bundle you up in the van. Don't want to be late for your event, do you?"

"No," the caterer agrees. "Ish an impor—impor ish a big 'un."

As I gape in powerless horror, Fourth Aunt bundles him into the minivan, then goes for the next caterer, ushering her in with a soothing voice. I turn to Nathan, who is gaping at Fourth Aunt and Ma like he's seeing them for the first time. Shame shoots through my entire being. What he must think of my family right now.

When Nathan catches me looking, he schools his expression into something more neutral. "Well, your mom and aunt are . . . doing their best?" he says.

"They just drugged these people," I hiss.

Nathan nods slowly. "Yeah . . ." He swallows, then takes Ma aside. "Ma, ah . . . can I ask, what was in that drink? I just want to make sure that there's nothing dangerous in it."

"Aduh, of course nothing dangerous," Ma says. "Aiya, better don't ask such questions lah. You kids don't understand, we have to get Erjie back!" Her voice cracks then, and she glares at us through her tears. "We do anything to get her back." Though her voice is slightly wobbly, the desperate strength behind it is clear.

"Oh, Ma." I go to her and put my arms around her frail shoulders. "We'll get her back. I promise. Just—please don't drug anyone again, okay?"

Big Aunt is standing there staring as Abi and his driver carry the caterers and load them up into his minivan. It takes a while for her to regain her voice, and when she finally does, it comes out hoarse and wobbly, barely louder than a whisper. "I—you—you drug my chefs."

"It's okay, Dajie," Fourth Aunt quickly says, linking her

arm through Big Aunt's. "We had to do it. They were never going to allow us all to tag along as part of their team, don't you see? We would've been back on square one, with just you getting inside Kristofer's house, the rest of us stuck outside, and what good is that going to do?"

Big Aunt takes a shuddery breath, looking unconvinced.

"And Sanjie is right," Fourth Aunt continues. If I weren't so shocked myself right now, I would be surprised by the fact that Fourth Aunt just agreed openly with Ma. "Our priority is to save Erjie. Nothing else matters. We would do anything for her. Anything!"

That seems to do the trick. Big Aunt nods slowly, her lips thinning into a firm line. She looks like she's regained some of her resolve. "Please—" she calls out to Abi, who's grunting as he lifts one of the caterers over one shoulder. Big Aunt hesitates for a second, emotions warring on her lined face. "Be careful. Don't hurt them."

"Yep, don't hurt them, got it," Abi huffs, out of breath, right before he carelessly drops the caterer onto the seat of his minivan. The caterer's head lolls forward, the momentum causing his upper body to sag forward, and we all squeak and rush toward the poor guy, pushing him back upright.

God, could this whole thing feel any shittier? I feel like the worst kind of human right now. Despicable, awful. I couldn't possibly feel any crappier than I do in this moment.

Then Fourth Aunt opens her mouth and proves me wrong.

"Right. Now we just gotta undress them." Ignoring Big Aunt's, Nathan's, and my horrified expressions, Fourth Aunt winks at us. "Don't you worry, I've got plenty of experience undressing people."

Sure enough, it seems like only moments later, Fourth Aunt

starts flinging pieces of clothing in our direction. Nathan catches the first one—a chef's jacket—and almost drops it with a shiver. "It's still warm." He grimaces as he holds it up.

The mention of the warmth unnerves me. I get a flash of Ah Guan's body, remaining warm for hours after we thought he had died. Before I can react, a pair of pants scythes through the air and smacks me right in the face. "Argh!" I bat them away frantically, as though they were a cobweb that I just walked into. Nathan bends over and picks them up.

"Last piece," Fourth Aunt calls out, and flings an apron at us. "That set should fit you, Nathan." She winks again before moving to the next caterer.

The flurry of uniforms flies out of the minivan in a steady stream, Nathan and I doing our best to catch them all before they fall to the ground. Before we're even done gathering all of the clothes, Fourth Aunt climbs out of the van, wipes her brow with flourish, and spreads her arms with a wide grin. "Ta-da! Uniforms for everyone. You're welcome."

Are we supposed to applaud her? My mind warbles wildly at me. I suppose, as macabre as this whole thing is, Fourth Aunt has technically done something extremely vital, and she's right. We now have uniforms and can finally get into Kristofer's house to save Second Aunt.

Second Aunt. Right. Second Aunt, who is in the clutches of people who go around snatching little middle-aged ladies from their front lawns. The thought of this bolsters me. I can't lose sight of the true purpose here: saving Second Aunt. It's not about getting rid of a dead body this time, or outwitting the mafia. It's about saving one of our own. And, I realize with a sudden rush of fierce love, Ma and Fourth Aunt are right. I would do absolutely anything to save any one of them. Drugging an entire catering company and putting on their uniforms? That's nothing compared to the lengths I would go to when push comes to shove.

My grip on the uniform in my hands tightens. "Thank you, Fourth Aunt. I'll go change now." I stride around to the other side of the van for some modicum of privacy without looking back at Nathan. I can't bear the thought of looking at him and seeing disapproval, or worse still, disappointment. I'm not a good person. I'm not as kind as him, as giving, as pure, as—

"Mind if I join you?"

I startle, my shirt already halfway unbuttoned. Nathan stands before me with a crooked half smile.

"So, this is kind of . . . out there, huh?" He starts unbuttoning his own shirt.

"Yeah." I focus on taking off my shirt, unable to meet his eye. I feel so ashamed for dragging him into yet another of my family's messes.

"You okay?" He takes off his shirt, and now he's standing before me with his stupidly perfect abs on full display.

I take a deep breath and avoid looking at his abs because they're so distracting. This is the time to do it. I have to say this. I have to give him an out. "You can sit this one out. I won't hold it against you."

"What? Meddy, look at me." His eyes are somber, his jaw clenched, but—I realize with a start—not with anger. With worry. A lump forms in my throat. "Hey, we're a family now. And you and your aunts—you're exactly the kind of family I have always wanted to have. The kind of family that would burn down the world to protect one another. Do you realize what a privilege it is to be included in your family?"

It's as though he's just given my lungs permission to breathe.

Air sparkles through my body, bringing it back to life. Tears sting my eyes. "I just didn't want you to—we're always dragging you into these dangerous situations—"

"And I know that if I were to one day be kidnapped while doing Tai Chi, you'd rain down hellfire on everyone and everything to save me." Nathan pulls me close, and I bury my face in his chest, inhaling the warm, comforting scent of him. "We're going to be okay, Meds. We'll get in there, we'll find your aunt, and we'll get out and—I don't know—repay these poor caterers somehow, and then we'll be out of here, and this whole thing will be the best dinner party story ever. Can you imagine the Johnsons' faces when we tell them about this?"

Somehow, he's always able to make me laugh, even in the worst moments. "I don't know, I'm sure Bryce would come up with some scandalous story to top it off."

Nathan snorts. "He can try." He shrugs on the chef's jacket and buttons it up before spreading his arms. "How do I look?"

"Annoyingly sexy. How do you make even this shapeless outfit look good?"

"Talent, baby." He winks.

"Gross," I laugh. But when I've shed my clothes and put on a caterer's uniform myself, I look down and think that yeah, maybe this will work after all, and we'll be back in LA before we know it, trading stories with our friends over dinner.

13

Abi takes charge of the minivan full of drugged caterers, driving it away from the Ritz and parking it someplace where no one would accidentally stumble upon the unfortunate load. Meanwhile, his chauffeur drives the rest of us in the catering van to Kristofer's mansion. Along the way, we go over our plan. Once again, we come up with a list.

1. Go inside Kristofer's house as caterers. (Check. Well, almost checked. We're halfway to achieving this point, good job, everyone.)

2. Big Aunt takes care of the food preparation while the rest of us go through the house to find Second Aunt.

3. Find Second Aunt. *(How? I don't know, how I know? You have to thinking! Thinking very hard. If you are kidnapper, where will you keep the Denzel in distress? . . .*

maybe a cellar of sorts. A wine cellar? Ah, yes, good thinking. You see? You can do anything, just need to thinking hard.)

4. Give Second Aunt caterer's uniform that we have saved for her and leave the premises as caterers. *(Ooh, this very good idea, just like James Bun. James Bond. Yes, James Bun, that what I say.)*

5. There is no step 5, but Ma insists that we can't end with Step 4 because 4 is an unlucky number. *(Is mean death, you want this to end with death?)* Hence, Step 5. What is Step 5? *(Step 5 is, you and Nathan make grandkids.)* Focus, Ma.

"I feel good about our plan," Fourth Aunt says. "A solid five-step plan, easy to follow."

Nathan grimaces. "Well, except we don't have any of the important details. Like how to find Second Aunt—"

"Like Meddy suggested, she's probably in the wine cellar," Fourth Aunt says with confident simplicity.

"Right . . . but then how would we get into the wine cellar without anyone noticing, and what if she's not in there . . ." Nathan's voice trails off as he takes in the myriad expressions around him. Fourth Aunt is sneering at him like, *What kind of moron can't find his way down to the wine cellar?* Ma is looking like she's this close to wailing, and Big Aunt is looking like a North Korean dictator who's just been told that his parade was canceled due to bad weather. "Ah, you're right. It's a piece of cake. We'll find her. Somehow." He gives a half-convincing smile, which is enough to assuage Ma and the aunties for now.

What little confidence I have is shaken as we arrive at the

perimeter of Kristofer's estate. Like Julia Child's estate, his is surrounded by impossibly high walls topped with barbed wire. But as the front gates yawn open to let our little van trundle in, I see that his has even more armed guards strolling across the grounds. There are at least a dozen of them, and I don't care what Julia Child says, I can't imagine these men carrying toy rifles. Those rifles look real as hell. I gulp audibly and have to remind myself to keep breathing. It's okay, Meddy. It's going to be okay. You've been a photographer for so long, you know that people in the service industry are next to invisible. You've seen how Big Aunt and Second Aunt and Ma flit through weddings, practically unseen by the hosts and guests alike. This is just the same. In your black caterers' uniforms, you are all invisible.

We're stopped as soon as we enter the gates. Two guards, one of them with a large German shepherd, approach the van, gesturing to the driver to roll down his window. As the German shepherd sniffs around the van, the first guard says, "Name?"

Big Aunt leans forward, putting her face close to the driver's window. "Caterers from the Ritz." She gives him her most motherly smile. "We've got the food for tonight's feast."

The guard nods and says, "Open the back."

Nathan does so, and we all hold our breath as the German shepherd leaps into the back of the van and smells the foam boxes noisily.

"What do you have in there?" the second guard asks, standing behind the dog.

"Food," Ma says.

There's a pause. "Right . . . what kind of food?"

Oh god, just come up with something! my mind shrieks.

But my mouth refuses to open. Apparently, the rest are just as tongue-tied when faced with a rifle-toting guard and a trained German shepherd. The pause stretches, and the guard shifts his weight, his hand traveling down toward his rifle. "You don't know what kind of food—"

"Tch!" Big Aunt snaps. "How many times must I go over the menu with you useless lot? I've told you, tonight we are serving the roast suckling pig, yes? Did you lot forget that already? And to go with it, we've got pearl shrimp dumplings, and whole steamed bass, and garlic scallops cooked in their shells—have you prepped the scallops?" The barrage of questions is fired without any pause for breath.

"Um, ah . . ." My mouth opens, but nothing coherent comes out.

Big Aunt rounds in on me. "You see? Unprepared. That's what you all are. Pay cut, all of you. Now, when we go inside, first thing I'm doing is checking the scallops, and if they're not cleaned, one of you will be *fired*."

Even the guards have leaned back, wearing the horrified expressions I know so well. "Um," one of them says, "that's . . . uh, well, everything looks to be in order. Go around the corner to the east wing of the house. You'll find the service entrance there." He shuts the back door of the van quickly and thumps on it twice to signal to the driver to go. We all breathe a sigh of relief.

"That was really quick thinking, Big Aunt," Nathan says, wiping his brow.

Big Aunt sniffs. "Lucky for you all, I think very fast on my head. You see, this what you get when you working as head chef. Something go wrong—something always going wrong, no event has perfect record—the most important thing is, quickly think: How I solve this?"

Nathan gives her a sheepish smile. "I feel like I should've reacted faster, because you're right, nothing ever goes perfectly, and being in the hotel business, I for one should've known that. But I just—I froze. I'm sorry. I'll do better next time."

Ma leans over and pats him gently on the arm. "Is okay, Nathan, is because you not use to breaking into other people house, ya? Because you such a good boy. But Meddy—" She levels her gaze at me, her eyes narrowing. "Meddy should know better. She seasoned criminal already."

"What?" I cry.

Ma holds up her index finger. "Kill Ah Guan, hide his body, lie to police . . ."

"Okay, okay, I get it."

"But Nathan, he innocent boy." Ma smiles at him and pinches his cheek.

"Thanks, Ma." He beams at her. The little suck-up.

The van stops and for a moment, we all freeze, expecting more guards to storm us. But the only person present is a harried-looking man dressed in all black, who rushes up to our van and calls out, "Ayo, cepat. Don't block the door. Other vendors are due to arrive."

Sure enough, behind us, another van pulls up, this one with the words "Bella Flowers" painted on its side in curly gold font. "Right, let's do this," Fourth Aunt says, and we all look at one another and nod. Nathan opens the back door, and we climb out and start unloading the boxes of food.

Big Aunt approaches the man. "We're from the Ritz."

The man gives an exaggerated sigh and rolls his eyes.

"Yeah, I can see that." He frowns down at his checklist and draws an aggressive check mark. "Go through that door and to the right and you'll find the kitchen. Do not go into any other room. Next! Flowers? Did you get my note about the hydrangeas—"

Big Aunt nods at us to follow her. We each carry three huge foam boxes, with the exception of Nathan, who's carrying five to show off to my family. As soon as I step inside Kristofer's house, the blast of AC cools me down, a reprieve from the sweltering tropical heat outside.

None of us breathes a word as we march as quietly and professionally as we can down the hallway. The boxes I'm carrying go right up underneath my eyes, covering half my face, and I'm ridiculously thankful for their presence. They feel like a shield, hiding me from any suspicious eyes. We pass by several doors, a couple of which are slightly open, and each time we near one, Big Aunt slows down and glances into the room. The first one is apparently a storage room filled with skis and surfboards. The second one is a pantry stocked with sacks of rice, beans, and the usual staples. The third and fourth doors are firmly closed. Big Aunt hesitates, stopping and staring at the third door until someone behind me calls out, "What's the holdup?"

I startle and turn around to see a scowling florist, face red under the weight of a massive vase of flowers. "Hey, can you guys stop snooping around and just keep going, please?" she snaps.

"Oh, yeah, sorry. Of course." I move forward, nudging Ma, who is in front of me. Ma nudges Fourth Aunt, who nudges Nathan, who thinks better of nudging Big Aunt.

But just at that moment, the door opens and two women

wearing servers' uniforms walk out. They pause when they see us, and one of them says, "Are you headed for the kitchen? Follow me, I'll take you there."

Right, so these two rooms whose doors were shut are presumably the helpers' bedrooms. We follow the helper, who leads us around a corner, and suddenly, we find ourselves in a magnificent kitchen. There are huge picture windows all around, as well as a skylight, and the entire room is bathed in glorious sunlight, the white and gray marble counters and floors gleaming invitingly. Big Aunt gives an audible gasp and stands stock-still. This is probably the kitchen of her dreams. We file around her and put down our boxes on the counter with relief. Behind us, the florists are led toward the living room to set up their floral structures.

"Dajie, don't just stand there," Ma says, patting Big Aunt's arm.

Big Aunt starts. "Oh, yes." Still, her gaze roams the kitchen with lascivious admiration as she puts down her boxes. "Look, they got all the best equipment." She shakes her head slowly, her eyes wide. "Wah, La Cornue's Château Line oven. You know, this one cost as much as Mercedes. And look, they even have wood burning oven."

Sure enough, there's a round pizza oven covered with emerald-green mosaic tiles in one corner of the kitchen. There are also two massive refrigerators, which Big Aunt tells us are "smarty fridges," a cooker with eight stoves, and a humongous, gorgeous kitchen island with beautiful brass lamps hanging over it. Big Aunt rubs her hands together, her eyes glinting, a small smile playing on her lips. She looks like the oldest grandson on Chinese New Year morning, knowing he is going to get the biggest red packets from all the relatives. The tip of her tongue darts out, moistening her lips. I suddenly feel as though I'm intruding on a private moment.

"Okay." Big Aunt claps once, with renewed authority. "Open the boxes."

We all hurry to do as she says, and box after box is opened to reveal all sorts of delicacies. There are sea cucumbers, golden abalones as big as my fist, scallops in their shells (cleaned, thank goodness), tiger shrimp, lobsters, Kobe beef steaks, all of them pristinely packaged.

"Wah," Big Aunt says with each reveal. "*Wah. Wuuaaaahhh!*" Her excitement increases as she studies the ingredients, the rest of us forgotten in the moment. Indeed, I wonder if she even remembers why we're here in the first place.

"Hokkaido scallops!" she practically shouts. "Ooh, you know how long I have wish to cook these? They say they taste so sweet, almost like lychee."

"Um, that's great, Big Aunt. So uh, should we start looking for Second Aunt?"

Big Aunt's mouth drops open, and for a split second, she looks as though she's torn, like, *Hmm, Second Aunt or Hokkaido scallops?* Then she slowly, with great reluctance, lowers the bag of scallops, muttering, "Yes, yes, we should."

"Actually," Nathan says, "you should stay here and cook, Big Aunt."

"I should?" Big Aunt says with naked hope.

Nathan nods. "Yeah. If we all went to look for Second Aunt, who would do the cooking? If the food isn't ready on time, they'll know something is wrong."

Big Aunt's head bobs forward and back so fast that it's practically a blur. "Yes. Exactly. Good boy. Yes, very true!" She turns to the rest of us, not even bothering to hide her huge

grin, and claps once. "Right. So, you all spread out and looking around—wait, you take this." She bustles through the
kitchen, opening cupboards. "Aha. Yes, here we going." She
takes out a whole stack of silver trays, places them on the
kitchen island, then locates champagne glasses. "Champa-
gen," she says to us.

Nathan quickly locates a crate that we brought with us and
opens it. Inside are dozens of bottles of champagne and wine.

"Ooh!" Fourth Aunt wiggles her eyebrows and pounces on
a champagne bottle, but Ma snatches it out of her hands.

"No time for you to be drunk," Ma scolds.

Fourth Aunt levels a flat gaze at her. "Really? You're going
to judge me for drinking alcohol? What was in that stuff you
gave to the caterers, hmm?"

Ma's mouth drops open in shock-horror. "I give that to you
because I trusting you. Now you throw it back in my face?"

"I'm just saying, you're not one to judge."

They glare at each other until I pluck the champagne bottle
out of Ma's hands. "Cut it out, you guys." We get a few of the
champagne bottles open and pour them out into flutes and
place them on the trays. Now we each have a tray of precariously balanced, fragile, priceless flutes of champagne. Great.

"Don't carry like that," Big Aunt scolds, tapping my right
hand with a wooden spoon. "Not both hands like that, that
not how server carry tray. You have to carry like this, see." In
one smooth motion, she takes the tray out of my hands and
places it on her palm, as confident as though the tray were
empty.

"Uh, yeah, unlike you, Big Aunt, I don't have over forty
years' experience as a chef, so I don't know if I can manage
that."

The others nod in agreement. "Yeah, and I don't think this is something that will make or break our disguise, Dajie," Fourth Aunt says.

Big Aunt tuts. "Everything worth doing is worth doing the Asian way—that is, with high accuracy."

"That's not how the saying goes," I pipe up.

Big Aunt plops the tray back in my hands with a huff. "I tell you how to do things right, you all don't want to follow, is fine. Don't later come to me, cry-cry because your cover is blown away."

"We'll do our best, Big Aunt," Nathan says. Of course, he's somehow managed to carry his tray exactly the way Big Aunt has shown us. Big Aunt nods with apparent fondness at Nathan. I've never even seen her look at her own son with such affection before. How is Nathan so effortlessly, infuriatingly good at everything? If Second Aunt weren't in danger right now, I would've been tempted to stick out my foot and trip him. Big Aunt waves us away, already turning her attention to her beloved scallops.

Nathan, Ma, Fourth Aunt, and I nod at one another and then file out of the kitchen together, walking super slowly to avoid the flutes from falling off our trays. It's a lot harder than it looks, balancing these trays. My respect for servers has sky-rocketed in the last few minutes. They're not only heavy, they're also fiendishly hard to balance. Every step I take, the champagne in the flutes sloshes around like a turbulent sea. A glance at Fourth Aunt's tray confirms my fears; Fourth Aunt never just walks, she sashays. And all that hip-swaying has caused a third of her champagne to spill out onto her tray. God, I hope she doesn't run into anyone who might take notice of her sloppy tray.

We all pause when we get to the living room. It's stupidly huge, and calling it a "living room" feels ridiculous. It's more like a ballroom, and it is so large that it doesn't just have one chandelier but ten. *Ten* chandeliers. I've been in proper hotel ballrooms that can fit easily into this "living room." The floors are made of patterned gray marble so shiny that they reflect the lights like a pristine lake, and hung up on the walls are oil paintings, no doubt priceless. The room is filled with people bustling about, carrying floral structures and vases, putting up exquisite draperies here and there, and red Chinese lanterns all around. Cherry blossom trees have been shipped in, eight of them placed throughout the room. They're in full bloom, their branches covered in clouds of delicate pink flowers. Even though the decorating team isn't done, the room already looks stunning.

As we stand there hesitating, a woman who's unpacking a box of Chinese lanterns glances up and barks in Indonesian, "What're you standing around for? These drinks for us?"

"Uh." I hesitate. "No? They're for the guests."

She snorts. "Right, well get out of our way, please. Clearly you're not supposed to be here. Go on out there to the garden. The boss is out there with some of his business partners." She jerks her head toward a huge set of glass doors leading out to an expansive backyard. Outside, the Olympic-sized pool glitters in the bright sunlight, and I spot a handful of people swanning around.

"Thanks." I nod to Ma, Fourth Aunt, and Nathan, and we walk away from the stressed-out decorator and into a far corner of the living room, away from the hustle and bustle. "Okay, so we should definitely avoid going outside because that's where Kristofer is."

"This house is a lot larger than Google Earth made me think it would be," Nathan sighs, looking around us.

He's right. I'd thought that Google Maps had given me a good idea of the size of Kristofer's mansion, but coming inside is like entering a separate dimension where it's much larger than it should logically be. As we glance around us, I can feel our spirits dropping. From our vantage point alone, I can spot three different staircases. There's a grand staircase that winds up to what I would assume are the bedrooms, but next to the grand staircase are two others, leading down. My mind scrambles in increasing panic, trying to figure out where Second Aunt might be. Upstairs or down? To make matters worse, the surly decorator is still glancing our way and muttering to herself as she angrily sorts out the paper lanterns.

"We're still being watched," I mutter to the others.

"Okay, we gotta act fast," Nathan says. "Ah, choose which direction to go . . . upstairs?"

"Aiya," Ma says, "if we all go up, they will be wondering why. Better we split up—"

"Uh-uh," Fourth Aunt says. "I've seen the movies. We are not splitting up. That's how they kill us."

"Why you so ridiculous?" Ma snaps. "We splitting up, only way. Come, Nathan, you with me."

"Wait, what?" I have to stop myself from grabbing Nathan's arm as Ma herds him away.

"Don't worry," he murmurs, "I'll look after her."

It's not Ma I'm worried about, I want to say. But there's no time to argue, and before I know it, Nathan and Ma are already halfway up the grand staircase and I'm left on my own with Fourth Aunt.

"Alright, well." Fourth Aunt shrugs. "Let's go, kiddo. Second Aunt isn't going to save herself."

I can only nod, not trusting myself to reply. Is it weird for a couple of servers to walk down to what must be the basement? I guess it is, but we don't have many other options, and it's not like we could turn around right now and go back up, not without attracting the attention of the decorator, who obviously hates her job. We walk as confidently as we can past the decorator, who frowns at us as we go, and together, Fourth Aunt and I walk down into the darkness of the basement.

14

As it turns out, the basement isn't like any other basement I have ever seen. First of all, after the darkness of the stairwell, there is a sudden glow of light, and what greets us is . . . the pool. Or rather, the sides of the Olympic-sized pool, which are made of glass, like a giant aquarium. It's a disconcerting sight, made more so by the realization that the pool was designed to allow people to watch anyone swimming inside it from the basement. It's kind of creepy. Thankfully, no one is currently swimming. A few paces away from the huge tank are lounge chairs and coffee tables.

"Phew," Fourth Aunt whistles as she places her tray down on one of the tables. "This is something else, isn't it? Kinky."

"Ew, Fourth Aunt."

"What? I like it. I can just imagine myself swimming in this pool and giving some hot guy a good show while he watches from the basement."

Oh god. I stop myself from gagging at the thought of my aunt doing some sex dance while some creep ogles her from the other side. Please, universe, make her stop talking.

"You know, the more I learn about this Kristofer, the more I like him."

"Uh, you mean the man who had Second Aunt kidnapped? You like that man?"

"Tch, okay, that part we can work on. But come on, look at this place. Sexy, isn't it? Something about this whole place feels so carnal. So—so virile."

"Oh god. Please, Fourth Aunt, stop, ew, ew. Argh." I shake my head, trying to dislodge the words "carnal" and "virile"—words I never, ever want to hear coming out of Fourth Aunt's mouth again. Gah, too late, this terrible moment is forever seared into my brain. "Anyway, we need to keep looking." I hurry away from the eerie blue light of the tank to the far end of the basement, which is shrouded in darkness. Normally, I would be more hesitant, wary of the dark, but right in this moment, all I can think of is getting away from Fourth Aunt's sexual fantasies.

I must have crossed some sort of threshold unknowingly because the lights turn on abruptly. "Oh!" I squawk in surprise, stopping in my tracks. In front of me, lights blare on row by row, revealing a massive collection of sports cars. "Holy crap."

"Whoa." Fourth Aunt hurries over, her tray of drinks entirely forgotten. She stops in front of a neon green Maserati and whistles before reaching out to stroke it.

"Fourth Aunt," I hiss. "Don't. Touch. Anything!"

"Meddy," she sighs. "Sometimes I wonder if you're truly related to me. How can my own niece be this boring? Live a little, sweetie. Your ma isn't here to guilt-trip you into being a mini version of herself. When was the last time you stroked one of these beasts, huh?"

My mouth opens and closes, and I sputter for a bit before I manage to spit out, "Never. And it doesn't matter because it's not ours. What if you set off the car alarm?"

Too late, Fourth Aunt is already stroking the Maserati like it's a favorite pet, purring at it lovingly. "Oh, my baby, look at you. Here, Meddy, take a pic for me. Do it for the 'gram."

"Okay, the last thing we want is photographic evidence of us being down here."

But she's shoving her phone in my face, ignoring my protests as usual. With a cry of frustration, I snatch the phone from her, balancing the tray of drinks in one hand and swiping furiously at her phone screen to get to the camera app. I take a picture and hand the phone back to her.

"Now do a video for TikTok." She struts over to a Rolls-Royce and, to my horror, drapes her entire body over it so her back is arched and her boobs are thrusting up.

"Oh god." I close my eyes, willing this nightmare to end. When I came into this house to save Second Aunt, the last thing I envisioned myself having to do is shoot raunchy TikTok videos of my auntie. I just. I can't. I keep my eyes away from her as I hit Record. Fourth Aunt winks at the phone.

"Hi, lovelies," she croons. "Isn't this car a beauty? Oof, nothing better than riding a rough, powerful engine under—"

"Okay, that's enough." I hit Stop and hand the phone back to her.

Fourth Aunt frowns, straightening up. "I wasn't done, Meddy. My followers are voracious for content. You should know, being a young person and all. Though you wouldn't know it from the way you behave," she mutters.

"We've got more pressing matters to attend to instead of your TikTok followers."

"God, Meddy," she groans, throwing her arms up. "I swear, youth is wasted on you. You should've been born a middle-aged auntie."

I grit my teeth and stalk away, hoping like mad that she will follow me. Fortunately, minutes later, I hear her high-heeled footsteps clacking across the floor toward me. I let my breath out. Okay. Now what?

There are a few doors around us. One of them is obviously a garage door leading outside. I go to the farthest one and lean closer to it, listening. There are noises inside. Sounds like someone's watching TV. Interesting. Fourth Aunt, who's arrived at the same door, listens intently before gesturing at me to walk away from the door. When we're sufficiently out of hearing range, she waves at my tray.

"Bring that closer."

I do so, wondering what she's up to, and she dips into her cleavage and takes out a packet of brown powder. I wince. "Ma's concoction?"

"Hey, it's never failed us before." She divides the contents of the package among the four champagne flutes and stirs it with her index finger until everything is dissolved. She pauses and quirks an eyebrow up at me. "You gonna whine about it being unhygienic?"

I shrug defensively. "I mean, no." I kind of was.

She unbuttons the top two buttons of her top, until the lace trimming of her bra is showing, then smiles at me. "Showtime."

God help us.

Fourth Aunt knocks on the door. The noise behind it stops

abruptly. Sounds like the TV's just turned off. A moment later, a male voice calls out, "What is it?"

"Refreshments." Fourth Aunt winks at me again, her mouth open in a barely repressed laugh. Should she be enjoying this quite this much? There's no time to dwell on Fourth Aunt's obvious delight at the situation, however, because the next moment, the door swings open.

"Oh." The uniformed man standing behind it is clearly not expecting us. He peers around our shoulders, checking the rest of the basement, then frowns at us. "What—"

Before he can finish the rest of the sentence, Fourth Aunt smoothly takes a champagne flute from the tray and pushes it at him with a coy smile. "Here you go. Happy Chinese New Year!"

"Uh—" The man, who has raised his hand instinctively, looks surprised to see the champagne glass suddenly in his hand. I totally empathize with him. The number of times I've ended up holding something I didn't want because Ma or the aunts just thrust it in my face . . .

"It's from upstairs. The big boss." Fourth Aunt jerks her chin up to indicate the floor above us. "He wanted all of his employees to know that he appreciates each and every one of you."

"I don't know—drinking on the job—"

Fourth Aunt giggles, the sound making me cringe because argh, the last thing I wanted is to witness my auntie flirting. "Oh, a big man like you. It's just one little glass of champagne, you won't even feel it." She waggles a playful finger at him. "And I'm stopping you at one, mister."

Okay, ew.

But it works on the security guard, who, with a reluctant smile, lifts his glass to his lips. "Please thank him for me. I really wasn't expecting anything like this."

"He's full of surprises. Bottoms up!" Fourth Aunt places the tip of her finger underneath the champagne flute and gently but confidently coaxes it up.

The guard drinks it all up in one swallow. When he's done, he gives a small burp. "Huh. I thought these posh drinks would taste a lot better, to be honest. But don't tell Mr. Kristofer that."

"I won't." Fourth Aunt takes the glass from him and hands it to me without even looking at me. Her eyes are locked on the guard, studying his every movement. "But it's a nice treat, isn't it? You feeling happier? Looser?"

The guard shrugs. "It's okay."

"Oh, big guy like you," Fourth Aunt says with a coquettish smile. "Here, have another."

"Fourth Aunt." I don't really know what to say beyond that. I hope she gets that I'm trying to hint at her not to make the poor guy overdose.

As usual, Fourth Aunt ignores me. She pushes another glass into the guard's hand with a wink. "I won't tell if you don't."

The first glass of spiked champagne must have loosened the guard up a bit, because he drinks the second one without much resistance.

"So," Fourth Aunt says, leaning against the doorway. "What super-secret, vitally important thing are you working on in there?"

"Oh, you know. Security and stuff." His words are coming out noticeably less enunciated.

"Really? Sounds very important. You must be such an essential member of this household."

"Oh yeah, without me, things would come to a . . ." A crease appears between the guard's eyebrows as his voice trails away. "Wow, it's going straight to my head."

"Oh dear. Maybe you're not such a big guy after all. Come here, let's get you to a chair before you—oh." She pauses as the guard tips over like a fallen tree and slumps to the floor with a thump. She grimaces. "That's going to leave a bruise. Poor kid. Why didn't you catch him, Meddy?"

"Uh . . ." I gesture madly at the tray of drinks in my hand. "Because of these?"

Fourth Aunt tuts like she's disappointed that I'm unable to catch a full-grown adult male while also balancing a tray of champagne glasses. But then she shrugs. "Oh well. Young people heal fast. Come on." She steps over him and sashays into the room.

With one last furtive glance behind me, I follow her, closing the door as gently as I can.

Ahead of me, Fourth Aunt is staring at a wall of screens. "Jackpot."

"What is it?" The words are out of my mouth by instinct before I see the screens and realize there wasn't a need to ask because it's obvious what they are. Security camera footage. Fourth Aunt is right; we really have hit the jackpot. There are over twenty screens, lined up into a neat rectangle, each one showing different parts of the house. Bedrooms, swimming pool, garden, nothing is unwatched.

Already, Fourth Aunt has taken a seat in front of the screens and is rubbing her hands. Before I can stop her, she puts her hand over the mouse and clicks on it. Noise bursts out from the speakers—what sounds like gunshots and shouting—and we both jump.

"Turn it off," I hiss, and she scrambles to do so. Blessed silence. We both breathe out slowly. "Did that come from one of the camera feeds?" My nerves are so frayed by now that I feel as though my entire body is about to unravel into electric wires. Gunshots and shouts. That's not a good sign. We need to—

"Ah, there it is." Fourth Aunt points at one of the screens at the bottom, which, instead of showing the usual bluish-tinted security camera footage, is paused in the middle of a Netflix movie.

Thank god. I nearly sag onto the floor with relief. Then I feel silly for even thinking that the gunshots could have come from real life. Of course they're from a movie. What was I even thinking? I'm too anxious, too far out of my comfort zone, and my mind is flitting about like a frightened butterfly. I really need to get a grip of myself. Taking a deep inhale, I stand next to Fourth Aunt and study the screens one by one.

"It's weird that they have cams in the bedrooms as well," I mutter. "Feels like a real breach of privacy, doesn't it?"

Fourth Aunt shrugs. "My guess is that they get turned off in the evenings." She pauses, a wicked grin melting across her face. "Or maybe not. Maybe Mr. Kristofer is into that kind of thing. The more I learn about this guy, the more I like him."

"Fourth Aunt," I groan. "You really need better taste in men."

"Hey, I know what I like, and I'm not going to apologize for it."

A movement in one of the rooms—looks like a gym—catches my eye. My muscles turn to stone as I recognize Nathan and Ma walking inside, carrying their trays of drinks and looking around. When it becomes clear that the gym is empty,

Nathan says something and starts to leave, but Ma stops him. What's going on?

"Sorry, Fourth Aunt, can I just—" I take the mouse from her and click on that screen, turning on the sound receiver.

Ma's voice floods the room. "—still no grandbaby. You can tell Ma if there is problem, you know."

Oh. My. God. Tell me that my mother is *not* cornering my poor husband in the middle of a literal heist to grill him about grandbabies. Oh, who am I kidding? Of course she is.

"Um, there's no problem, Ma, I swear. Anyway, I think we should—"

"Aiya! If there is no problem, then why no grandbaby? Hanh? What you two waiting for? I tell Meddy, don't you go on those birth control pill, later they will dry up all her eggs. You know that happen, right? My neighbor's daughter's friend's cousin, she taking birth control pill all the time, and now her eggs are dry up. Like powder!"

"Uh, I don't think that's scientifically possible . . ."

Ma tuts. "Hanh, this one I hear from my WhatsApp group. So I know, is definitely real. You listen to me, I know all this thing. You don't know because you and Meddy never watch the videos I forward to you kids. They are all very edumacational, you really should watch, you know, tell you real thing about the world."

I squeeze my eyes shut with frustration. The number of scam videos that Ma and the aunties forward to the family WhatsApp group chat is unbelievable. Years ago, I watched them dutifully but stopped when in one of the videos, an elderly Chinese uncle said, "To avoid getting cold and flu viruses, gargle with boiling hot water." I made Ma and the aunties promise that they would *never* gargle with boiling hot water, and they tutted and said of course they would never do such a silly thing. But then why forward that video? The mind boggles. Anyway, I decided then that it was better for my mental health to not watch any more of these viral scam videos, and of course, right now is the time that my mother chooses to bring them up. Sometimes, I just cannot with her. Okay, a lot of the times.

"I'll ah—I'll look them up when we're not in Kristofer's house looking for Second Aunt?" Nathan says with a touch of panic in his voice.

Ma sighs. "Always an excuse with you kids. Never a good time to talk about it. Then when can we talk about it?"

"Uh. Okay, Ma. I promise you, once we're out of here safe and sound, we'll all sit down and you can talk to us about all of your concerns. How does that sound?"

"Dang," Fourth Aunt says, "he's good."

He really is. Despite my frustration at Ma's awful timing, I'm also proud of Nathan for handling this with so much kindness and respect. If I were him, I wouldn't react half as well. I would be tearing out my hair and going, *Are you freaking serious? Right now is the time you're choosing to bring this up?*

"No wonder she wanted to be paired up with him when we split up," Fourth Aunt laughs.

Gah, that's so true. I hadn't even thought of that. So all that time, while we were frantically trying to come up with a way to save Second Aunt, Ma was like, *Ooh, good opportunity for me to corner my son-in-law.* I am going to need to have a serious talk with her when all this is over.

But my frustration toward Ma is short-lived because just then, I spot it. Or rather, I spot her. Second Aunt. "There!" I cry, pointing at a screen in the far right corner. "Oh my god, there she is."

To my relief, Second Aunt is not in a dungeon. In fact, it looks like she's in a luxurious guest bedroom, complete with a four-poster bed and plenty of space to move around in. She's using the space well, standing in front of the vanity mirror and—of course—doing Tai Chi. I move the cursor over to her screen and switch the sound over to Second Aunt.

"Carry the tiger over the mountain." On the screen, Second Aunt moves her arms up languidly, gently. "And now turn . . ."

My breath releases in a relieved huff. "She sounds totally fine. They haven't harmed her." My muscles feel loose, and it's only then that it hits me how frightened I'd been this whole time. How worried I was for Second Aunt's safety. Seeing her in that bedroom doing Tai Chi, speaking calmly, fortifies me. She's okay! Maybe Abi and Julia Child have been telling the truth all along, that they're not triad leaders but legit business-people. And maybe, as Julia Child insisted, it's not really kid-napping, but more like a very insistent invitation. Okay, that sounds ridiculous. It's very definitely kidnapping. But still. She's okay!

I straighten up, grinning, feeling like we've just come out of a very dark tunnel at long last. "Let's go get her."

Fourth Aunt gets up and holds up her fist at me. "We did great work, kiddo."

I bump her fist. "Yeah, you were brilliant." I glance at the poor guard, who's still out on the floor. Poor dude never really had a chance against Fourth Aunt. I take out my phone and send Nathan a quick message to let him know that we've found Second Aunt and are headed toward the guest bedrooms right now.

We're both in high spirits as we walk out of the security room and up the stairs. Even before we reach the ground floor, the sounds of people chatting and laughing drift down to us. It sounds like the guests have started to arrive, which is even better for us as it'll give us more cover. Yes! And if things go badly—knock on wood—surely it would be a lot harder for Kristofer to capture us. He wouldn't want his guests witnessing any sort of violence. My heart soars. We're almost in the clear.

"Has Nathan replied?" Fourth Aunt says as we reach the top of the stairs.

My reply is sliced short by a loud gasp. The shout that follows stabs right through my guts. "What are you doing here?"

Time stops. Slowly, painfully, Fourth Aunt and I turn. They say your whole life flashes before you when you're about to die, but what flashes before my eyes is my future. Specifically, how there probably won't be one. Because there, standing one arm's length away from us, staring with open-mouthed shock, is the man who masterminded it all, the man whose house we've broken into, the man that even Abi is fearful of. Kristofer Kolumbes.

15

It feels like I'm staring into the face of my doom. And that face looks like Tony Leung's. Which is to say, handsome and well-groomed, with a clear undercurrent of potential deadliness. Have I ever been so terrified in my life? Well, okay, probably yes, like for example when I was stuck in the car with Ah Guan. And then later when I thought I'd killed him. And there was that time with Staphanie—

Okay, so I have been terrified a lot of times in my life. A lot more than normal, that's for sure. But it doesn't get any better. It's not like riding a bicycle, where you learn a skill and that skill stays with you for life. It's more like riding a unicycle, except the unicycle is made of broken glass and razor blades. Okay, so maybe that made no sense and maybe my brain is just babbling on and on to distract from the fact that Fourth Aunt and I are probably about to die horrific deaths. How do the mafia kill people here? Guns? Machete?

"Please—" The word chokes out of my throat, wobbly with unshed tears.

"I can't believe this!" Kristofer roars, his whole face turning red.

I squeeze my eyes shut. This is it.

"Mimi Chan. It's you. I would recognize you anywhere. Waduh!"

Okay, there was a lot more joy in that statement than what I was expecting. Unless the thought of torturing and killing two people sparks joy in Kristofer, which is entirely possible. Still, curiosity overcomes my terror and I crack open one eye. Kristofer is beaming, his eyes alight with sheer joy, his grin so wide that it covers half his face.

"Who invited you here? Ah, it must be Robert. That sneaky, wonderful bastard. I can't believe he even had you dressed up as one of the help," Kristofer laughs. I swear he's this close to clapping and skipping around like a little kid. He holds out his hands to Fourth Aunt. "Mimi Chan in the flesh. Wow."

Fourth Aunt hesitates for just a split second, her gaze darting to me. Like me, she's probably suffering from whiplash—thinking we're about to get killed one second, realizing she's run into a fan the next. But she recovers far better than I do. In the next moment, the unsure expression on her face is quickly replaced by her usual feline confidence. She raises her chin ever so slightly, and the corners of her pursed, plump lips quiver into the hint of a smile. Coolly, she places one hand on Kristofer's outreached ones as though she were offering him a priceless jewel.

Kristofer Kolumbes laps it all up, his eyes never leaving Fourth Aunt's face as he eagerly jerks her hand up and down in an enthusiastic handshake. "I can't believe it. I still can't.

What are you doing here? I thought you'd moved away from Jakarta."

"Oh, I came back for Chinese New Year," Fourth Aunt says airily, pulling her hand back and sparing him another cool smile.

Kristofer gasps. "Oh my goodness, are you—" He lowers his voice and steps closer to Fourth Aunt. "Are you here to give a private performance? That Robert, he is truly the best friend I could ever ask for. I can't believe he invited you here to perform for me."

"Yes, he's a good friend indeed," Fourth Aunt agrees. "But listen, I'm not actually here to—"

"You know, this is perfect timing because I've just had a whole new Bang & Olufsen sound system installed in my house, including . . ." He pauses for effect. "A vintage Neumann microphone."

You could practically see the sun rising behind Fourth Aunt's eyes. In one moment, her face goes from mild disinterest to delighted shock. It's as though there are tiny, invisible hands pulling up her face. Her eyebrows go up, her eyes open wide, her cheeks defy gravity. "Bang & Olufsen? Vintage Neumann microphone?"

"Yep. My family's very into karaoke. I even had an electric stage built into the center of the living room. It's hidden in the floor, all I have to do is hit a button, and it'll rise slowly and majestically up." He raises his palms to illustrate, and Fourth Aunt's expression turns from bright to blinding. She's probably already seeing herself on this stage, grabbing the vintage Neumann microphone and belting into it.

"That's really nice," I pipe up, "but we kind of have other engagements?" I grin at Fourth Aunt and try to signal to her

208 ◆ JESSE Q. SUTANTO

with my eyes that we really should get going. Who knows how long our luck is going to last?

But I'm too late. Fourth Aunt is already caught in the promise of the kind of performance she's dreamed about forever. For as long as I've known her, she's complained about the lack of a budget for proper equipment. Even after the family wedding business picked up, Fourth Aunt is still unable to fit the costs of the high-end equipment she wants into the budget that she's given. To be fair, if Fourth Aunt had her way, she would blow everything on ridiculously expensive equipment, and as Ma pointed out, "She sing at wedding, not at rock concert. No need the best equipment." And now, here it is, finally. Her chance to sing and hear her voice being amplified into the most exquisite sound.

"Excuse me, Kris," Fourth Aunt says, "I need a word with my assistant." With a small nod at Kristofer, she links her arm through mine and pulls me to one side. "I'm doing it."

I sigh. I knew it. "I don't know . . ."

"It'll be a great distraction. You need to use that time wisely." She speaks louder. "You need to make sure my social media is kept up to date, okay?"

I don't feel great about this, but to be fair, it's not the worst idea. Fourth Aunt is right that it would be a fantastic distraction. And she'll sing enough songs to give me time to get Second Aunt, reconvene with Nathan and Ma, and get the heck out of here. It just might work. So against all my better judgment, I nod. Fourth Aunt closes her eyes and takes a deep, gratified breath. It's as though the lines on her face melt away and I'm seeing Fourth Aunt at her peak, as a young woman with a world of promise. Then she opens her eyes and turns back to Kristofer.

"Come! I am ready to sing."

"Wonderful!" Kristofer holds out his arm, which Fourth Aunt takes with confidence, and the two of them stride down the hallway.

I'm about to slip away, but just then, Kristofer glances back at me and frowns. "Come, you must record the famous Mimi Chan performing at my house. I have many friends who are fans of Mimi, and I won't pass on this chance to really rub it in!" He throws his head back and laughs, and Fourth Aunt does this fake *Hohoho* laugh.

"I'm sure your guests will record it," Fourth Aunt says when they're done laughing.

"Pfft!" Kristofer snorts. "My guests? Trust me, they'll be too busy gawking at you to record you. No, I don't want to leave it to them." He snaps his fingers at me without even bothering to look at me. "Follow us, and keep your camera trained on her."

I shoot Fourth Aunt a panicked look, and she shrugs. This is fine. Things are still very much under control. I can wait until everyone is entranced by Fourth Aunt's singing before sneaking out of there and finding Second Aunt. Yep, this is totally okay.

It feels as though half of Jakarta's population arrived while Fourth Aunt and I were down in the basement. Even before we reach the living room, the noise spills out, and it's overwhelming. Laughter and shouts of "Gong xi fa cai!" fill the air. Names being boomed out with overly joyous proclamations.

"Harun! Wah, it's been so long. How are you?"

"Waduh, Herman, you look so healthy. How have you been?"

And so on and so forth. My mouth cracks open when we

get to the living room. The party is in full swing, with throngs of people milling about and greeting one another and drinking champagne. The decor team has done an amazing job; the cherry blossom trees and the red lanterns transform the living room into something completely magical. Big Aunt has evidently been hard at work, because on one side is a long table filled with platters of delicious-looking dishes. There are plates of golden-fried seafood noodles that signify longevity, braised abalones swimming in rich sauce, black pepper beef in lettuce cups, and a dozen other dishes that I can't believe Big Aunt has whipped up in such a short time. She's even prepared eight huge plates of nian nian you yu—Chinese salad that everyone will mix together using their chopsticks as they chant a rhyme for a good year ahead. Big Aunt is clearly in her element. That makes one of us, at least.

In one corner of the room, a live band is playing a contemporary version of traditional Chinese New Year songs, the beat fast and catchy and nearly impossible not to dance to. Kristofer leads Fourth Aunt through the crowd, pausing now and again to greet his guests. When they get to the center of the room, he says something to Fourth Aunt, who nods. Then Kristofer leaves her and approaches the live band. He gets to them, climbs up onto the stage, and pats one of the musicians on the shoulder. The man, who was playing a violin, starts and, recognizing Kristofer, quickly stops playing. The music comes to a standstill, and Kristofer smiles and nods at the band as he takes their mic. The chatter in the room disappears, leaving an expectant hush.

"Hello, everyone!" He's so comfortable on stage. Even from my vantage point deep in the crowd, I can see the lively gleam in his eyes. He's a natural; he adores the limelight. And everybody is reacting to his energy, smiling up at him. "I'm so honored to have all of you here, my closest friends. Every year, I throw this party to honor our friendship, and to let all of you know that you are practically my family."

A murmur of agreement goes through the crowd, and a few people cheer and call out, "Love you, Dage!"

Laughing, Kristofer raises his hands and nods. "Love all of you too. We've all had a great year, haven't we?"

They all cheer and whoop.

"And we're about to have an even better year ahead. Xin nian kuai le!"

Everyone applauds with enthusiasm.

"And now, I have a surprise for all of you. We have among us a national treasure. Remember when we were ambitious, hot-headed twenty-, thirty-year-olds—you old farts remember those days, eh?"

A ripple of laughter and nodding heads goes through the room.

"Ah, those were the days. I remember, when I was in my thirties, I heard this song on the radio. What were the lyrics?" He closes his eyes and hums a tune for a second. "Ah yes, 'Let the wind tell our story, it's fleeting as the days I spent with you.'"

His audience is nodding along appreciatively with nostalgic smiles.

"Sang by a rising young star, Mimi Chan. I used to listen to her songs and think of my teen years." Kristofer's eyes grow wistful. "Of the love I left behind."

Someone in the crowd whistles, and Kristofer laughs. "Well, enough of that. Are you ready for my surprise?"

Everyone cheers.

"Presenting the voice of my—of our youth. Mimiiii Chaaan!" He points a hand to the center of the room, where Fourth Aunt stands, and all of a sudden, Fourth Aunt starts ascending.

For a second, I wonder if Fourth Aunt is having a Rapture-esque moment and is being called to the heavens by the angels, but then common sense kicks in and I realize, of course, that it's just the electric stage slowly rising from the floor. Fourth Aunt looks a bit taken aback at first, her eyes widening, but then she looks around at the room, the sea of eyes all trained on her, and it's as though she feeds off their attention. Her back straightens, her chin lifts, and she unfurls like a blooming flower. Along with the stage, a standing microphone rises from the floor, and Fourth Aunt grabs hold of it like it's a long lost lover.

"Helloooo, Jakarta!" she croons into it, and I finally understand why she was so keen to get to sing into this particular microphone. Kristofer hadn't been exaggerating about his sound system. Fourth Aunt's voice, already pretty nice on its own, is amplified in a powerful and yet silky way through the microphone.

Everyone claps. Whistles tear through the applause, and I can't help but smile. Fourth Aunt has told me, time and again, what a big deal she'd been in Indonesia, but when it comes to Ma and the aunties, I can never tell what's real and what's been stretched for maximum drama. But now I see that she wasn't stretching the truth at all. She really was somebody back here.

The music starts, and Fourth Aunt closes her eyes and begins to sing. Everyone, me included, is entranced. She sounds as smooth as oil, as rich as chocolate. It's nearly impossible to tear my eyes away, but somehow, I do. And of course, as soon as I look away from Fourth Aunt, Kristofer catches my eye. I guess he's been glaring at me this whole time, because when we make eye contact, he gestures for me to start filming Fourth Aunt. Right. I sheepishly take out my phone and aim it at Fourth Aunt. Kristofer nods gruffly and goes back to enjoying the song, his gaze growing soft and faraway as he's no doubt transported to the days of yore. I can't tell from this distance, but it looks almost as though he's getting teary-eyed. Yep, I'm right. He really is getting a bit teary-eyed. Who would've thought that such a scary dude could be so sentimental? But then again, who can blame him? Fourth Aunt's song is at once hopeful and sorrowful, and even though I don't quite under-stand all of the Mandarin words, I catch enough to know that she's singing about a lost love, and deep inside me, I feel my heart clench at the sadness in the song.

I wait for a minute longer for Kristofer to really get im-mersed in Fourth Aunt's performance. By then, more than a handful of people are wiping away a tear. This is it. This is my chance to slip away. I keep my phone aimed at Fourth Aunt as I begin to inch away, just to give the impression that I'm still shooting in case Kristofer checks on me. Summoning all of the subtlety I've learned from years of experience as a wedding photographer, I melt into the crowd, keeping my eyes trained on my phone to avoid eye contact with anyone else, while using my peripheral vision to guide me. I'm about halfway to the door when a scream slices through Fourth Aunt's golden voice.

"That's her!" someone shouts.

Fourth Aunt opens her eyes, looking dazed, as though she's just been shaken away from a heavy dream. The music falters and stops.

A ripple goes through the crowd as someone scythes through

them with ruthless efficiency, elbowing and shoving people out of their way. When I finally catch sight of the person, every muscle in my body freezes. Because it's Rochelle. The girl my mom and aunts accosted.

Rochelle points an accusatory finger up at Fourth Aunt. "*You*," she yells. "You attacked me. You stole my title deed!"

"What's going on?" Kristofer calls out, hurrying over to Rochelle.

"Ah Gong," Rochelle calls him. Grandfather. Oh god. In the hectic confusion of yesterday, I'd somehow failed to remember Rochelle is Kristofer's granddaughter. "This woman and her crazy family—they attacked me."

A gasp shudders through the crowd.

"What?" Kristofer says. He glances up at Fourth Aunt and hesitates. "But why would Mimi Chan do that?"

"Okay, first of all, don't say 'Mimi Chan' like she's someone famous, Ahgong." Rochelle rolls her eyes. "And second of all, they attacked me because they wanted to steal the title deed from me. You know, that title deed I was telling you about? The whole reason you—you know, did the thing?" Rochelle raises her eyebrows meaningfully.

"What?" Kristofer says again, obviously mystified. He frowns and shakes his head. "No, that was—that whole mess has to do with Abi, not Mimi Chan. I don't understand—"

The dread in my stomach has been building up this whole time, as Kristofer inches his way to the truth. Any moment now, he's going to put the pieces together and realize that his beloved Mimi Chan is none other than Second Aunt's sister, and then what's going to happen to us? Fourth Aunt catches my eye, and I know then that she's thinking the exact same thing I am. She gives me the slightest nod. *Go, Meddy.*

I nod back at her, a lump knotting in my throat. I'm going to go. I have to get to Second Aunt, even if it means leaving Fourth Aunt here, in the middle of this mess. I have to trust that she'll be able to get out of this somehow. As I turn to leave, I hear Fourth Aunt's voice, once more amplified by the microphone.

"Someone's been indulging in too much champagne, eh?" she calls out. "Hit it, band!"

A lively, jaunty tune starts up, and Fourth Aunt starts singing in this frantic, powerful voice, trying her best to drown out Rochelle's shouts of, "It was her. I'm telling you!"

I chance a glance back. Kristofer has taken out his phone and is talking into it. I don't know what he's saying, but his face is deathly serious. His gaze shifts and locks on mine. He stops talking. My blood freezes. He knows.

I turn from him and run.

16

I push my way through the crowd without any regard for personal space. A few people grunt and hiss, "Watch it!" but I don't pause, I don't look back. It feels like forever before I finally make it to the door. I burst out of it and close it behind me. I run down the hallway and make a quick turn to the left, and there in front of me is a staircase leading up. Yes!

I rush up the steps, taking them two at a time, and just as I reach the top, I hear one of the doors cracking open. Without thinking, I dive in and push the door shut behind me.

"Meddy!"

I gasp. "Nathan! Ma! Oh my god." I throw my arms around them and squeeze.

"How did you know we were here?" Nathan says.

"I—I didn't, I was running and I heard the door creaking open and it—I don't know, it sounded suspicious? Like, someone who's trying to hide would open a door like that." I realize I'm babbling and tell myself to stop.

Ma pats my cheek. "Ah, you so smart, Meddy. My daughter so cunning, ya? She can tell who is bad guy just by the door opening."

"In this scenario, we are the bad guys," Nathan reminds her.

Ma tsks. "Obviously no lah."

"Okay, we don't have time for this." I gesture at them to listen. "Second Aunt is in one of the guest bedrooms. Fourth Aunt is in the living room, performing, but Rochelle is also down there and she recognized Fourth Aunt, so we're in a bit of a bind. We need to find Second Aunt and get her out and then find some other way to get Fourth Aunt out."

Nathan and Ma gape at me. Then Ma goes, "Hanh? Fourth Aunt performing?" She snorts, shaking her head. "Aduh, that woman, no shame. No understanding why we are here. She see the stage, she has to go on it, such attention hole, you see what I say? Attention hole!"

"Actually, it wasn't her fault. We ah—we ran into Kristofer and he recognized her and sort of pushed her into performing." Okay, well, she could've said no, but I choose to leave out that tiny little detail for now.

Ma snorts again. "He recognize her? Hanh! She will be boasting about this for year and year, you just wait and see. Will be unbearable."

"Uh. Right. Anyway, my point is, things are pretty bad, and we need to move fast."

"How you know Second Aunt in guest bedroom?" Ma says.

"Ma!" I throw up my hands. What part of "we need to move fast" does she not understand? "I'll explain later, okay?

Come on." I open the door a little and peer outside, half expecting a whole army of guards to rush through the door. But the hallway is empty. Huh. Maybe I'd imagined Kristofer's knowing look after all. Maybe he was looking at me like that because he was annoyed that I wasn't capturing Fourth Aunt's performance from a close enough distance? Well, anyway, there isn't time to linger. I gesture to Nathan and Ma to follow me.

Slowly, we creep out of the room. I wince at every sound we make; our footsteps, something I've never thought much of before, sound thunderous in the silence. Even my own ragged breathing seems deafening to me. Stay calm, I tell myself. We're so close to rescuing Second Aunt. So close. We'll find her in one of these rooms, set her free, and go. Of course, as soon as we're fully out in the hallway, it hits me that the room that Second Aunt's in is probably locked. How are we going to get her out without a key?

Doesn't matter. All we need to do is find which room she's in and then figure the rest out. Right. One step at a time.

"Aduh, this house so big, how we going to find her?" Ma complains.

I shush her. I look down the hallway at the doors on either side of us. They are all identical, and there are six doors in total, including the one we just came out of.

"My guess is they're all guest bedrooms," Nathan says, reading my mind.

"How do you know?"

He shrugs. "Well, the room we were in was one. And a house this size probably has a lot of guest rooms. It makes sense to put them all together on the same floor."

"Ah." That does make sense. "And I'm guessing any guest

they might have would be downstairs at the feast, so these rooms should be empty, except for the one Second Aunt's in."

"Yep." Nathan gives me a half-confident smile. "That's a bit of luck. Come on." He straightens up and brushes invisible lint off the front of his caterer's shirt before approaching the first door on the right. He knocks twice and says, "Room service." When there's no reply, he takes a deep breath and opens the door. My blood is a deafening roar in my ears. I'm half expecting someone to start screaming about an intruder, but there's nothing. The room's empty. And Nathan's right, it's a guest room. He closes the door gently and cocks his head toward the next room.

But before we can get to it, Ma has marched right up to the next door and knocks on it. "Room service," she calls out, and without waiting for an answer, she turns the knob and flings the door open.

"Wait," Nathan says, rushing toward her.

I run to catch up with them, but once I get inside the room, I freeze.

Because against all odds, we've found Second Aunt. She's standing right in front of a beautiful picture window, her arms raised in a Tai Chi move. For a second, we gape at each other, and then Ma darts forward and envelops Second Aunt in a fierce hug.

"Erjie!" The questions spill out in rapid Indonesian. "Are you okay? Did they hurt you? We were so worried."

"Wait, Sanmei—"

"What is all this?" a gruff, male voice booms. Ma stops speaking. We all turn around, and there, standing behind us, are three tall, broad-shouldered guards.

"Don't move!" one of them barks.

"What? Were you two here the whole time?" Ma cries. She glares at Second Aunt. "Why didn't you tell us there were guards?"

"I was about to, but you were speaking over me," Second Aunt snaps.

"But you were doing Tai Chi," I babble. I have no idea why it matters that she was doing Tai Chi. Pretty sure my brain is just misfiring because, holy shit, there are three guards in the room and they look ready to pounce on us and do god knows what.

"Yes, I was teaching them how to do the Tai Chi. They were enjoying it, too, weren't you, boys?"

The guards nod. One of them cocks his chin at us. "Hands up."

"Oh, are we doing the Tai Chi together?" Second Aunt says eagerly.

The guard gives Second Aunt a look. "No, lady. Tai Chi time is over."

Every sense in my body is screaming, nearly in full panic mode. I can't let all of us be captured. Not now that we've finally found Second Aunt. What would happen to us? This can't be how this journey ends, with all of us captured and under the mercy of Kristofer, a man I'm sure doesn't have much mercy to spare. Images flash through my head, each one grislier than the last. Our bodies dumped into unmarked graves. Our bodies stuffed into suitcases. Our bodies—

As though reading my mind, Nathan glances over his shoulder back at me. Our eyes meet. He doesn't need to say a word. I understand him completely, and I hate it. I hate what he's conveying to me. *Run. We'll handle these men.*

I can't do that, I can't leave Nathan and my mom and Second

Aunt behind. I've already left Fourth Aunt on her own, and that had been awful. I won't be able to forgive myself if I abandoned them too.

Nathan gives a small shake of his head, his gaze unwavering, his jaw hard. *Run. Get help.*

I'm the one nearest to the door. I'm the one who has the best chance of making it out of here and calling for help. My whole body is resisting it, but I know this is the only way out. The only way that we can have a fighting chance. Taking a shuddering breath, I give him the smallest possible nod.

"Love you," he mouths, and before I can change my mind, he leaps at the nearest guard. The guard, caught unaware, staggers back, but manages to stay on his feet. Another guard pounces on Nathan. I hesitate. I should help. I should pick up something—a vase, maybe—to hit the guard with—

"*Go!*" Nathan roars at me.

The animal rage in his voice reaches deep into the primal instincts inside me, and before I know what I'm doing, I turn and run. Shouts ring out of the room, Ma and Second Aunt yelling, "Get him! Hit his pen-ees!"

I stumble down the hallway, the sound of my ragged breathing flooding my ears. My first thought is to crash inside one of the other guest rooms and hide there, but just as I place my hand on one of the doorknobs, my survival instincts kick in. What the hell am I doing? The absolute last thing I should do is hide in one of these rooms. They're the first place the guards would check if Nathan fails to—to—

No. I can't let myself think the worst. I force myself to keep going, hating myself the whole time, torn between turning back and helping them and going forward. I reach the stairs and climb up to the next floor, fear and adrenaline making my breath come out in a wheezing gasp. There are only two doors on the third floor. The one on my right leads to what looks like the master bedroom, a lavish room with its own seating area and expansive balcony and—ew—a hot tub built right into the floor, next to the bed. Okay, did not need to know this about Kristofer. I hurry back out and choose to go inside the other room instead.

This room turns out to be Kristofer's study. I close the door behind me and lock it before leaning against it and taking a second to catch my breath. Okay, Meddy. Think. *Think really freaking hard.* Okay. Things have definitely gotten out of control. I don't know what to do. Silent sobs shudder through my entire being and I slump to the floor, covering my face with my hands. That was so stupid. Why did I leave them? There were four of us and only three guards. We could've taken them. Well, I don't know if we could've. But we could've tried, at least.

But of course we couldn't. Because I wouldn't have done anything to endanger . . .

My hands go to my belly, cupping it protectively, feeling painfully aware of the tiny thing growing inside it. Tears streak my cheeks. I wouldn't have pounced on the guards like I might have before because I wouldn't be able to forgive myself if anything happened to this little peanut growing inside me. The past couple of weeks or so, as my breasts got sore, I thought it was just my period coming, but now I know it isn't. Not now that my period is almost a month late. I was going to tell Nathan in Bali. I'd had it all planned out. A beautiful sunset dinner at a cliffside restaurant, followed by a waiter presenting him with a takeaway box. Inside the box would be a baby's onesie. Or maybe a baby bottle, or a pacifier? Whatever it was, it would indicate *baby to come*!

And now, I don't even know if we'll ever get out of Jakarta alive. I squeeze my eyes shut as tears pool inside them. Did Nathan suspect it? Maybe he did, and that was why he'd shouted at me to run. To leave him, Ma, and Second Aunt behind. Even though I understand that I couldn't have done much good back there, that I had to protect myself and my— my baby—it still feels awful to abandon them.

No, I remind myself. I haven't abandoned them. I've been given a chance to save everyone. Right. With shaking hands, I take out my phone. Whom to call? The cops, obviously. Screw Abraham Lincoln and Julia Child not wanting to get the cops involved.

Hah. Now there's a sentence I never thought I'd say.

I'm about to dial 911 when I realize that that's probably not the emergency services number here in Indonesia. What's the number for 911 in Indonesia?

Don't panic. Just Google it. Right.

I do a search for "police number Indonesia." 110. Great. I call the number and swallow as I lift the phone to my ear. It rings once and is immediately picked up. I'm in such a state of panic that it takes me a second to realize that the person on the other end is speaking rapid, formal Indonesian.

"Sorry, uh, can you—" What the hell is the word for "repeat" in Indonesian? In the end, I settle for, "Can you say that again?"

The operator repeats herself, slower this time, and I get the gist of her question: What is your emergency?

Oh god. It's in this moment that I realize I have no clue what the word for "kidnapping" is in Indonesian. "Uh, my aunt, she was—uh, she was taken." But I've used the word "ambil," which technically should be used on objects, not people, as in "ambil the bag" and not "ambil the aunt."

"Do you mean that your aunt was picked up?"

"No, not picked up. Like, she was taken. Diambil." My voice is getting louder. Oh, the irony of the situation. I'm always telling Ma that repeating herself louder doesn't actually help her get understood, and now I'm doing the exact same thing. "Kidnapped!" I blurt out in English, hoping against hope the operator understands it.

"Kidnapped. Diculik?"

"Yes! Diculik, that's it. Yes, my aunt was diculik and you need to—ah, mail people before my whole family is killed."

"I thought you said your aunt was kidnapped, but now it sounds like your whole family has been taken as well?"

I sputter wordlessly for a second, hurling myself over the mental hurdle of getting myself understood in a language I'm not used to speaking. I've taken for granted the fact that I've gotten comfortable with just listening to Indonesian and not speaking it, and now that I'm under the haze of panic, everything I know about the language has gone out the window. Of course, even if I were relaying the information in English, it would still take a lot of explaining, because how the hell do I convey to anyone what just happened?

In a halting, broken Indonesian, I say, "It's a long story. My aunt was diambil—diculik, then we tried to get her back by uh—we entered the kidnapper's house and now we're stuck in here and you need to get us out."

There's a moment's silence. "So your aunt was kidnapped, and instead of calling the police, your whole family stole into the kidnapper's house to get her out, but now you're caught?"

"Yes! That's exactly right."

The operator gives a long, tired sigh. "You do realize that prank-calling 110 is a jailable offense?"

"No, wait—this isn't a prank, please. I—" I struggle to think of the words for "I swear."

"Mhmm." Even through the phone, I can practically hear her rolling her eyes. "And where is this kidnapper's house located?"

"It's—I don't know the address, but it belongs to Kristofer Kolumbes Hermansah."

She cackles. She actually cackles, like a demented witch. "Oh right. Of course. Yes, Mr. Hermansah, the guy who owns all those hotels and malls and schools and all those charitable organizations? He kidnapped your whole family and you want us to storm his house, am I right?"

"Well. Yes!" I cry desperately.

"Listen, count yourself lucky that I'm in a good mood and I won't be pressing charges for this prank call. But do it again and you'll be looking at prison time." With that, the call is so abruptly disconnected that it takes a second for me to realize she's hung up.

I stare at the phone for a second, swallowing the urge to scream. I shake my head, trying to clear it, and instead, dial Abi's number. He picks up after the first ring and doesn't even let me speak.

"Do you have her? Is she alright? Tell me she's okay!"

"She's fine." I hesitate. "Ah, well, she was fine. But Abi, listen, we didn't manage to get her out. Things got bad." My voice comes out shaky, and I have to pause to take a deep breath. "Everyone's been taken, including Second Aunt. Everyone, that is, except me, and I'm stuck in a room and they'll probably find me soon. Well, and Big Aunt, but she's all the way down in the kitchen and I have no idea what she can do anyway, there's only two of us against all of them." My voice breaks, tears catching in my throat.

"This is going too far. I shouldn't have allowed this to happen. I knew it, it's time for war."

"Wait, but if you go to war, what if he hurts them—" I realize I'm speaking to a disconnected line. This time, the shriek tears itself out of me before I clasp my hands over my mouth. I squeeze my eyes shut, feeling my hands trembling against my tear-stained cheeks, and gasp in and out. I try calling Abi again, but it goes straight to voicemail.

What have I done? What the hell does "war" even mean? What else can it mean? An all-out fight, of course. Bloodshed. And who can tell what Kristofer will do when faced with that? He's got hostages galore; he doesn't have to face Abi in a war, all he has to do is bring out Nathan, Ma, Second Aunt, and Fourth Aunt and threaten their lives to coerce Abi into admitting defeat. And then what will happen?

I can't bear it. This can't be real. I can't possibly be in a situation where I'm about to lose literally every member of my family. Everyone I love. (Well, minus Big Aunt, but really, what are the chances she's going to make it out of here safely?) I feel like a caged animal, awaiting the return of the hunter who caught me, knowing that things are about to get much worse. I sag against the wall, hopelessness taking over, making my limbs feel heavy.

But deep inside me is a kernel that refuses to bend. A tiny

ember burning brighter and brighter until I find my legs shifting under me, pushing me back up. I'm not just going to sit here and wait for Kristofer's men to find me. No matter how futile, no matter how outnumbered I am, I need to keep trying. Isn't that what my family has always done for me? Even when we all thought that Staphanie and her family had everything on us, we refused to let them win. We're fighters. And after everything, the least I can do for my family is try.

17

I stand up and look around, forcing myself to count breaths as I take in my surroundings. Maybe there's something here that I can use.

Sturdy, dark-colored shelves line the walls, each of them holding leather-bound books. The room is dominated by the largest office desk I have ever seen. It's as big as a six-seater dining table, with a chair behind it that's so large it's practically a throne. This is where Kristofer conducts his business. Maybe I can find something useful. I don't know what, but no harm in looking.

I hurry behind the desk and study it. There are two framed photographs on it. One of them is a black-and-white shot of Kristofer and his wife on their wedding day. He's smiling into the camera, she's smiling up at him. The other is a more recent picture of his wife. She looks like she's in her fifties and is lying back on a sun lounger, squinting slightly from the bright sunlight as she laughs into the camera. She looks so gentle and sweet and not at all like the kind of person who would be married to a literal kidnapper.

Maybe I could go to her for help? I observe the picture again, noting the smile lines around her eyes and mouth. She would definitely be sympathetic.

A loud rumble from outside the house interrupts my thoughts. Thunder? I rush to the window, but the sky is clear. More rumbles, like roars deep from the belly of a tiger. I glance down and freeze. Oh god. There's a whole cavalcade of Jeeps and cars and little trucks, all of them filled to the brim with men. Men hanging out of the windows, their hair flying in the wind, hooting and jeering as the vehicles drive up to the front of the house. The front vehicle, a large Hummer, stops, and Abi appears from the top like the world's worst jack-in-the-box. He raises a hand, and all the cars start honking.

The noise is deafening. Even from where I stand, three floors up and behind a closed window, the honks from a dozen cars are so loud I feel my eardrums vibrating. I clap my hands over my ears and grit my teeth, willing the cacophony to die down.

People rush out of the house in a confused flurry. When enough of them are gathered out front, Abi lowers his hand. The honks stop. After all that noise, the sudden silence rings in the heavy air, almost painful in its own right. Abi raises a loudspeaker to his mouth.

"Greetings, honored guests. I'm so sorry to disturb your celebration, but I have business to attend to with the master of this house." His voice is silky soft, and somehow, that's even more terrifying than if he'd been screaming into the loudspeaker. There's a quiet, cold rage that's undeniable, and even from this distance, I shiver, my survival instincts telling me to get far, far away from here.

I don't care what they've told us. This is not normal business practice. This is very clearly mafia shit. I didn't think I could feel any more terrified, but there's some noise from the crowd of guests down below and they begin to part like the Red Sea. Kristofer is slicing through the crowd, flanked by guards. But then they go a bit farther away from the house and I can now see that the people flanking Kristofer aren't guards but my family.

My breath rips out of me in a choked gasp. "No!" But no one can hear me, and I can only watch as Nathan, Ma, Second Aunt, and Fourth Aunt are pushed forward by Kristofer and his men to act as his shield. The only consolation I have is that they look largely unharmed. They're glaring at Kristofer, and Ma's and Second Aunt's hairdos are all messed up, but I can't spot any bruises on them, and they're all walking normally and not limping, so that means they're okay, right?

"Thank you for coming to my Chinese New Year feast, Abraham Lincoln," Kristofer calls out. He raises his arms and turns back to his guests. "Abraham Lincoln Irawan, everybody!"

A slow, confused scatter of applause starts and peters out almost immediately.

"I'm so honored that you've come to my humble abode. Unannounced." The coldness in Kristofer's voice is palpable. The skin on my arms breaks out into gooseflesh.

This is not going well. Or maybe it's going as well as those two psychopaths downstairs want them to go. Clearly, they're not down there negotiating for a peaceful exchange. They're here, as Abi had repeatedly said, for war. And I don't know what that means, exactly, but Abi is here with what looks like a hundred men raring to cause havoc and injury, and my family is caught right in the middle of it. I can't just stand here and do nothing.

Think, Meddy!

I force myself to gulp in air and step back from the window. Taking that step back is one of the hardest things I've done. Everything inside me screeches to stay put so I can follow what's happening, but I know that standing here watching isn't going to do anything. I rip my gaze away from the window and look around the study once more. Think! Is there anything in here that I can use against Kristofer? I dart back to the desk and fling open the drawers one by one. I grab papers and scan the words on them before flinging them over my shoulder. Papers flit around the room like dust motes, and still I don't find anything useful until I reach the last drawer. Which is locked.

Primal rage takes over. It's locked because there's something valuable in it. I know it. I take the handle in both hands and yank as hard as I can, nearly squishing my fingers in the process. With a yelp, I let go. My frustration boils over and I kick the drawer with an enraged shriek. Then I gather my shirt, wrap it around the handle to give myself a better grip, prop one foot against the table, and pull again, this time putting my entire body weight behind me.

It doesn't budge.

I'm sweating, panting like an animal. Panic is so close to taking over all of me, but I force myself to stop and think. Clearly the lock is made of some strong metal. But the desk itself is wood. Maybe . . .

I crouch down onto my hands and knees and peer underneath the desk. And sure enough, the bottom is wood. Yes! The fury and anxiety inside me give me renewed strength, and with a huge bellow, I push the desk over. It falls with a floor-shaking thump. Adrenaline surges through my veins, and I don't even wait for the dust to settle before I aim a swift kick at the bottom of the drawer. The thin wood cracks. I take a breath and kick again, and this time, the heel of my shoe goes right through the wood sheet. With a victory cry, I scramble to it and rip away at the crack, ignoring the sharp pain of splinters digging into my palms. I wiggle my fingers deep inside the drawer until they find a sheaf of papers and pull them out of the crack.

Okay, what is it? What's so important about these documents that Kristofer had to keep them locked away?

In the silence, my ragged breath sounds so loud. I flip through the papers, scanning the words as fast as I can, which isn't very fast at all, given they're all in Indonesian.

To: Kristofer Kolumbes Hermansah
Date: 12th October 2019
Re: Complaint No. 7612-HUX

Dear Mr. Hermansah,

In accordance to *something-legal-something-something*, all developmental work at the property at Jln. Cideng Raya Nomor 10, Jakarta Utara, is halted until further notice. Please refer to *something-more-legal-speak*. If there are any complaints, *something-something-something*.

Okay, clearly, my understanding of Indonesian legal documents is abysmal. Am I missing something here though? This just sounds like a notice to stop building something. Why did it need to be under lock and key? I go to the next document.

Complaint Number: 8253-TSG
Date: 8th August 2015

To: Kristofer Kolumbes Hermansah

Your complaint regarding the property at Jln.
Tulodong No. 1, Jakarta Selatan, is currently under review.
A *something-something-official* officer will be in touch
with you in the next ten business days.

Another complaint? But this one looks like it came from Kristofer. I'm so confused right now. I take out my phone and open up a search window. I pause for a second, unsure what to look for. Finally, I Google the address "Jln. Tulodong No. 1, Jakarta Selatan."

The first hit is the official website for a huge skyscraper. The byline says: Jakarta's Premier Office Building. I click on the site, scroll down the page, which is filled with impressive pictures of the eighty-floor steel and glass structure, all the way to the bottom, where there is a line saying: Owned by ABLIN Corp.

ABLIN. Abraham Lincoln.

So the property at Jln. Tulodong is a skyscraper owned by Abi, and when he was in the middle of building said skyscraper, Kristofer had lodged a complaint to the building regulations ministry to sabotage him. I Google the address on the other letter, and sure enough, it comes up with a hotel that's owned by Kristofer's company. I sift through the other documents, all of them in the same vein. Complaint after complaint after complaint. These two men consistently, doggedly reporting each other to the regulations board to try to disrupt each other's businesses. And, more than that, there are other documents—ones showing how Kristofer had tried to outbid Abi on a plot of land, another showing that Abi had made a merger with a company Kristofer had been eyeing, and so on. They go back as far as thirty years ago.

Hopelessness threatens to crush me. This war was a long time coming. I'd had an inkling before coming here that there's history between Abi and Kristofer, but I hadn't known, would never have guessed, how deep their hatred toward each other runs. It was inevitable, then, after decades of subterfuge, for things to escalate to this point. I can't see any possibilities that would lead to the two men backing down.

But right on the tail of hopelessness comes the anger in a surprisingly strong wave. My hands ball into fists, paper crackling underneath them. These two men. These two selfish, childish, petty men. No, not men. They're boys. Boys who think the world is their playground, who think that sabotaging each other's businesses is part of playtime. Maybe it was. Maybe when it all started, they were legit rivals. But over the years, it has festered into something more, something resembling hatred, and now they've dragged my family into this twisted game of theirs. How dare they? They must not care for anyone else but themselves. Bastards.

I storm out of the study, a battle rhythm pounding in my

head. But as soon as I get into the hallway, uncertainty clutches at my stomach. What am I doing? What's my plan? Am I about to go down and tell Kristofer and Abi off?

Yes.

In Kristofer's own house?

Uh-huh.

Surrounded by his men?

Okay, maybe I need to rethink this for a bit. What I need is some form of protection. A weapon. I gnaw on my lower lip. It feels as though my mind is moving so fast, crashing in every direction, that I can't even really tell what makes sense and what doesn't. Yes, I need a weapon. I glance back at the study, then think better of it and go instead into Kristofer's bedroom. I'm willing to bet that Kristofer is the kind of guy who sleeps with a gun under his pillow.

The master bedroom is, as one would expect, exquisite. I rush past the chaise lounge and baby grand and go straight to the bed, pulling the rows of pillows off frantically. Nothing. No guns. Damn it. Bedside tables! I wrench open the drawer from the left bedside table and find only a couple of paperback novels and a pair of reading glasses. Really? Kristofer's the kind of guy who reads in bed? I run to the other side of the bed and yank out the drawer of the other table. This one contains a hardcover book. With a cry of frustration, I pick up the book, intending to fling it across the room—let Kristofer come back to a destroyed room, then—but something flutters out from between the pages.

It's a letter, written in shaky handwriting, as though whoever wrote it was a millennial who's always on their phone and has forgotten how to handwrite. Or maybe they were in pain.

My dear Kris,

Thank you for being a wonderful husband and father.
You have done your duty, I have no complaints as
your wife for the past thirty-six years, aside from your
snoring. I know you have learned to love me over the
years, though never quite as passionately as I loved
you, but you did your best, and you took care to
never let the children see. But I know, and you know,
that your heart was never mine. I used to hate her for
it, but now I am thankful to her. Because the love you
had and still have for her has made you the best
husband I could have wished for. Go to her, my love.
Well, not right away—what will people think? Wait a
year, then go to her. With flowers. Don't be a fool.

Love,
Marjie

I gaze down at the letter in my hands for what feels like an
eternity. Marjie. Those photos I saw in Kristofer's study. The
wedding picture where he was looking into the camera and his
bride was gazing with open adoration up at him. "Though
never quite as passionately as I loved you." A thin sob catches
in my throat. This is a letter from his wife. His dead wife. Telling him that she knew for over thirty years that he had always
been in love with someone else. God, this is awful. My heart
aches for this woman I have never, and will never, meet. Something tells me that if she were still around, we wouldn't be in
this situation right now.

"Marjie," I whisper, "what the hell do I do?"

As though she were in the room with me, I feel a sense of calm wash over me, even if only for a moment. I close my eyes, calming my mind, calling it to stay still and not thrash about. I need to save my family, yes, but me panicking isn't going to achieve that. Don't be a fool, Marjie told Kristofer, and yeah, I hear you on that, Marjie. My breath releases in a long sigh. In spite of everything, I feel sorry for Kristofer. The letter has shown me a new side of him. Poor Marjie, loving someone for over thirty years, knowing that she was never his first choice. And poor Kristofer, in love with another woman this whole time. That's a long time to pine for someone. He must've been in his teens when he fell in love with her.

Teens.

Julia Child's words flash across my mind like lightning. *We were teens, the three of us, and living together at our guardian's house. Kristofer was a strapping lad. You should've seen him. But, of course, he turned out to be a petty child.*

The years of rivalry with Abi. Kristofer going out of his way to actively sabotage Abi's business. It's not a normal way to behave, not even toward a business rival. There has to be something more personal behind it, and this is it. A love triangle.

Of course. When they were teens, Kristofer must have been in love with Julia Child, but then she dated Abi—

No. He wouldn't have dated her, because Abi had always been in love with someone else. Second Aunt.

So Kristofer was in love with Julia Child, but he thought that she and Abi were an item, when in reality, Abi was mooning after Second Aunt. Kristofer must have had a fight with Julia Child after that, and they'd gone their separate ways, and since then, the three of them have been in this toxic rivalry that has bled into their businesses.

Could this be true? Could all of this mess really have been born out of this strange love—not love triangle but love square? It seems too ridiculous to be true.

Who am I kidding? Literal wars have been fought, countless lives ended, over sillier reasons. Love is perhaps the only thing worth fighting over. And it isn't just love, is it? For years, they've lived in a tenuous peace, Julia Child avoiding Abi and Kristofer while the two men kept their battles strictly to business. Years and years of passive-aggressive acts, and it only came to a head because of me and my family. If we hadn't come here, if Fourth Aunt hadn't called Abi to join our Chinese New Year celebration, if we hadn't let Rochelle take the special red packet, if we hadn't body slammed her for it . . . Every step of the way, our involvement was what pushed this conflict into erupting. In a way, this mess we're in is very much our own fault. And it's time I clean it up.

18

The noise outside of Kristofer's bedroom has reached a fever pitch. Shouts and thumps can be heard vaguely even from all the way up here. My pulse leaps into a gallop and I race down the stairs. The noise becomes even louder as I approach the ground floor, and my stomach plummets when I finally catch sight of the front door. The crowd of guests are crammed in and around the doorway. I run up to them and try to slip through the crush of bodies, but no one is budging. They're all riveted on what's going on outside, many of them hooting and cheering.

"Get them!"

"Show that gangster who's boss!"

Oh god. Of course, Kristofer's guests are thugs, just like him.

"Excuse me," I shout, "I need to go through—" Nobody pays me any attention.

I try to pry in between two people, and the one on my left, a woman in a ruby-red gown, actually snarls at me. Good grief.

And the noises coming from outside. More thumps, followed by breaking glass, people shouting and chanting, and for the love of god, what is happening? I would scream, except that nobody would hear me above the din. Are Nathan, Ma, Second Aunt, and Fourth Aunt okay? And Big Aunt? Big Aunt!

I turn away from the crowd and sprint toward the kitchen. Surely, she's not still in there. Surely, she would've heard all the noise and chaos by now and gone out to see what was—

Nope. Big Aunt is indeed still in the kitchen, a KitchenAid mixer on full blast, pots and pans bubbling and sizzling on the stoves, and she is moving like a demon through the mess. She's deep in her own world, completely oblivious to the outside world.

"Big Aunt," I call out. She doesn't hear me. "Big Aunt!" Still nothing. *"Big Aunt!"* This time, I stride to the giant KitchenAid mixer and yank the plug out of the electric socket. It dies with a sad whir.

"Wha?" Big Aunt whirls around, her mouth halfway open. When she sees me, she goes, "Aduh, Meddy, quick, fix the mixer. Otherwise later my meringue not set. Ayo, cepat."

"No, listen, Big Aunt, stop. Stop!"

She puts down the whisk she's using to whip something on the stovetop and gapes at me. My tone had been so sharp it cut like a knife, slicing through the layers of propriety, going straight to the bone.

"What happen?" Her voice is quiet, somber. She's prepared for the worst possible news.

"They're outside, and it sounds like they're fighting."

"Second Aunt?" Her face is so lined with worry it resembles a walnut.

"She's fine. Well, she was fine. Kristofer has them all. Nathan, Ma, Second Aunt, and Fourth Aunt, and I saw him take them outside. Abi's arrived with all these men and it sounds like—god, I don't even know. Like some sort of fight is going on, and our family's out there on the front lines and I can't get through the crowd."

Big Aunt groans. "Aduh, Meddy, how many time your ma and we all teach you how to get through crowd at dim sum restaurant? You have to be firm. 'I have reservation. My family already waiting inside!' and then just go in." Her hand slices down firmly, like a cleaver. "Cut through the crowd, like a shark."

"Okay, this is slightly different from a dim sum crowd." But is it, really? The crowds at the San Gabriel Valley dim sum places have been known to get very territorial, especially when they sense that the lunch carts are running out of the good stuff.

Big Aunt tuts and wipes her hands down on a kitchen towel briskly. "Come, follow me. I show you how to do." At the last minute, she grabs a large wooden spoon from the counter and marches out of the kitchen, with me hot on her heels.

"These people are probably really dangerous, Big Aunt." I don't know why I feel the need to remind her of this. It's clear they're dangerous; they kidnapped Second Aunt, for crying out loud. But still, I feel like I need to tell Big Aunt not to scold them like naughty kids.

"Hah!" Big Aunt slaps her palm with the wooden spoon. "If only I have feather duster, then I really show these boys their place."

Ah, the feather duster. It's like every Chinese parent's go-to weapon. When I was little, Ma told me that when Chinese people have babies, the hospitals bestow upon them a feather duster and tell them to use it liberally. Ma never used one on me, but I've seen my aunties use it on their sons, chasing them around the house with it as my cousins grab their butts with both hands and dart around, squealing.

I'm about to beg Big Aunt not to spank Kristofer or his men when we get to the crowd. Somehow, it seems even bigger than before, swelling and replicating in numbers. The noise is deafening, everyone cheering or booing or generally shouting. My steps falter, but Big Aunt charges ahead without pause. The wooden spoon moves in a blur, rapping someone's shoulder one second, whacking into another's elbow the next.

"Awas!" she shouts, as she thwacks her way into the crowd with deadly precision. "Minggir!" It shouldn't work as well as it does. The wooden spoon is merciless, sure, but a crowd this enthusiastic and tightly packed shouldn't move apart so easily under Big Aunt's assault, but somehow, as though everyone's survival instincts kick in, sensing a greater danger behind them, the crowd splits apart.

I scurry after Big Aunt, sticking as close to her as possible, terrified that the warm bodies around me will close in, separating me from Big Aunt and, worse, trapping me in the midst of this half-rabid group. As we scythe our way deeper into the crowd, the noise becomes so loud that I feel it in my veins, pounding like war drums. The heat becomes unbearable, the energy of over a hundred people crushing up against one another hot on my skin. I hate this, god, I hate every moment of this, but I have to keep going, keep my eyes locked on Big Aunt's back. One foot after the other. One step, then another, and another.

And somehow, we do it. We break out of the yelling throng in a sudden burst of cool air. I suck in a desperate breath. It's all I have time for before my brain digests the scene in front of me. The fight.

No, the fights. Six, seven, eight men are struggling with each other on the ground, throwing savage punches and kicks, grunting, roaring like beasts. Abi and Kristofer stand on either side of the ring, shouting at the men. And a few paces away stand my family members, each of them with a guard holding on to their elbows, their faces tight with horror. Well, except for Fourth Aunt, who's cheering along with the crowd.

"Hit him in the neck!" she cries. "The neck, I said. Oh for—are you even trying?"

I follow her gaze to the man she's cheering on and oh god. All of my insides plummet. My heart forgets to beat, my lungs forget to take in air. Because the man that Fourth Aunt is cheering on is none other than Nathan.

Nathan, bloodied and shirtless, raising his fists up to protect his face, swaying a little on his feet. A man charges at him and I gasp just as Nathan dodges. He grabs the back of the man's shirt and shoves, using the man's momentum to fling him off. The man tumbles onto the dirt, but another man pounces on Nathan with an animal cry. Both of them fall onto the dirt, scrambling, and this is a nightmare. It can't possibly be real.

"Stop it." My voice comes out thin, swallowed immediately by the jeers around me. "Stop it!" I look around wildly. That's my husband. The person who always sees the best in others, the one who's done nothing but be supportive about spending our honeymoon visiting my ancestral homeland. And now this poor, sweet guy is rolling around in the dirt, literally getting beaten up by thugs.

Something overcomes me. Rage. Flowing hot as lava, filling up my entire being. Everything around me ceases to exist. The noise recedes to a background hum. I've had enough of this fucking thing. I march over to Kristofer. Neither he nor his guards pay any attention to me, a puny, weak female. I don't stop to think.

I'm so close to Kristofer I can practically smell him, I can see the little hairs on the side of his ears, and without any hesitation, I reach out and grab him by the collar of his shirt. Summoning all of my strength, I yank Kristofer down so we're face-to-face. I only have a few seconds before his guards are on me. The few words I'm about to say will be the most important words of my life. If I stop to consider what to say, I will lose the moment. So I pounce on the only things I know. The truth.

"You're in love with Julia Child." The words rush out of me like a raging river, unstoppable. "She's in love with you too. All these years. Your wife knew it. Abi never had a relationship with Julia Child. He was always in love with my aunt, Enjelin."

Hands grab my shoulders. I'm wrenched away from Kristofer, jerked back like a rag doll. I let go. Struggling might endanger this life growing inside of me, and I would never do anything to risk that. But I keep my eyes on him. I watch it all sink in; his expression going from anger to confusion to surprise and then something almost unreadable. An expression that comes from emotions layered one right on top of the other. Grief, joy, hope, embarrassment, all of them intermingling, fighting for control of his features.

"Wait." He holds up his palm. The rough hands gripping my shoulders stop pulling, though they remain there, firm. Kristofer takes a step closer to me. "What do you—how do you know?"

My natural instinct is to answer him. That's just the sort of person I am. But I wrestle my stupid instincts to the ground. Instead, I make myself raise my chin with defiance. "I'm not telling you anything until you tell your henchmen to get away from my husband."

Kristofer's eye twitches a little, but then he turns to the men in the center, purses his lips, and blows a short, shrill whistle. As though they're robots whose switches were turned off, four of the men immediately stop fighting. They drop their hands to their sides and leap back onto their feet. Nathan and the other men, presumably Abi's henchmen, slowly straighten up, looking confused. The crowd falls silent.

Every pair of eyes is now directed at us, the weight of everyone's attention almost physical, like ants crawling on my face. I resist the urge to hide.

Kristofer turns his full attention to me, and it's even more unsettling than having all these people staring at me. He has the kind of intensity that tears away at your confidence, because it's obvious when he looks at you, he's fully listening, absorbing not just everything you say but all of the minute details of your movements, reading your body language like a book. It's easy to see, in this moment, how this man has ascended to the top and become one of the largest business tycoons in the country. I falter. I don't know how to convince this man, this person who's probably heard it all.

But then I catch a glimpse of Nathan, Ma, and my aunties. And they're all looking at me with trust. Even Big Aunt. I would've thought that their main reaction would be: Oh crap, who put Meddy in charge? But no, they're all looking at me with hope shining in their eyes, filled with utter confidence that I'm about to solve everything. And knowing that bolsters that little kernel of defiance inside me. Kristofer's cynicism has nothing against me, because I'm about to tell him the most valuable thing anyone has ever given him. I'm about to tell him the truth.

"I read your wife's letter." I ignore the flare of anger in his eyes and plow on. "She said to seek 'her' out. The woman you've been in love with ever since you were teenagers."

Kristofer sucks in a painful breath. "You don't know what you're—"

I shake my head, my frustration spilling out. "I talked to Julia Child. She said things—they didn't make sense at the time, I thought that you were just business rivals, but now I get it. The way she talked about you, she was bitter."

"Hah!" Kristofer snorts. "That's because we're competitors."

"No, it's much more than that. There was a lot of emotion in it, a lot of history. Look, I—my family, we run our own business too. I know what it's like to come across a competitor. This was much more than that. This was personal." I take a deep breath, ignoring the look of cynicism on Kristofer's face, and raise my voice, louder and louder, so every word rings clear and true. "She loved you. And you loved her."

There's a collective gasp from the people around us. Kristofer blanches. "That's not true—"

"Your wife knew. Marjie, she said as much to you. You were a good husband, but she knew there was someone you left behind. The one that got away." My voice breaks as my gaze strays to Nathan. Despite everything, a small, sad smile touches his mouth. It's a smile that speaks of years of loss, when we were both apart from each other. A smile that speaks of confidence. He completely trusts that I will make things right again.

I force myself to look at Kristofer again. "I know what it's like to have that person, the one who got away, because that's my husband. And I was lucky, so lucky, to have been given a second chance, but you and Julia Child never had that, did you? You two broke up and you got married and you were a wonderful husband and father and you moved on, but there's always been a piece of you that was left behind with her."

Kristofer's hands clench and unclench. He glares at me as though I'm the only person who exists in this whole world, everyone else forgotten. His upper lip curls up. "We didn't break up. I gave her all of me, and she took my heart and she cheated on me with that scumbag." He shoots a poisonous glance back at Abi.

"No, you were mistaken." This is it. The root of everything. "She didn't. There was nothing going on between her and Abi, and I know this because Abi was, and still is, in love with my aunt."

Kristofer's mouth snaps shut. He opens it, drawing a breath, but doesn't say anything.

"It's true."

I turn to see Abi stepping forward. He spits at the ground and glares at Kristofer. "There was never anything between me and Julia Child. We were close, yes, but all we did when we spent time together was talk about you and Enjelin."

"You're lying," Kristofer snaps. "I saw the two of you walking, holding hands."

"Apa? Holding hands?" Second Aunt demands in a pterodactyl screech. She wrenches her arms free from the guards holding her back and takes a murderous step toward Abi before the guards catch her again.

"No, Enjelin, I swear to you, I never—" Abi pauses, his

mouth dropping open as realization apparently sinks in. "You and Julia Child—you had the same haircut. All the girls did, at the time. It was this really round bob, kind of like a helmet?" He sees the expression on Second Aunt's face and quickly adds, "A beautiful helmet. And you're about the same size—well, you're much curvier, of course—but from behind, it would be a challenge telling you apart. I mean, of course I would've been able to tell you apart from every other girl, but Kristofer must have seen you and me together and thought it was me and Julia Child."

Second Aunt narrows her eyes and sniffs.

Ma frowns at Kristofer. "You can't even tell your own girlfriend apart from Enjelin?"

The expression on Kristofer's face is basically the teethgritted, cringe emoji. "I—it was from behind, and—you're lying," he hisses at Abi. "It was Julia, I know it was, because she had this green silk scarf on."

"Oh, ah." Abi grins sheepishly. "That might have been my fault. I might have borrowed the scarf from Julia Child to give to my beautiful Enjelin."

"Hanh!" Big Aunt booms. "You. I knew you were a thug. You gave my sister a stolen scarf?"

Abi's head whips to face Big Aunt, his eyes wide with fear. "Um. I didn't have any money at the time. We were all just trying to survive, and I wanted to give her something nice."

"I mean, it's kind of romantic, if you think about it," Fourth Aunt mutters.

"Romantic?" Big Aunt hisses. "This is very bad behavior. I was right about you all along."

"You bastard," Kristofer says, his face taken over by cold, deadly anger. He takes a step toward Abi, and it's all I can do to stop myself from running away, because every inch of Kristofer is oozing quiet rage. I can easily picture him killing Abi with his bare hands right now. "You—"

The rest of his words are drowned out by a terrific noise from the sky, an endless staccato of rapid gusts of wind. We all look up, and my mouth drops open. A helicopter is flying toward us, the noise swelling exponentially as it nears, the wind whipping our hair up. It's hard to breathe, the air slamming into my face, and I raise a hand to shield my eyes from the glare as the helicopter lands in the middle of Kristofer's expansive front lawn. I've never seen a helicopter in real life before, and it's jarring to be so close to one now, to see just how huge it really is, how impossibly large the wingspan is, and above all, how deafening it is, a continuous roar so loud that I can't hear my own thoughts. The door opens, and all thought leaves my mind, because it's her. Julia Child, wearing an expression as murderous as Kristofer's.

19

A man jumps out of the helicopter and holds out a hand to help Julia Child down, but she swats it away like an irritating fly. Halfway down, she turns and shouts something at the pilot, and the chopper is turned off. We all breathe a sigh of relief as the buffeting winds die down and the overwhelming noise recedes. Julia Child strides across the lawn toward us, her expression still one of complete and utter ire.

When she's a few steps away from me and Kristofer, she stops and crosses her arms in front of herself. "Well?"

Kristofer gapes at her, and I honestly can't decipher the expression on his face. Awe? Terror? Admiration? Love? All of the above?

He doesn't seem ready to start speaking anytime soon, so I rush to fill the silence. "Ah, uh, thank you for coming, Tante Julia." I look at everyone and add, "I called her. When I was upstairs. I told her to come quickly because—uh—"

She barely spares me a glance. "You said you had something deadly important to tell me. What is it?"

"I—uh—" I'd had it in mind to do this big, dramatic reveal: *He loved you!* But now, faced with Julia Child in the flesh, the connection between my brain and my mouth is severed, reducing me to a stammering mess. How do I convince her? How do I bridge this gap that has spanned over thirty years? Whom did I think I was breaking the news to—

"Aiya!" comes a familiar shout. Ma is flapping her hands wildly. "He in love with you!" As usual, Ma probably thinks she's speaking in a normal voice, but in truth, it's loud enough to be heard across the lawn.

"What?" Julia Child and Kristofer say at the same time.

"Aduh, all this time," Ma continues, "from when you two are teenager, Kristofer in love with you. Even while marry to wife."

"I loved my wife very much," Kristofer roars.

"No one's saying you didn't love your wife, dude," Fourth Aunt pipes up with a roll of her eyes. "It's possible to love more than one person at a time. Ask me how I know."

"Hanh!" Ma snorts. "Is because you hussy."

Oh god. "Um, not that we're calling you a hussy, obviously," I quickly say.

"No, of course not," Ma says. "You two just in love with each other, but then Kristofer get jealous of you and Abi."

"Even though nothing happened between us," Abi calls out. "Because I only ever had eyes for my beautiful Enjelin." He gazes with naked adoration at Second Aunt, who blushes prettily, grinning hard.

Kristofer looks back and forth between Second Aunt and Abi before finally turning to face Julia Child. His expression is unreadable, but his jaw is working like he's grinding his teeth.

Julia Child shakes her head. "You let your jealousy get in between us."

He drops his gaze. "You were spending so much time with him, and . . ." His voice trails away and he shakes his head. "No, you're right. I have no excuse. I was a jealous, insecure kid. You were the most beautiful, the most intelligent person I have ever known, and I didn't understand why someone like you would give me the time of day. I didn't think I was worthy of you, and so I assumed—"

"But is also his fault," Big Aunt adds, "because he steal Julia's scarf. If he not do that, then you not think that Enjelin is Julia."

Second Aunt glares at Big Aunt.

Kristofer clears his throat. "To be fair, I was already paranoid and jealous even before that. If it hadn't been the scarf, it would've been something else. I see it now." He turns back to Julia Child, his voice softening, becoming hoarse with emotion. "I was the one who ruined everything. I accused you of cheating. I lashed out at you, at everyone. I was alone for years. I was in my twenties when I met Marjie, and I would've ruined that, too, except by then, I was a little bit more mature. We worked through my issues together. She made us go to counseling, and I learned to be a better partner. I—I thought of you, sometimes, but I was determined to be the best possible husband to Marjie. I never knew that she was aware of—" His voice cracks. "Of my feelings for you."

Someone pushes through the crowd. Rochelle. She places a gentle hand on Kristofer's back. "If it makes you feel better, Ah Gong, Ah Ma never held it against you."

He blinks at her. "How do you know?"

"She told me," Rochelle says with a shrug. "I was her favorite grandkid, didn't you know? She told me all sorts of stuff. She said you always have a special place in your heart for your first love, and she knew, but didn't mind because you were faithful. She said she would've probably gotten along really well with Julia Child."

I glance at Julia Child, who's smirking a little. "Sounds like I would've gotten along with your Ah Ma, kiddo."

"All this time," Kristofer whispers, "I was mistaken."

"Tch, you cannot say that," Big Aunt thunders. "No regretting. Look at everything you build." She gestures at the massive mansion behind us, the rolling grounds around us, and the crowds watching us. "You have beautiful family, big business, maybe all this not happen if you have gone down different path."

Kristofer nods. "I don't regret any of it. I regret other things—not being a better husband, not treating you well in the past, but I don't regret marrying Marjie."

"And I don't regret not marrying you," Julia Child says simply.

A flash of hurt crosses Kristofer's face, and a corner of Julia Child's mouth quirks. She adds, "I didn't mean it that way. I just meant . . . if I had married you, we wouldn't have grown as people. Your wife was a force of good in your life, and I've grown too. I built an empire all on my own, no husband needed. You learned how to soften, how to bend, and I learned how to stand firm. And if we'd ended up together as teens, I don't think either of us would've grown into the people we are now."

Big Aunt nods sagely. "I think you two will make even better match now."

"Oh yes," Ma chirps happily. "I can see in your face, you still love each other, ya? Is all in the eye. The way you look at each other, wah, such fire. I see in Meddy and Nathan, you see how they look at each other?"

"Like they're always undressing each other mentally," Fourth Aunt mutters. "It's really quite disturbing."

"What?" I squawk, dropping my gaze from Nathan immediately. "I do not look at Nathan like that." To deflect, I add, "You mean the way Second Aunt and Om Abi look at each other, maybe."

And it's true. Abi and Second Aunt are smiling at each other, everyone else forgotten for the moment. It very definitely looks like they're mentally undressing each other, which is somewhat unnerving to watch. "You come to rescue me," she's saying. "I thought you say you outnumbered?"

"I would throw everything I have at him, even if it means utter defeat, if there's even a slightest chance of rescuing you, my love."

My skin crawls at the melodramatic profession of love, but I can't stop staring at them. I've never seen Second Aunt like this before, and it's kind of a treat.

"Ah, I'm a Denzel in distress and you are my knight in shiny armor," Second Aunt murmurs.

"Oh god, please get a room, you two," Fourth Aunt snaps. "Nobody wants to see that."

Kristofer and Julia Child are now standing face-to-face, looking at each other. I don't quite know how to describe their expressions. It's a bit shy, and very uncertain, but also hopeful. Slowly, carefully, Kristofer holds out his hand, palm up. I'm close enough to see that his fingers are slightly trembling, and this time, when I look at his face, I see the years stripped away from it, the cynicism and bitterness torn away, revealing the innocent, hopeful core of him.

Kristofer is the first to speak, his voice coming out soft and gravelly, hoarse with emotion. "I'm sorry."

The hint of a smile tugs on Julia Child's mouth. "Hmm."

"I was an insecure fool. But that was my problem, not yours. I shouldn't have let my insecurities come in between us."

Julia Child smiles, and it's a real smile this time, not a knowing smirk or a sarcastic twist of the mouth but a true expression of joy. "I've waited years to hear you say that."

There's a hush, then Julia Child lifts her hand gracefully and places it on top of his. Our breath collectively releases as one, as though the earth resumed its exhalation. And somehow, I know that Marjie is smiling down at them, maybe even snorting a little. I can see her shaking her head at their stubbornness.

Someone hoots, and suddenly, everyone is cheering and clapping. It feels like the atmosphere has lightened, the weight of a storm breaking and sunlight finally streaming down on us. The heaviness on my chest releases, and I can finally take in a deep breath. I feel as free as a bird.

Kristofer and Julia Child look around with sheepish, embarrassed grins, still holding hands. "Let's go back inside," Kristofer calls out. "Let the feast continue!"

I close the distance between me and Nathan and fling myself onto him. His strong arms close around me, and his familiar scent envelops me. I squeeze my eyes shut, gratitude and relief flooding my senses as I hold my husband tight in my arms. Twice now, in the past two days, I thought I'd lost him. I'm never letting him go again.

"You did it, Meddy."

A laugh, wobbly with tears, bubbles out of me. "You make it sound like I did everything, but it wasn't all down to me, you know."

Nathan grins and presses his lips to my forehead. "Most of it was. The rest was down to Ma and the aunts. All I had to do was sit back and let you guys handle everything."

I laugh again, and this time it's less teary. I hit him in the arm. "If Ma heard you say that, she'd scold you for sitting on your ass this whole time."

"Okay, to be fair, your mom did corner me for like half an hour grilling me about everything and making sure I was treating you right."

"As she should." My cheeks hurt, I'm smiling so wide.

Nathan's eyes soften before he pulls me close and kisses the top of my head. "We're okay," he murmurs into my hair, over and over again. And I know he's right. Somehow, we've made it through all the craziness, all the danger, and we're together again. We're okay.

20

"Are you sure about this?" Jems asks as he helps to lug my suitcase down the stairs.

"Yeah," I mutter, following after him. I check that I have my passport, as well as Nathan's, with me. When we get to the bottom of the stairs, Jems sets my suitcase down. Nathan rolls his suitcase next to mine.

"Well, that's everything," I say.

Jems checks his watch. "You guys have time before we need to head for the airport. Let's have some snacks first."

The three of us head toward the dining room.

"You guys all packed?" Elsa says, sliding out of the kitchen while carrying a tray of freshly brewed coffee. She sighs loudly. "I can't believe you're leaving already. You just got here like two days ago? Have some local coffee, it'll help change your mind."

"Oh, yes," Sarah agrees, "this is a new blend I just sourced from Kintamani. You're going to adore it."

Nathan and I laugh and reach for a cup each. My cousins aren't wrong; as soon as the scent of the coffee hits my nose, it's as though my muscles are unlocked, my whole body relaxing. I breathe in deep, closing my eyes. Truly, there's nothing better than Indonesian coffee. Beside me, Nathan takes a sip and gives an appreciative sigh.

"This coffee tastes sinful," he says. "Like a rich dessert, but not too sweet."

Elsa grins at him. "The secret is a spoonful of melted palm sugar." Then her smile wanes and she frowns at me. "Now, what can we do to convince you not to leave so soon? I hardly had any time to catch up with you, Meds."

I squirm inwardly. How do I explain to my sweet, wholesome cousins that the reason why I've persuaded Nathan to leave Jakarta is because I'm not fully convinced that the whole mess with Abi, Julia Child, and Kristofer Kolumbes is behind us? I mean, sure, they had that whole beautiful moment yesterday where everyone reconciled and everything seemed fine, but I've spent enough time with the three moguls to know that they're (1) hot-tempered, (2) used to getting their way, and (3) very definitely gang leaders. And I'm not sticking around to watch shit hit the fan the next time one of them gets jealous over this or that. Call me cynical, but I've been in enough mishaps with my family to know to jump ship the moment there's any sign of trouble. Plus, it's not just me that I have to protect.

"I'm sorry, but work came up, and you know how it is." I force a smile. Nathan squeezes my hand.

Elsa looks hurt. "Was your stay here really that bad? And you were hardly ever in the house! I mean, I know there's much to improve about the place, but still—"

"No, not at all," Nathan hurriedly says. "I loved my time here. I was actually really blown away by the city. It's just—"

Nobody looks convinced, and it makes my stomach sink. I hate the thought that I'm leaving my cousins this way, with them under the wrong impression that we think we're somehow superior. I put my coffee cup down and clasp Elsa's hands. "We'll come back soon, okay? You're right, we've hardly had any time to catch up, and there's so much to talk about. I—"

The rest of what I'm about to say is drowned out by a series of sharp honks.

"Is that our hired car, maybe?" Nathan says, standing up, but before he can get to the front door, shouts pierce through it.

Oh god. I forget to breathe. I'm too late. I should've insisted on flying out last night instead of waiting until the morning to leave the country. And now, the tenuous truce among the trio must have imploded and they're here to—

"Eh, buka pintu!" Ma calls out from outside.

As though on instinct, Nathan rushes to the door and does as he's told. He's barely unlocked it when it bursts open and Ma hurries inside, her arms laden with gift boxes piled high over her head.

"Ma, let me help you." Nathan grabs the boxes, grunting. "Oof, what've you got in these?"

"Oh, so many thing, many, many thing." Ma breezes inside. Behind her is Big Aunt, carrying shopping bags bursting with items.

Elsa rushes forward to take the bags from Big Aunt, and behind Big Aunt saunters in Fourth Aunt, also carrying bags and boxes. I hurry to help Fourth Aunt, but she gives me a side-eye and says, "Get out of my way, Meddy."

Geez, okay. I meekly obey, standing to one side as my family streams in, followed by a handful of men carrying yet more gifts. Finally, when the men have set the gifts down, they go out, and in strides Kristofer with Julia Child. Behind them are Abi, with Second Aunt on his arm, looking very smug and regal.

"What's all this?" Jems says, gaping at the mountain of gifts that have just been deposited on the marble floor.

Elsa is staring at Kristofer. "Wait, hang on, are you—" She gasps. "You are! That's Kristofer Kolumbes Hermansah. And you're Julia Child Handoko! Oh my god. Where's my phone?" She darts away like a frightened rabbit.

"What's going on?" I can't seem to stop wringing my hands. They're here, all of them. The house we're in, which seemed so big when we first arrived, now feels shrunken, the walls closing in around us. What would we do if things went bad? Where would we go? How would we protect everyone we love?

Julia Child shoots Kristofer a meaningful side glance and he clears his throat. "Ah, we're here to ah, bai nian."

"Bai nian?" Jems echoes. He looks around at us.

I'm as surprised as he is. Usually, the younger members of the family go to the house that belongs to the highest member in the family hierarchy to bai nian. Traditionally, this would be the oldest member of the family.

"But—you're our elders, and uh, not to be disrespectful, Om Kristofer, but we're not related. And you're our elders," he blurts out again. "Even if we were related, we'd have to bai nian to your house, not this way around."

Kristofer levels a cold gaze at him. "Is that a problem?"

"No. No, of course not! Not in the least," Jems babbles. He scratches the back of his neck, his gaze frantically moving from us to Kristofer to the aunties and back again.

"Jems," Big Aunt says, "go make coffee for everyone."

"Yes!" Jems practically runs out of the room. "Right away."

Big Aunt shoots a glance at the other cousins.

"I'll prepare some cakes," Elsa says. "There's plenty left from yesterday."

"I'll help!" Sarah says. And with that, they all scurry away, leaving me and Nathan with Ma, the aunties, and the strange trio before us.

"So." My mind comes up blank after that one word. "You all look like you had a busy morning."

"Yes, well." Kristofer clears his throat again. "I—we—wanted to apologize to you and your family for the . . . the everything."

Julia Child nods. "We've compensated the caterers at the Ritz."

"Overcompensated, more like," Abi mutters. "They said it was more than a year's salary."

"Those hardworking, talented chefs deserved more after what you had us do to them," Big Aunt snaps.

Abi drops his gaze. Julia Child nods. "Yes, I deeply regret that it had to come to that, and I hope that our compensation goes a long way to . . . ah, reviving their spirits."

I can't help but feel some relief that those poor caterers that Ma and Fourth Aunt drugged are at least being compensated.

"Hmph," snorts Big Aunt. "They never calling me Mami again."

Ma pats Big Aunt's shoulder, looking very guilty. "We will explain to them that we are the one who drug them, not you."

Big Aunt nods sadly. "Still, a trust is betray, cannot be earn back so easy."

"But price was worth it," Ma says. "Now we have Erjie back."

Big Aunt sniffs and side-eyes Second Aunt like, eh, is she really worth it? Then she smiles. "Yes, price was worth it."

It feels as though my heart has melted into sweet milk chocolate. Big Aunt is actually looking at Second Aunt with true affection.

Second Aunt returns the smile. "I still can't believe you all do such crazy thing to save me."

"I think Natasya just wanted an excuse to drug people. It's kind of her thing," Fourth Aunt mutters. Okay, I guess this beautiful moment is just that. A moment.

Ma narrows her eyes at Fourth Aunt. "You just jealous because I always saving the day, all the time."

"Hardly!" Fourth Aunt laughs. "Who was the one who came up with the idea of knocking them out in the first place?"

"Ah," Second Aunt holds up her index finger. "But Meddy was the one who figure out, Julia Child and Kristofer were children sweeties."

"Childhood sweethearts," I correct her.

Color blooms in Kristofer's cheeks. "I wouldn't call us—I—"

Julia Child cocks an eyebrow at him. "Didn't you say that one of the lessons you learned from Marjie is to stop being embarrassed of your own emotions?"

Kristofer's voice trails off and he adjusts his collar. "Yes, well. Good job putting the pieces together."

Ma grins so wide her whole face is 80 percent grin. "My Meddy is so smart, ya?" She shamelessly looks at Kristofer, then Julia Child, and repeats herself. "So smart, kan? My daughter. She went to UCLA, you know."

"Ma," I groan. "Not the time."

"Well," Julia Child says, "your mother is not wrong. It takes a certain amount of acumen to deduct these things, and god knows, no one else around us figured it out." She gives a rueful laugh. "To be fair, we did spend decades of our lives actively trying to take each other down, so that might have been somewhat misleading."

"But no more," Second Aunt chides. "You all working together now. Ya kan?"

"Ya?" Big Aunt says, and suddenly, my mother and aunts are all staring expectantly at Abi, Julia Child, and Kristofer.

Under the assault of their gazes, the three tycoons stand no chance.

"Yes, my love," Abi says. "Of course. From now on, we will cooperate with one another. A new era."

"I think it'll bode well for all of our businesses," Julia Child says.

Big Aunt narrows her eyes at them. "And what is this business? Hanh? Because we also run our own business, but we don't have henchmen and war and this kind of thing."

"It's all legit, right?" I quickly say. It's hit me that maybe, at the end of the day, I don't want to know what these people really do for a living. Maybe it's for the best that we're kept in the dark. "I'm sure it's all aboveboard. Real estate and uh, stuff like that."

There's a beat of hesitation, then all three of them burst out into fake laughter, half quailing under Big Aunt's unforgiving stare.

"Oh yes," Abi says. "We're all just businesspeople. We do a bit of everything. Trade, manufacturing, land development."

The problem with that is my brain immediately goes:

Manufacturing=Creating drugs/firearms/whatever other illegal goods.

Trade=Selling aforementioned goods.

Land development=Pablo Escobar-esque development of forests into hidden drug factories.

As though reading my mind, Julia Child says, "We would be more than happy to give you all a tour of our companies when you're free."

I immediately start to refuse, but Nathan beats me to it. "I would love to, actually."

I gape at him. What the hell is he on? Catching my eye, he shrugs. "I've read up on your companies, and they sound incredible. And yeah, very legit. I would love to get a tour."

"Ah, my son-in-law." Ma beams up at him and pats his shoulder. "He is very good businessman, I tell you, right? He own very nice hotel in America. You all have to come and stay there, we give you room upgrade, free minibar."

Of course my mother would invite the three people who have had Nathan and Second Aunt kidnapped to stay at Nathan's hotel.

"Sounds good," Kristofer says. He nods at the suitcases near the door. "And I see you're leaving?"

"Yeah." I can't say it fast enough. They may have come to assure us that they're all lovey-dovey now, and sure, they've come bearing a ridiculous amount of gifts, but I'm still keen to get away from them. They're too rich, too powerful. Nothing they do has any real consequences to them, and I don't feel safe being around them. Unlike my mother and aunts, who seem entirely comfortable, chattering excitedly about all the stuff they've just been given. "We loved our stay here, but I'm tired of traveling."

"Yes, Meddy," Fourth Aunt says with a sly sideways glance. "You should stay off your feet. What with all this panicking and running around, you must be exhausted. Don't overdo it."

A beat of silence follows, everyone's attention on us. Say something! My mind yells, but it doesn't come up with any suggestions. Then, as though the penny's suddenly dropped, Ma gasps, both hands flying to her mouth. "Meddy!"

One look at her face is all it takes for Nathan to get it. All at once, he's at my side, his hands on my arms, his eyes shining with tears. "Really?"

"Uh—" This is so not how I'd wanted to break it to him, in front of all these people. I'd come up with a plan B. We have a layover in Dubai for a couple of days on our way back to LA, so I'd made a reservation for a romantic dinner at the Burj Khalifa. I was going to tell him then. But when has anything gone to plan, especially when my family is involved? Frustration scratches at me, but then I take a deep breath and let myself fall into this moment, embracing all of it. I should've known better than to wait this long to tell Nathan. Because of course, Ma and the aunties would find out one way or another. And this is just the way it's always going to be in my family. No secrets from one another.

I let the smile spread across my face as I take in Nathan's expression, memorizing every detail on his handsome face, the way his eyes are open so wide, hope written clearly on them. "Yes."

The room erupts in cheers. I have to shout to be heard. "But it's early days yet, and it's really way too soon to celebrate—"

I laugh as Nathan sweeps me off my feet, his arms firm around my waist.

"Oh my god, Meddy," he whispers, kissing my cheek, my forehead, my chin.

"Aiya, don't lift her like that!" Ma wails, tapping Nathan's back frantically. "You put her down. Must be gentle. She carrying my grandbaby!"

"Okay, okay, I'm sorry," Nathan laughs, putting me down ever so gently.

My mom and aunts are suddenly around me, all of their hands on my belly, cooing at it. Oh god, is this what the next nine months are going to be like?

"Baby ah, this is your Ah Ma!" Ma shouts at my belly. "Aduh, so excited to see you. You be good, ya? I buy you so many presents."

"You'll hurt the poor thing's eardrums, shouting like that," Fourth Aunt scolds her.

"She has to talk loud, otherwise baby cannot hear under Meddy belly fat," Second Aunt says.

"Geez, thanks, Second Aunt."

"Tch, not saying you fat, just saying, belly got lots of fat, is good for baby."

"Not enough fat, you too skinny, Meddy," Big Aunt scolds. Before I can react, she reaches out and pokes my right breast. "Look at this, chest so flat, got no milk for baby. Is okay, I cook you confinement food, very nutritious. Later you will have so much milk."

I look up at the ceiling. I guess part of me knew that this is what it would be like, but now that it's actually happening, it's still overwhelming. But then when I look back at them, these women who have spent their lives raising me, doting on me and making a fuss over me, it hits me that I don't want any different for my child. Nathan catches my eye and smiles, and I know that he's thinking it, too, that as crazy as my mom and aunts drive us, we wouldn't have it any other way, and it's a lucky baby indeed that gets born into this family.

ACKNOWLEDGMENTS

This book spells the end of the Aunties series, and I have so many feelings around this. I don't even know where to begin. It is no exaggeration to say that *Dial A for Aunties* changed my life. It propelled me to a world that I did not think was possible, and so much of it was made a reality by my loyal readers. Publishing is such a roller coaster. It all depends on numbers, and those are so unpredictable. So when *Dial A for Aunties* came out and so many of you fell in love with the aunties and recommended it to your friends and family, it made it possible for me to continue writing about these chaotic women.

I am not exaggerating when I say that this book would not have been possible if not for you, dear reader.

I would also like to thank my publishing team at Berkley for being the best possible house to bring the aunties to life. My editor, Cindy, has been so supportive and flexible, I truly cannot fault her in any way. I am always boasting to my friends about how wonderful she is, and I know how lucky I am to be her author. My team at Berkley has worked tirelessly to bring the aunties to as wide an audience as possible, and for that, I cannot thank them enough. My agent, Katelyn, was the one who made all of this possible. I sometimes think about what my life would be like if I had been with a different agent, and it is a very bleak picture indeed.

I wish I could be more eloquent with my acknowledgments, but truly, I am so overcome with emotion at the end of this epic journey. This is so much more than I ever thought was possible, and the past two years have shown me that the sky is the limit. And it is all thanks to you, dear reader, and so I hope that you stay with me throughout my journey in writing, whether it be with the aunties or other meddlesome auntie characters that are to come. I am so grateful to have been able to share in this journey with you. Thank you for letting me and the aunties be a part of your life.

THE
GOOD,
THE BAD,
AND THE
AUNTIES

◆ ◆ ◆

JESSE Q. SUTANTO

READERS GUIDE

QUESTIONS FOR DISCUSSION

1. *The Good, the Bad, and the Aunties* marks the end of the Aunties series. How do you think the characters have changed and grown throughout the series?

2. Do you think that Meddy's aunties will be a little more sedate after all of their misadventures?

3. How do you think Meddy's relationship with her mother and aunts will change after having a baby?

4. The aunties are immigrants, and in this book, they return to their motherland, Indonesia. What do you think it's like for immigrants and their children to return home after establishing a different life overseas?

5. What were some of the biggest cultural surprises you found in this book?

6. What do you think of Nathan agreeing to remain as a sacrifice while Meddy and the aunties go about trying to find the title deed? Is he being heroic or foolhardy?

7. Do you relate to Meddy's relationship with her mother and aunts?

8. Which auntie do you most connect with, and why?

9. If you were Nathan, would you be as accepting of Meddy's meddlesome aunties?

10. What will you miss most about the aunties?

Keep reading
for an excerpt from
Jesse Q. Sutanto's
next novel . . .

YOU WILL
NEVER BE ME

MEREDITH

I'm stalking my best friend. There's no use denying it; when I first started, I told myself we were so in sync that we were like the same person torn into two halves, and those two halves are linked by an invisible thread that is always pulling them back to each other, so of course we'd constantly be running into each other. Simpatico. That's what we always used to say. "Simpatico!" Followed by a wink, content and smug because out of almost eight billion humans in the world, the two of us have somehow managed to find our soulmates in each other, and what is that if not pure and beautiful magic?

And anyway, it's not really stalking, not like the kind you'd see in the movies, with the stalker prowling in all black (contrary to popular belief, black is *not* for everyone. It certainly does my skin tone no favors), a chloroform-soaked rag in one hand and zip ties in the other. I'm not trying to kidnap Bestie. It's more like . . . Stalking Lite. I just want to know how she's doing. I need to see if our earth-shattering fight has mauled her the way it has me. That's reasonable. And I sure as hell won't find out anything through her social media accounts, which are all glossed over with giddily jubilant content. No, if I want to see signs of the wreckage underneath, I need to see her in person, catch a glimpse of the tightness around the right corner of her mouth, or the way she'd lick her lips like a lizard does, a rapid twitch that does nothing to moisten them.

And that's why I'm sitting in my car around the corner from the twins' school, waiting for her car to appear out of the drop-off line. Damn it, I know it sounds bad; I'm literally parked outside of her kids' school. But this has nothing to do with her girls, even though I miss Noemie and Elea so much (and I'm sure they must miss Aunt Mer), and Luca misses little Sabine.

"Don't you, Luca?" I coo, glancing back at my eight-month-old son. "You miss baby Sabine, don't you, sweetie?"

He's too busy sucking on his toes to give me a reply. But I can tell. I know he misses Sabine. Sabine is two months older than Luca, and he hasn't spent a single day away from Sabine's side up until her mother and I had our catastrophic fight. It's not fair on the kids. Why can't she see that?

I tap the steering wheel impatiently, my eyes scanning each car as it leaves the school. Have I missed her already? I'm not cut out for this spy shit. What if she sees me? What if she recognizes the car? I was careful-ish. I'd switched cars with Clara this morning, telling her that I had plans to drive up to Griffith Park for a shoot and needed her four-wheel drive. Of course, I've driven my sister's car a few times, so maybe Bestie will still recognize it. Maybe I should drive home. What the hell was I thinking?

But just then, I spot it. Her SUV pulling out of the school driveway. My breath catches in my throat, emotion welling up at the painfully familiar sight of her car. I can practically smell the inside of her car already—her Miss Dior perfume, the girls' raspberry shampoo, and homemade kale chips. Then, as it drives past, I catch sight of her face, her eyes hidden behind her oversized Chanel sunglasses and her hair falling in loose mahogany waves down her shoulders, and tears rush to my eyes (behind my similarly oversized Jimmy Choos). Damn it, but I miss that bitch, Aspen. A bitter snort tumbles out of my mouth at her name. Aspen. I gave that to her. What's in a name? Well. A name is the beginning of your brand, so what's in a name? Everything. In a way, you could say I made Aspen into who she is today. She owes me everything.

Eight Years Ago

I know it's in vogue to hate LA—the dry heat, the fake cocaine-and-wheatgrass-and-matcha-fueled cheerfulness of everyone, the way that the checkout girl at the supermarket looks like she just stepped off a runway—but honestly? I love it. I can be as manically cheerful as the best of them, and I don't even snort coke (except when I'm trying to lose weight, but ever since I started doing the celery juice fast, I haven't done any lines). Back in Ohio, I was always "too much," but it turns out that in LA, you can never be "too much." Everyone here loves me, some people—I won't name names—even describe me as their "happy pill."

I'm being invited to so many parties that some evenings, I

would literally spend just five minutes at each venue, just enough to make the rounds (*Hi, sweetie! Oh my god, you look FAB! Ah! Omg it's been too long! We must catch up soon. We MUST! Oh, let's take a selfie, you look AMAZING!*), kiss cheeks, and make sure we're photographed before I make my exit (*Sorry, gotta run, Chell is celebrating her birthday at the—yes, we MUST catch up soon! Okay, love you, bye! Bye! Kisses!*), then zip down the 405, billboards grinning and winking at me like we're all in on some great secret, to another party, glitzier than the one before, then to another party, more exclusive, then another, and another.

(Do you hate me? You mustn't. I'm just a girl trying to make it big. Trying to *thrive*.)

It's at one of these parties that I meet her. Ryleebelle. I only notice her because among the skinny, shimmering LA bodies and glinting fake smiles, she looks so out of place. Picture this: a non-skinny Asian woman in an ill-fitting black dress (black is less cruel to her than it is to me, but still. Who wears an LBD to a party in LA, for fuck's sake?), both hands clasped around a martini glass that she's holding against her chest like a shield. Too much eye makeup. A terrified look on her face. I'm about to glide past her when she glances up and I catch the look that crosses her face.

Pure and unadulterated admiration. Imagine a fan being called backstage after a BTS concert. That's the look on her face. More than just a fan. A worshipper. It seizes me (do not try to tell me that it wouldn't have seized you too).

I give her a kind smile. I'm gracious, generous. I like to help. There's a special place in hell for women who don't help other women, etc. When she sees my smile, the relief that goes through her face is that of a drowning person who's just been thrown a lifeline. I go to her.

Pause for a second. I need you to fully understand what a huge favor I'm doing here. Because the other thing about her is that she looks very clearly like an Asian person from Asia, and not even the right parts of Asia, not the ones that inspire weeaboos or Koreaboos. I was born and raised in Ohio, and I'd had to learn a long time ago how to fit in, which parts of my Asianness to highlight and which ones to hide. One of the things I quickly learned to do was to dissociate from other Asians who weren't conforming. It might sound cruel, but you know what else is cruel? High school kids in Ohio. It was a long and brutal road for me to become The Right Kind of Asian. The kind that doesn't bring anything with a face on it for lunch. (One time, Raj Singh's mom packed him a fish head curry in fifth grade. I looked Raj up on Twitter the other day; he is now an alcoholic. I bet I can trace everything that went wrong in his life back to that fish head curry. It smelled dope though, I'll give his mom that.)

So for me to now approach this plump—okay, she's not plump, but her collar bones aren't jutting out the way that LA likes them to—this non-skinny Asian woman is a huge risk for me to take. She has everything to gain from catching my eye; I have next to nothing to gain from being kind to her.

Anyway, so I go to her with a kind, empathetic smile, and say, "First time at one of these things?"

The "one of these things" we happen to be at is a rooftop mixer for model/actor/singer/social media influencer wannabes, with agents and photographers prowling among us like sharks. She's actually quite pretty under the heavy makeup, but like I said, not skinny, so obviously she's not a model. I bet she has a luscious voice and thinks she can win *America's Got Talent* or whatever horror talent show they've got going on nowadays.

She gives me an apologetic smile. "That obvious, huh?"

Only the slightest hint of an accent in her voice. And it's actually a nice accent, not one that would get her made fun of. A point in her favor. One less thing to change. "Only because I've been in exactly your position before."

"Really? You?" She gives me a once-over that's overflowing with admiration. "I don't believe that."

I brush imaginary lint off my sequined dress. "Hey, I'm from Ohio, so when I first moved here, I was probably the epitome of uncool."

"I know," she says. Seeing my look of surprise, she adds, "I know you're from Ohio. I follow you on YouTube and Instagram. Your beauty advice is amazing. I'm such a fan."

Clearly she hasn't taken my beauty advice to heart though. Is that a mean thought? Damn it, one of this year's resolutions was to stop being so mean, and it's not even February yet.

As though she's read my mind, she flushes a little and says, "I know, I probably have too much makeup on. I know your mantra: less is so much more! But when I get nervous—god, it's like a tic—some people bite their nails, I dab on a little bit more makeup."

"Let me guess: you were *very* nervous tonight?" Oh my god, why am I being so catty?

Instead of telling me what a bitch I am, she laughs. A full-on laugh-shout from deep in her belly. And I find that I really like her, this woman who doesn't mind laughing at herself.

"Dude, I was so nervous, I almost chickened out of coming

here tonight. I mean . . ." She gestures at everyone else around us, and I see them through her eyes. How ridiculously, painfully beautiful and fashionable everyone here is. How stunningly blond. "I don't belong here, do I? I can't believe I moved all the way to America thinking I might make it."

"Hey, just because you don't fit in yet doesn't mean you won't ever fit in. I wasn't always this fabulous. You should see my middle school photos. I wore mom jeans. Like, seriously, I was a twelve-year-old who wore mom jeans and thick glasses."

She's laughing again, and there's nothing I like more than making people laugh, so I keep going. "I mean, where the hell did I even get those jeans, right? They don't make them in kid sizes. They're called mom jeans for a reason."

"Well, you've come a really long way."

"It's been a hell of a journey." The unspoken question between us: Am I going to take her on that journey? Make her my mentee? Maybe this can be my good deed for the year.

"I'm Ryleebelle," she says, holding out her hand.

I take it. She has a surprisingly strong grip. I like her. And I promise it's not just because she follows my YouTube and Instagram accounts. In that moment, I make a decision. I'm going to help her. "No, you're not," I say.

She blinks. Laughs hesitantly. "Sorry?"

"What are you trying to be?"

"Huh?"

"Singer? Actor? No offense, but obviously not a model."

"Oh. Right! Um, singer. Well, trying to be."

"So you're on YouTube?"

She nods eagerly. "Yeah, I'm Ryleebellesings on there."

Ryleebellesings. Dear god. "And how many subscribers do you have?"

"About five thousand."

"Change your name and you'll probably get another five thousand." Okay, I mean, I don't know that for a fact, but I'm willing to bet money that her name is holding her back.

Her eyes widen. "But—"

"No one is going to take Ryleebelle seriously." I tilt my head, appraising her. "I'm thinking . . . some sort of plant? Not a flower, ugh. A tree name. Rowan? Hmm, you don't strike me as a Rowan. Oh, I know! Aspen."

The moment I say it, I know we both feel it. The click. The puzzle piece slotting into place. It fits. The uncertainty melts away from her face and she gazes at me with wonderment. She really does look quite pretty. After my makeover—or rather, my makeunder—she's going to look stunning.

"Huh," she breathes out. "I like it. Aspen. It sounds so . . . American."

I know exactly what she means. In many Asian cultures, people like to give their kids Western names. But they don't have a good grasp on Western culture, so then they reach for the "fancier-sounding" ones and make the spelling "unique" and that's when you get atrocities like Ryleebelle. They don't get that like makeup, with names, less is more. And because Aspen gets it, I know she's going to get everything I'll do for her. She'll get that I am giving her the most valuable gift. The gift of fitting in.

Photo by Donny Wu

Jesse Q. Sutanto is the author of the bestselling Aunties series, *Vera Wong's Unsolicited Advice for Murderers*, and *I'm Not Done With You Yet*. Her young adult titles include *The Obsession* and *Well, That Was Unexpected*, and her children's fantasy series is *Theo Tan and the Fox Spirit*. She has a master's degree from Oxford University and a bachelor's from the University of California, Berkeley. She currently lives in Jakarta with her husband and two young daughters.

Ready to find
your next great read?

Let us help.

Visit prh.com/nextread